THEY HAD BEEN ON COUNTLESS ALIEN WORLDS, FACED MANY SURPRISING DANGERS . . .

But neither Kirk nor Spock was prepared for what came through the alien door.

In strolled a tall, overweight, nearly bald man dressed in a billowy green shirt and loose gray pants, the legs of which were tucked into the tops of his tall black boots. He had a wide, cherubic face and an even wider black handlebar mustache. He had hooked his thumbs under his belt, and he swaggered like a king at his coronation.

Kirk recognized him instantly. "Harry Mudd!" he exclaimed. "What the devil are you doing here?"

Look for STAR TREK Fiction from Pocket Books

Star Trek: The Original Series

Star Trek: The Next Generation

Star Trek: Deep Space Nine

Star Trek: Voyager

STAR TREK®

MUDD IN YOUR EYE

JERRY OLTION

POCKET BOOKS
New York London Toronto Sydney Tokyo Singapore

An *Original* Publication of POCKET BOOKS

POCKET BOOKS, a division of Simon & Schuster Inc.
1230 Avenue of the Americas, New York, NY 10020

A VIACOM COMPANY

STAR TREK is a Registered Trademark of Paramount Pictures.

This book is published by Pocket Books, a division of Simon & Schuster Inc., under exclusive license from Paramount Pictures.

ISBN: 0-671-00260-0

First Pocket Books printing January 1997

10 9 8 7 6 5 4 3 2 1

POCKET and colophon are registered trademarks of Simon & Schuster Inc.

Printed in the U.S.A.

For Kathy,
who makes marriage fun

Acknowledgments

I'd like to thank a few people for their help and support while I wrote this book:

John Ordover for letting me play in this particular niche of the *Star Trek* universe in the first place.

The Eugene Wordos for encouragement, inspiration, and brainstorming.

And Marybeth O'Halloran for background and cookies.

Chapter One

"DEARLY BELOVED," said Captain Kirk.

Someone in the back of the observation lounge snickered, and Kirk looked up to silence the offender. Not that he blamed them, of course; two less likely mates than Lieutenant Nordell and Ensign Lebrun would be hard to find even on a ship with as large a crew as the *Enterprise*. Still, they had chosen to wed, and as captain of the ship Kirk had the dubious honor of officiating. No matter what he thought about their chances together, he wanted no disruptions to mar their ceremony, so he eyed the thirty or so people— mostly from engineering and security—who had come to wish their friends well, and when he was satisfied that he had cowed the group into silence, he continued to read from the vows that Ensign Lebrun had written.

"We are gathered here in this fragile bubble of life amid the vastness of space to witness the union of two people in the bonds of holy matrimony," he read. He wasn't sure how he liked that "fragile bubble" line, either. The ship was indeed in a vast and largely uncharted region of space, and the multicolored whorl of an incandescent nebula beyond the viewports provided ample proof of that, but the *Enterprise* was hardly fragile. However, Kirk supposed he could allow Lebrun a bit of poetic license for the sake of romance. She and Nordell would need all the romance they could get to make up for the stormy courtship they had endured on their way to the altar. So he smiled and kept reading while the brilliant stars shone in on the happy couple.

They looked blissful enough. Nordell wore his dress uniform, its deep red jacket festooned with medals received in his three years of Starfleet service, and if he felt any discomfort in the seldom-worn clothing, his silly grin betrayed none of it. Lebrun had forgone the uniform in favor of a traditional white wedding gown, and while it was a bit of a shock to see the normally quite butch security officer in chiffon and lace, Kirk had to admit that she had never appeared more beautiful. Her short brown hair shone radiantly beneath the jeweled tiara, and her high cheeks and wide, green eyes also seemed to glow with a light of their own.

Their attendants, Chief Engineer Scott and Yeoman Rand, wore their dress uniforms as well. And the witnesses behind the wedding party were also decked out in various degrees of finery. Smiles abounded. Everyone seemed excited at the prospect of this wedding. So why did Kirk feel such a sense of impending doom?

He had made it through the "Marriage is a precious thing" section and had just reached the line "If anyone knows a reason why these two should not be joined together, speak now or forever hold your peace," when the intercom chimed and Lieutenant Uhura's voice came over the speaker: "Captain, we're receiving a subspace transmission from Admiral Tyers, priority two."

Everyone in the observation lounge, even the nervous couple, burst into laughter, and Uhura said, "Did I say something funny, sir?"

"As a matter of fact, you did," Kirk told her. "I'll explain later. Tell the admiral I'll be with her in a moment." If it was priority two, then Tyers could wait long enough for Kirk to finish what he had started. He turned back to the wedding party and said quickly, "I think we can safely assume that the admiral is calling on other business. So do you, Simon Nordell, take this woman to be your wife, to love her, honor her, and obey her, in joy and in sorrow, in sickness and in—"

"Wait a minute," said Nordell. "What's this 'obey' stuff? I didn't agree to that."

"Yes you did," said Lebrun.

"I never—"

"You agreed to a traditional exchange of vows," said Lebrun, shaking her bridal bouquet for emphasis until a yellow daisy snapped off and fell to the floor. "'Love, honor, and obey' is traditional."

"It's also demeaning," Nordell protested.

Scotty bent down to retrieve the flower and handed it to Lebrun, who absently stuck it back in the bouquet. "Look, I'm going to say the same thing," she told her husband-to-be.

3

He set his jaw stubbornly. "Well I'm not."

The people gathered behind them fidgeted nervously. Kirk cleared his throat. "The admiral is waiting," he said. "Do you want to try this again later?"

Nordell shook his head. "No, we can work this out." He looked over at Lebrun. "How about 'Love, honor, and cherish'? That's traditional too."

She frowned. "I like 'obey.'"

Nordell said, "Of course you do. You're a security officer. But I can actually keep my vow if I say 'cherish.'"

Someone laughed, and this time Kirk was glad of the interruption.

After a moment's thought, Lebrun nodded. "Okay, I guess we can cherish each other." She turned back to Kirk. "Is that all right with you?"

Kirk held out his hands palms forward and said, "Far be it from me to object."

"Good." She smiled at Nordell, and he smiled at her as if nothing had happened. Their ability to recover after arguments was just as amazing as their propensity to get into them in the first place.

Kirk shook his head and read the modified vow again for Nordell, who repeated it without hesitation, and a moment later Lebrun made the same vow to Nordell. Kirk began to hope that the rest of the wedding would actually go off smoothly, but that hope died when it came time to exchange the rings. Nordell turned to Scotty for the band he was to give Lebrun, and Scotty pulled from his pocket a monstrous blinking red-and-green jewel that looked more like it belonged in a warp engine than on a woman's hand. Obviously Nordell wasn't expecting that; he looked at the thing in Scotty's palm as if it might explode at any moment, and his mouth opened and closed like a fish's.

Lebrun had no trouble finding her voice. "You didn't," she said threateningly.

"I didn't!" Nordell protested.

Amid growing laughter, Scotty said, "No, I did. And here's the real item." He held out a more traditional ring, a single diamond on a gold band, and with that and a brushed gold band passed from Yeoman Rand to Ensign Lebrun, they completed the ceremony.

At last Kirk said, "I now pronounce you husband and wife," and Nordell and Lebrun kissed enthusiastically while everyone applauded. "Now if you will excuse me," Kirk said when they came up for air, "I'll go see what the admiral wants."

He took the call in one of the conference rooms adjacent to the observation lounge. The admiral looked up from her desk when Kirk activated his viewscreen, and said, "Trouble, Jim?"

Kirk grinned. "I hope not. But you never know. I was performing a wedding for two of my crew members."

"Ah," the admiral said. "Extend my congratulations." She glanced down at her desktop full of papers, then looked back at Kirk again. "We have just received word that Prastor and Distrel, two planets in the Nevis system, have declared peace. We want you to go investigate."

Kirk narrowed his eyes, puzzled. "You want us to investigate a *peace treaty?* Why?"

"Because Prastor and Distrel have been at war for twelve thousand years, that's why."

"Twelve millennia of interplanetary war?" Kirk

asked, horrified at the very notion. "I'm surprised there's anything left."

Admiral Tyers read from her briefing papers. "From what the survey teams report, their battles are almost entirely hand-to-hand."

"They would have to be," Kirk said. "Either that or they breed like rabbits."

The admiral grinned. "They are apparently quite humanoid in that regard. But we don't know very much about them. Their leaders have spurned diplomatic overtures from every peaceful race who have ever encountered them, and the common people are just as unsympathetic toward xenologists."

"Open hostility or just uncooperative?" Kirk asked.

"It depends on the situation," Tyers said. "They were very polite about it when they rejected the offer to join the Federation, and a bit less so when the Klingons and the Romulans got pushy with their respective invitations. They have the technology and the attitude to enforce their will, so the rest of the galaxy reluctantly left them alone to fight one another until the heat death of the universe, if that was what they wanted." She shrugged. "So you can see why this declaration of peace of theirs caught everyone by surprise. We want to find out what happened, and why."

Kirk nodded. He could think of two very spooky possibilities already. What if the Nevisians had decided to band together and take over the rest of the galaxy? Or what if someone even more warlike than they were had conquered *them?* They might have simply gotten tired of fighting and decided to bury the hatchet, but it would be dangerous to make that assumption.

"We'll look into it," Kirk said.

"Good. I've already given the coordinates to your navigator. You're only a day away at warp seven. I'll expect a report in a day and a half."

Kirk nodded. "You'll have it."

When the admiral signed off, he leaned back in his chair and closed his eyes for a moment. Maybe he was buying trouble, but he had a bad feeling about this. People who had been at war for twelve thousand years weren't likely to end it gracefully.

All the more reason for the *Enterprise* to be there, he supposed. If Kirk and his crew could help forge a lasting peace—and maybe even bring the two planets into the Federation—that would be a significant accomplishment.

He heard a cry of surprised indignation from the observation lounge, followed immediately by loud laughter. He got up and went to the door in time to see Nordell, his face covered in cake, smear a slice of it all over Lebrun's mouth and cheeks. Then to even louder cheers, they began licking it off one another. Kirk sighed. They were going to have an interesting life together, there was no doubt of that.

Chapter Two

THE DATA COMING IN from long-range scans intrigued Science Officer Spock. He had seen plenty of multiple stars in his travels, but unlike most double stars in the galaxy, the Nevis system's twin suns orbited one another in nearly circular paths. Normally the eccentric orbits of multiple stars prevented planets from developing in their habitable zones, but the Nevis suns' unusual stability had allowed a full range of them to form, including two class-M worlds that had either been colonized by humanoid life or had evolved it on their own long ago.

Now, as the *Enterprise* dropped out of warp and made its final approach, Spock wondered how fortunate the Nevisians had actually been. A single inhabited planet might endure a few centuries of war, but international commerce nearly always overshadowed the reasons for fighting within a few generations at most. Conversely, two planets separated by light-years of space couldn't afford to carry on a protracted battle. Warp-drive starships were too expensive, and the potential gain from conquering one's enemy was too small to make it worth the effort. Only two planets in one star system could marshal the necessary resources and reap the economic gains to make warfare a stable way of life.

Spock remembered another situation like this one. Vendikar and Eminiar VII had fought for five hundred years before the Federation discovered them. They would not have stopped then, either, had not the *Enterprise* been caught up in the hostilities and been forced to end their war for them in order to escape. Spock and Captain Kirk had broken the Prime Directive prohibiting interference with the development of a society, but no one who understood the situation had faulted them for their actions. Five hundred years of war without hope of an end was unthinkable; anyone would have done the same in their situation, even had their ship not been in danger. But this— twelve millennia of constant battle. . . . Spock came dangerously close to feeling emotion when he thought of how many lives had been lost, all for nothing.

But now the two planets had ended it without fanfare. Spock wondered what had precipitated such a dramatic shift in their behavior. Speculation would be pointless, since he would no doubt find out as soon as the *Enterprise* made contact with the Prastorian and Distrellian planetary governments, but he was definitely curious.

"Visual onscreen," said Captain Kirk, and Spock routed his optical sensors' data stream to the main viewscreen. Then he turned around in his chair to observe the larger picture himself. On the wall monitor beyond the navigation and helm control stations the two stars glowed brightly near the outer edges of the screen, and their planets shone along an erratic line running diagonally between the two. The *Enterprise* had entered the system slightly above the plane of the ecliptic. Prastor was the closer of the two inhabited planets, though even at impulse speed the difference in distance was insignificant.

"Lieutenant Uhura," Kirk said, looking over his shoulder at the communications officer. "Hail both planets. Let them know we're here."

"Yes, sir," said Uhura. She pressed the well-worn keys on her console that sent the standard hailing message, a multifrequency, multiply modulated burst transmission containing the ship's name and registry number. Practically anyone who was listening on radio, subspace, or even optical frequencies would at least know that someone was trying to communicate, and as soon as they replied Uhura would be able to tell what frequency and modulation method they used. She could then send a more specific message, and in that fashion she and the people she was trying to communicate with could zero in on protocols and language, and eventually establish a dialogue.

Uhura was good at her job. Within a minute of her first hail, she had a visual image on the viewscreen, and announced to the captain, "The Grand General of Distrel."

Spock took a careful look at the Nevisian. He was humanoid, but not close enough to the phenotype to be mistaken for human. His steely blue eyes weren't as deeply recessed into their sockets as normal, giving him a bug-eyed, scrutinizing look. His narrow face and small nose compounded the effect. His mouth was round instead of wide, and his ears, which attached much lower than usual, were deeply convoluted, with separate overlapping sections like petals on a flower.

His most remarkable characteristic, however, was his reddish gray hair, which stuck straight out from his head to a distance of at least four inches. It was coarse and heavy and extended in all directions, even from his tall forehead, shading his eyes and upper face and giving him an air of sinister watchfulness.

He was seated in an ornate chair at a dining table upon which a lavish meal had been laid out and partially served. A napkin was tucked into the collar of his billowy light blue shirt. Evidently the *Enterprise*'s hail had caught him at dinner. He apparently ate well, but his body seemed leaner and more muscular than Spock would have expected from a planetary head who dined that way regularly. His physique was not due to high gravity; Distrel had less than one standard g at the surface. Evidently the affairs of state left him time to exercise; that was a good sign. It meant he would have time to deal with the new problems that would undoubtedly develop now that his society had made such a dramatic change.

"I am Mesparth El Vuk Cevich Benat," said the Grand General. His deep, resonant voice carried an undertone that Spock recognized as quiet amusement. Spock wondered if the multitude of names had anything to do with that. Surely the Grand General couldn't use them all on a regular basis. "Welcome to the newly formed Commonwealth of Nevis," he said. "You're late for the party."

The captain smiled and said, "I'm James Kirk,

captain of the *Enterprise*. We didn't know we were expected."

The Grand General laughed, his round mouth open in a wide O, revealing a double row of sharp teeth. "Oh, we knew someone from the Federation would show up before long. You've always taken an unusually strong interest in other people's business."

Kirk's smile grew a bit strained. "We want to congratulate you on your peace treaty. I hope we haven't disrupted your festivities."

"Not at all, not at all!" the Grand General said. "We don't plan to slow down for some time yet. Please come join us."

"We'd be honored," said Kirk.

"Good. The Padishah of Prastor is here as well, so it'll save you a trip."

He turned his head to the side, apparently listening to someone outside the camera's field of view. When he turned back to Kirk, he said, "Bring your lovely communications officer when you come. And anyone else you like, of course. There's room for an army here at the palace, especially now that we don't have an army of our own anymore, ha, ha!"

"Thank you," said Kirk. "I'll bring Lieutenant Uhura and some of my officers."

"Wonderful," the Grand General said. "We'll be expecting you." His screen image winked out, and the viewscreen switched back to the stellar display.

Kirk turned toward Uhura. "It looks like you've made a conquest already," he told her.

She should have been blushing, but she merely looked puzzled. "I don't understand how, sir," she said. "I'm not in visual range of that camera."

"You must have switched to wide angle by accident," Kirk said.

She shook her head. "No, sir, I'm sure I didn't."

That was easy enough to check. Spock retrieved the transmission log from the computer files and replayed the outgoing signal on one of his data monitors. It showed only the captain and a blurry background. "Confirmed, Captain," he said. "Lieutenant Uhura's image was not transmitted to Distrel."

"Then it must have been your voice," said Kirk.

"No, sir," Uhura replied. "I used the computer's standard hailing files. If he's responding to a voice, then it's the computer's."

Kirk laughed. "Well then, he's going to get a surprise when he actually meets you. I trust it'll be a pleasant one nonetheless."

The captain didn't seem concerned, but something about the situation still bothered Spock. "Captain," he said. "The request came from someone outside *his* camera's field of view. Unless his own communications personnel were in the same room with him, which seems unlikely at dinner, then neither he nor whoever spoke to him would have heard the computer's voice either. It seems likely that someone on Distrel knows the lieutenant, or at least knows of her."

"Hmm, that could be," said Kirk. "Well, then, we'll want to keep our eyes open for old friends. We could have a Prime Directive situation on our hands. But let's not buy trouble before we have to. There could be a perfectly logical explanation for it."

Spock was certain there was, but unlike Kirk, the fact that the explanation would be logical did little to reassure him. He planned to be extra cautious until he knew who had arrived on Distrel ahead of them.

Scotty tugged at his collar, trying unsuccessfully to stretch it out enough so it would stop itching. Twice in two days was too often for him to wear a dress uniform. But he couldn't very well have missed yesterday's wedding; Nordell was one of his best engineers, and despite his little joke with the ring, Scotty had been truly honored to be his best man. Today's reception on Distrel was less vital to him, but it was important to the captain to have his senior officers along for show, so here he was trotting down the corridor toward the transporter room while he tried to ignore how uncomfortable he felt in costume.

He met Chekov just outside the door. The diminutive Russian was smiling broadly, obviously as pleased to be wearing his finery as Scotty was displeased.

"Any excuse to celebrate, eh lad?" asked Scotty.

Chekov struggled to keep a serious tone in his voice, "Oh, no, Mr. Scott. It's my duty to teach these people how to party. After twelve thousand years of war, they've probably forgotten how."

Scotty laughed. "Well, if anybody can show them how to have a good time, it would have to be you."

They entered the transporter room. Dr. McCoy, Lieutenant Uhura, Spock, and the captain had already arrived. Kirk had decided that six people would be plenty for the first landing party, so when Scotty and Chekov came in he waved toward the transporter platform and said, "All right, everyone remember your manners."

"Well, that puts a damper on things," Chekov said quietly as he took up a position at the rear of the platform.

"Everyone but you, Mr. Chekov," Kirk said. "I know better than to ask the impossible."

"Thank you, sir." All but Spock laughed. Scotty thought he looked even more preoccupied than usual, but then again maybe it was just the contrast between his emotionless demeanor and the others' mirth that made him seem that way.

Kirk said to the transporter officer, "Energize, Mr. Vagle." Vagle slid the activation controls forward and the transporter room shimmered out of existence around them, to be replaced by a much larger room, this one full of people. It had stone floors and a high, open-beamed ceiling, tall windows along three walls, wide double doors standing open in the fourth wall, and a long banquet table running the entire length of it. The table was still covered with food but the meal was evidently over; the people—about a hundred of them, Scotty guessed—all milled about in small knots of conversation, laughing and telling stories like anyone at a large gathering. If the room hadn't been so big there might not have been space for six more people to suddenly materialize in their midst, but Vagle had found a sizable gap to put them in.

Evening light streamed through the north and west windows, illuminating the banquet hall with a soft, reddish light only partially offset by bright crystal chandeliers overhead. Scotty turned around slowly to take it all in. Heavy wooden construction, but smoothly finished; intelligent use of arches and canti-levered beams to enclose the immense space; and careful placement of banners and wall decorations to cut down on echoes. These Nevisians had good design sense. Scotty approved.

Physically all of them, men and women alike, had the same protruding eyes, narrow faces, and straight-out shock of stiff hair. The predominant hair color seemed to be reddish orange or brown. Nobody seemed to be going bald with age, but a few people, both men and women, were graying on top.

The women wore long, brightly colored dresses that flowed gracefully when they moved. The men wore blousy jackets gathered at the waist, and instead of pants they wore blue-and-white striped wraps that looked for all the world like kilts. A bit too long to be in style back home, Scotty thought, but he suddenly wished he had worn his own kilt instead of the standard dress uniform. Ah, well. Next time he would know.

Everyone, men and women alike, wore short swords belted around their waist. Scotty assumed they were ceremonial; the Nevisians obviously had a high enough level of technology to create much more deadly weapons, and after fighting for as long as they had he was sure they would have done so.

The sound of conversation dwindled as people realized that someone had just beamed into their midst. Scotty felt self-conscious under their scrutiny, but Captain Kirk merely smiled and said, "Hello, we're here from the *Ent*—"

"Captain Kirk!" boomed a deep voice from the left side of the room. Everyone in the landing party looked in that direction and saw the Grand General striding toward them, his hands outstretched in welcome. "I'm glad you could join us," he said. "I've heard so much about you." He grasped Kirk's arm just above the wrist in a lodge-brother style handshake and pumped it up and down vigorously, then turned to Spock. "Did the Vulcans send a delegation as well, or are you with them?"

"I am a Starfleet officer, currently assigned to the *Enterprise*," Spock said. "As such I do not officially represent Vulcan, but I can and do offer my people's congratulations on resolving your armed conflict."

"Oh, that," the Grand General said, waving his right hand dismissively. "Well, we had help. To tell you the truth, I never expected it to be so much fun."

"I would like to ask—" Spock began, but the Grand General had already turned to Uhura.

"And you must be the lovely lieutenant. Every bit as beautiful as advertised, I must agree."

Uhura dipped her head and said, "Thank you. But how did you know about me? I'm sure I've never been here before."

"And that's our loss," said the Grand General, "but we hope to become much better acquainted now that you're here. May I get you something to drink? Saurian brandy, perhaps?"

"Saurian brandy?" Scotty said, not realizing that he'd spoken aloud until the Grand General glanced over at him. Well, in for a penny, in for a pound, so now that he had the General's attention he asked, "How did you get hold of Saurian brandy? We were under the impression that you didn't trade with the rest of the galaxy."

"We didn't," said the Grand General. "But once we made peace it seemed like a good idea to try a few of your more notable exports, and I must admit our preliminary findings have been quite satisfactory.

You'll have to try the I'danian spice pudding, if there's any left." He waved the *Enterprise* crew toward the heavily laden banquet table. "Come, come, enjoy!" he said. "Food and drink first; there'll be time enough to answer all your questions later. And you must meet the Padishah of Prastor. Arnitas!" he shouted. "Where did Arnitas get off to?" He turned back to Kirk and said softly, "It still seems odd to give our ancient enemy free run of the palace, but since we're at peace it would have been rather inhospitable to do otherwise."

Maybe so, thought Scotty, but it probably would have been smarter, at least until they were sure the truce was going to last. Apparently, having never made peace before, these Nevisians didn't realize how much more fragile a state it was than war. He wasn't here to rain on their parade, however, so he said nothing. He stepped over to the table and examined the food, wondering what sorts of unusual flavors it might have. There were four or five different types of meat, dozens of baked breads and cakes and pastries, trays of sweet-looking confections, and bowls of fruit. Scotty picked up a pretty round fruit about the size of an apple that had purple and white stripes dividing it into sections like orange slices. Its skin felt hard under his fingers, but it gave a little when he squeezed. He wondered how a person was supposed to eat it.

Conversation had started up around them again, but many of the Nevisians closest to them were still watching the newcomers. Scotty considered asking one of them for advice—one of the best ways he had discovered to break the ice in this sort of situation— but he noticed that Dr. McCoy had stepped over to the table with him and was waving a medical scanner over the food, obviously checking to make sure nothing there was poisonous, so Scotty held out the fruit and let him scan that, too. He nearly dropped it when the instrument beeped and a red light glowed on its top. The beep stopped a moment later, though, and the light changed to green. Molecular diagrams scrolled across the device's tiny display window.

Puzzled, McCoy scanned the fruit again, then he took it from Scotty and scanned it a third time, slowly rotating the stripes one at a time past the business end of the instrument. It beeped and blinked red and green once for each stripe.

The Grand General noticed his interest and said, "Ah, I see you've found the Palkos."

"Is that what you call them?" McCoy looked up at his crewmates. "This is incredible. According to my readings, this little fruit contains one of the most powerful nerve toxins I've ever seen."

"Nerve toxin?" Scotty asked, his palms suddenly sweating. He wiped the hand he'd picked up the Palko with on his pants leg, good manners be damned.

"It's a binary toxin," McCoy said. "It's got two separate nontoxic components, one in each colored stripe. Individually, neither one is dangerous, but mix 'em and you'd be dead before you took a second bite." He took a tricorder reading of the Grand General and said, "So would you, but I assume you know that already."

Scotty couldn't help himself. "Good god, man," he said to the Grand General, "you put something like that on a banquet table?"

"Of course." The General took another Palko from the bowl, tossed it into the air, and caught it. "It's a delicacy."

"You actually *eat* them?" Scotty asked, incredulous.

"Oh yes."

"How?"

The Grand General smiled. "Funny you should ask." He rapped the Palko hard against the table, and the entire fruit burst apart like a flower opening up into alternating purple and white petals. "Now," he said, separating out one of each color, "if you were a Distrellian, you would eat the purple ones. And if you were a Prastorian, you would eat . . . ?" He looked at the *Enterprise* crew members like a schoolteacher waiting for a particularly easy response.

"The white ones," Chekov supplied.

"Wrong!" said the Grand General. The people standing nearby laughed, and he smiled at Chekov to take the sting from his outburst. But he was obviously quite sincere as he said, "The Prastorians eat the purple ones too. Which means half the fruit goes to waste. Unconscionable! We have tried and tried to convince them to change their habits, but to no avail. They are a stubborn people."

"And you are not?" asked a new voice. Everyone turned to see another Nevisian approaching from the banquet hall's wide double doors. He was smaller than the Grand General of Distrel, and a few years younger, dressed in bright red from head to toe. Even the gloves tucked into his hind pocket were red. He smiled widely as he drew closer, then said, "You must be our guests from the Federation. I'm delighted to meet you; I'm Fareen Berg Gren Orondo Arnitas, the Padishah of Prastor."

"I'm James Kirk, captain of the *Enterprise,*" said Kirk, "and these are some of my crew members."

Scotty noted that Kirk skipped the middle initial that he often used when introducing himself. Apparently he didn't want to make it look like he was competing for lengthy names with these people. It would be a losing contest anyway.

The Grand General said, "I was just explaining to our guests the nature of our conflict." He was still holding the wedges of Palko fruit in his hand; he popped the purple one into his mouth and bit down on it with obvious enjoyment. "Here," he said, deftly picking out the rest of the purple ones from the pile on the table and handing them around. "Try one. They're really very good."

Chapter Three

KIRK REACHED GINGERLY for a slice of the fruit. He glanced toward Bones, who shrugged and took one himself. "Just don't eat any of the white ones for at least a week," Bones told him, "and you ought to be safe enough."

Kirk popped the wedge into his mouth and bit into it. Tart juice squirted out as his teeth broke through the crunchy skin, and an unfamiliar vapor made him inhale involuntarily, drawing its cool, not-quite-minty aroma into his sinuses. The flavor was something like a fresh apple, only sweeter, and with a much stronger aftertaste. Kirk could see why it would be considered a delicacy. It was wonderful, but too potent to eat very much of at one sitting.

And it was half of a binary nerve toxin. Kirk would have considered these aliens dangerously insane if he hadn't seen—even eaten—similar things on Earth. Like fugu, the Japanese dish made from the poisonous puffer fish, which still killed two or three people a year.

"Worth fighting over, eh?" asked the Padishah.

A nasty suspicion had been growing in Kirk's mind since the Grand General had made his remark about "the nature of our conflict." This confirmed it.

"You mean *this*—which half of the Palko to eat—is what you've been fighting about all this time?"

"Yes," said both planetary leaders. The Padishah went on. "It was a matter of principle. The white bits aren't as tasty, you see, so there was no way we Prastorians were willing to switch over unless the Distrellians did so as well."

"Which wouldn't have solved anything at all!" exclaimed the Grand General. "The only thing that would have accomplished would be to make us all eat the inferior pieces."

Kirk didn't even try to keep the sarcasm from his voice as he said, "So you fought over who would have to eat the white ones. Did it ever occur to you to try a rotating schedule? Or divide up your own populations into purple and white regions?"

"We're not stupid, Captain," said the Padishah. "Every conceivable alternative was tried and dismissed millennia ago. According to our oldest records, our ancestors even tried to eliminate the Palko bush—drive it into extinction—but of course each side kept its own private seed stock and after a few years they replanted and the same conflict arose again."

Kirk could only shake his head. It seemed so pointless, but then he wondered if that really made their war any more horrible. Had *any* war ever been worth it? They were all about something equally silly.

Which god you worshipped, or how you worshipped the same god, or whether a leader was inherited or elected. Or in the case of the Klingons, simply because they liked to fight.

Chekov broke his train of thought. "So what made you change your minds now?" he asked.

"We received an offer that was too good to refuse," said the Grand General.

"From whom?" asked Kirk.

"A friend of yours, actually," said the Grand General. "A master of diplomacy. He seems to share your knack for zeroing in directly to the heart of the matter. I've made him my political advisor."

"Where is he, anyway?" asked the Padishah. "I haven't seen him for some time."

"He was here just a few minutes ago, when the captain first called. Said he had to go straighten his cravat, I believe. But you know how he is. Punctuality isn't one of his strong suits."

The Padishah laughed. "Hah. True enough." He leaned close to Kirk as if imparting a deep, dark secret. "He seems rather fond of Nevisian women. Disappears for hours at a time with them. I'd be concerned for their reputations if it weren't for his chaperone, but she keeps a close eye on him. That is, when the Grand General isn't occupying her . . . ah, her time."

The Grand General colored slightly, and said, "I am merely trying to ensure that she enjoys her stay."

"I'm sure you are," said the Padishah.

"Gentlemen," Kirk interrupted. "Does this mystery friend of ours have a name?"

"Well, yes he does," said the Grand General. "Three of them. Soon to be four, but please don't tell him that. I'd like for it to be a surprise. And that of course is why I can't reveal his name to you just at the moment. He said he wanted to see the look on your face when you saw him, and I don't want to rob him of the pleasure." He turned to one of the women standing nearby and said, "Mistrae, my dear, could I trouble you to find my advisor? Tell him our guests have arrived."

"Certainly, General," she said. She walked out through the wide double doors at the end of the banquet hall, her voluminous dress billowing around her like a cloud as she walked.

Kirk watched her go, wondering what kind of problem would return through those doors with her. He no longer believed that this would be a pleasant surprise. No slap on the back from an academy classmate, no sultry "Hello, James," from an old lover, nor even a haughty "Nya-nya" from some self-righteous ambassador who might have ridden on the *Enterprise* to his first gig. Not with this kind of setup.

He leaned over to Spock and said softly, "I've got a bad feeling about this."

Spock nodded solemnly. "If I had feelings, they would undoubtedly parallel yours."

But neither of them were prepared for what actually came through the doors. First came the woman, Mistrae, looking quite amused. Then eight young men entered, bearing long, slender trumpets. They took up positions in two rows flanking the doors, and when they raised the trumpets toward one another, purple and white banners unfurled from the shafts. The men blew an elaborate fanfare, then crisply snapped the trumpets downward to stand at attention.

And in strolled a tall, overweight, nearly bald-headed man dressed in a billowy green shirt and loose gray pants, the legs of which had been tucked into the tops of his tall black boots. He had a wide, cherubic face, and an even wider black handlebar mustache. He had hooked his thumbs under his belt, and he swaggered like a king at his coronation.

Kirk recognized him instantly, by his mannerisms as well as his appearance. "Harry Mudd!" he exclaimed.

For indeed it was. The same Harry Mudd who had trafficked in beautiful women, "wiving settlers," as he called it, and who had nearly destroyed the *Enterprise* in the bargain. The same Harry Mudd who had later found a planet full of androids, and who had nearly trapped the *Enterprise* crew there as enslaved subjects for the androids to "serve." Oh yes, Kirk knew this man, though he devoutly wished he didn't.

But if Mudd sensed any of his animosity, he didn't show it. He just smiled broadly at Kirk and said in his booming, exuberant voice, "Harcourt, please. Harry is so . . . uncivilized."

"That's true enough," muttered Chekov.

"Ah, Mr. Chekov," Mudd said. "Clever as ever, I see. And the lovely Lieutenant Uhura. Certainly the most pleasant aspect of either of my stays on board the *Enterprise*. Thank you for accepting my invitation." He bowed deeply as he approached her, then caught her right hand on the upswing and brought it to his lips in a gentle kiss.

Uhura smiled wryly and said, "Hello, Harry. Good to see you again. I think."

Mudd chuckled. "Ah, such warmth and affection from my dear old friends. It truly warms my heart."

He turned to McCoy, and fluttering his right hand near his breastbone, said, "Stay near, good doctor. I may need your services if I become overwhelmed with emotion. And Mr. Scott. Your engines still look to be in tune." Mudd turned last toward Spock. "I know better than to expect an effusive greeting from you, sir, so allow me to greet you warmly for both of us." He grasped Spock's right hand and shook it enthusiastically—for about a second, until Spock tightened his muscles and his arm became as rigid as a steel beam. Mudd continued to shake for a moment, his whole body quivering with the effort, then he stopped and let go, saying, "As always, you're a veritable pillar of friendship, Mr. Spock."

The Nevisians—and Dr. McCoy—laughed at Mudd's antics, but Spock's reply was direct and to the point. "How did you escape from the android planet?"

As punishment for his role in capturing the *Enterprise* for the androids, Kirk and his crew had left Mudd there when they escaped—with five hundred android copies of his nagging wife, Stella, to make sure he got into no more trouble.

"Well," said Mudd, turning to Kirk, "the terms of my stay there were that I would be free to go when I was no longer an . . . 'irritant' I believe you called it. Of course since I never *was* an *irritant*, it was a simple matter of arranging for transportation once I decided to take my leave."

Kirk knew how to interpret Mudd's statements. Arranging for transportation meant . . . "You stole another ship," he said.

"Nothing of the sort!" Mudd protested indignantly.

"The androids provided me with one the moment I asked."

"And what sort of deviltry have you been up to since then?"

Mudd looked to the Grand General. "Ah, such kidders. You can see why I love them so, can't you? Well, Kirk, my boy, sorry to disappoint you, but this is my first stop. I heard about these people's terrible misunderstanding, and I hurried here as soon as I could to offer my services."

Kirk was almost afraid to ask, but curiosity wouldn't let him not. "What services?"

"Why, the exclusive distribution of Palko fruit to the rest of the galaxy, of course. Only the white halves, to be sure, but that still nets a substantial profit, of which the Nevisians get a perfectly equitable fifty percent."

McCoy said, "You're selling half of a binary nerve toxin to unsuspecting customers? That's against—"

"Unsuspecting? Doctor, why would I let such an opportunity for profit go untapped? Of *course* I told my customers of the danger. That allowed me to triple the price I would otherwise have gotten."

Kirk supposed that was probably true. Only someone like Mudd would have thought of it, and only Mudd would have stopped an interplanetary war in order to make the deal, but it sounded as if he might actually be telling the truth this time. The truth according to Harry Mudd, of course. Kirk knew that stopping the war had never been his first priority—profit was Mudd's *only* priority—but the result was apparently the same.

"The only problem with all this, Harry," said Kirk, "is that you've violated the Prime Directive."

"Prime Directive?" Harry picked up another Palko fruit and rapped it on the table. When it fell apart into sections, he selected a purple slice and ate it.

"Starfleet's General Order Number One," Kirk told him, "forbidding interference with a society's development."

Mudd smacked his lips noisily, then said, "The key word there, old friend, is 'Starfleet.' I'm not a member of Starfleet. Your General Order Number One doesn't apply to me. But you, on the other hand, had better mind your P's and Q's." He leaned close as if imparting a secret, but his whisper could be heard across the banquet hall. "Your clothing, for instance, might start a fashion revolution. Haberdashery could become the dominant economic force and spark a political overthrow. Really, Captain, I'm surprised you're not more careful."

The Nevisians laughed, and Kirk took a deep breath. He had been trying to control his temper ever since he'd seen that the mystery "friend" was Mudd. What was it about that man that made him so angry? It would be easier to ask what didn't. The man *was* an irritant, a major one, and a liar and a cheat as well. Everything he stood for grated Kirk, but mocking the Starfleet uniform was just too much.

"It's you who should be more careful, Harry," said Kirk. "A man with outstanding arrest warrants on half a dozen planets shouldn't be needling a Starfleet officer. Even if I can't haul you in for violating the Prime Directive, I could arrest and detain you for plenty of other crimes—including a capital offense on Deneb-Five, if I remember correctly."

That one stung—Kirk could see Mudd start to sweat a bit, but the con man in him immediately went into damage-control mode. Rolling his eyes upward in a pained, I-can't-believe-it expression, he said, "Really, Captain, I'd have thought you were above the spreading of false rumors, for of course that's all they are." To the Grand General he said, "The Mudd family has been the target of slander for nearly four hundred years, ever since an ancestor of mine—a prominent physician—attempted to save the life of a national president who had been shot. He was prevented from performing his duties, and then falsely accused of allowing the wounded president to die. Mudds have had to endure these attacks on our character ever since, but we have learned to ignore them and continue our good work throughout the galaxy."

Kirk nearly gagged on Mudd's self-righteous schmaltz. He said, "What you did has nothing to do with Lincoln. I'm talking about forgery, smuggling, theft, unauthorized sale of technology, impersonating a—"

"All unproven," interrupted Mudd. "Every one of those . . . misunderstandings . . . has been cleared up. In the case of the Denebians, I have even made restitution at my own expense rather than prolong any bad feelings by insisting on a formal review in court."

"Rather than face the death penalty, you mean," Kirk said.

Mudd shook his head sadly. "Captain, if you don't control yourself I believe I may have to charge *you* with slander, simply to protect my good name."

This really was too much. Kirk unclipped his communicator from his belt and flipped it open. "Okay, Harry, I'll call your bluff. Kirk to *Enterprise*."

"Enterprise here." Kirk recognized the voice of Ensign Jolley, Uhura's backup in communications.

Kirk said, "I want you to search our latest Starfleet records on Harry Mudd. Look for outstanding warrants for his arrest."

"Yes, sir. Checking," said Jolley. Kirk and the others from the *Enterprise,* and the Nevisians as well, waited uncomfortably for the report, but Mudd merely smiled and ate another purple wedge of Palko fruit.

His smile faltered momentarily when a shrill voice from beyond the doorway called out, "Harcourt!" but he gave no other sign of discomfort when a hatchet-faced, red-haired human woman dressed all in black stepped into the banquet hall and screeched, "Harcourt Fenton Mudd, what have you been up to now? *There* you are, you elusive rascal. You should know better than to try to give the slip to me. I can track you through solid—" She stopped when she saw the *Enterprise* officers, then said more quietly, "Hello."

"Hello, Stella," said Kirk, squinting to see what number she was. This had to be one of the android copies of Mudd's ex-wife, still watching over him even though they had let him off the planet. That made much more sense than Mudd's version of the story. But if this was an android, it had removed the numbered necklace they usually wore to distinguish multiple copies of themselves. Could there be only this one?

Stella walked up to the group and eyed everyone coldly, but her expression softened incrementally when the Grand General took her hand and said,

"Ah, Estelle my dear, I'm so glad you could join us again. These are our guests from the *Enterprise.*"

"We've met," said Kirk.

The android—if that's who this was—made no objection to his statement. She merely turned to Mudd and said, wagging her finger in his face in time with her words, "Just when I was beginning to trust you, you sent me off on a wild goose chase. There was no Denebian slime devil in our quarters. I—"

Mudd laughed. "Of course there wasn't, my little fussbudget. I merely wanted to greet the captain without your matchless beauty distracting him. But now that you've arrived, I'm as grateful as ever for your presence." He looked straight at Kirk as he said that, and Kirk winced at the tone in his voice. Maybe marooning him with five hundred copies of her had been a bit extreme.

The Grand General certainly seemed taken with her, however. He continued to hold her hand, and his prominent eyes followed her every move. There was no accounting for alien taste, Kirk thought.

His communicator beeped, and he said, "Kirk here."

"No outstanding warrants, sir," Jolley said. "I do have an annotation from Vulcan planetary security that they would like to hire him as a consultant if he would consent to tell them how he breached their computer network, but that's the only current activity in his file."

Kirk turned to Spock, not bothering to wipe the incredulous expression from his face. "Vulcan would *hire* him rather than charge him with data piracy?"

Spock said impassively, "The best method for stopping piracy is often to hire the pirates. As distasteful as it may seem in this instance, it *is* a logical course of action."

"Logic be damned," Kirk said. "This man is a menace to the Federation, and whether or not you know it yet, Grand General, he's a menace to the Nevis system as well. I'd advise you to—"

"Vendikar," Mudd said quietly. "Eminiar VII."

Alarm bells rang in Kirk's mind. "How do you know about that?" he demanded.

"Tsk, tsk, tsk," Mudd said, shaking his head sadly. "Certainly you wouldn't want me to compromise my information sources. But if you keep ranting on with these slanderous accusations, I'm afraid I'll have to mention your unfortunate breach of discipline on those planets to the proper authorities."

Chekov pushed forward and said belligerently, "The captain didn't do anything wrong on Vendikar. He—"

"That will be enough, Mr. Chekov," Kirk said quickly. The last thing he needed was his hotheaded navigator complicating the issue. To Mudd he said, "All right, Harry, we'll do it your way. We've got time."

"Do what my way?" Mudd asked. "Time for what?"

"Time to let your true colors show." To the Grand General Kirk said, "Give him enough rope and he'll eventually hang himself with it. But he has a knack for taking everyone around him down, too. I'd suggest keeping an eye on him."

The Grand General smiled. "I keep my eye on everyone, Captain. Including you. But really, I must insist that you put aside your differences while you are here. Distrel and Prastor are celebrating the end of millennia of war; certainly you and Mr. Mudd can find it in your heart to make peace as well, can't you?"

Mudd grinned at Kirk. "I have no quarrel with you, Captain, even though you stranded me—quite illegally I might add—on a planet full of androids. Forgive and forget, I always say." He held out his hand to shake.

Kirk stared at the proffered hand, then looked up at Mudd's face. His cherubic baby cheeks and thick handlebar mustache seemed like a mockery in themselves even without the silly grin to go with them. Could Kirk actually shake hands with this con man? It looked like he would have to, for Mudd showed no sign of dropping his arm any time soon, and the longer he waited the worse it made Kirk look. So Kirk reached out and clasped Mudd's sweaty hand. "All right, Harry," he said. "Let's give it a fresh start. And may the best man win."

Chapter Four

LIEUTENANT UHURA'S ATTENTION drifted toward the other Nevisians in the hall. She was glad of the distraction they provided from Mudd's and the captain's argument. Not that it was unimportant, but she hated conflict and there wasn't much she could do about this one anyway. Besides, this was a perfect opportunity to learn more about another alien race. Even though they looked almost human, the Nevisians would no doubt have plenty of fascinating differences to intrigue a xenophile like Uhura. She loved to learn the customs and mannerisms of the beings she met in her travels. That was one of the reasons she had joined Starfleet in the first place.

She turned away from the group around the banquet table and sought out the nearest friendly face. It was sometimes dangerous to assume that a smile meant someone was approachable, especially with a race that differed so much from humans in facial characteristics, but the woman the Grand General had called Mistrae had smiled and laughed before at all the right times, so Uhura figured she was safe enough to assume at least no hostility in the expression. She stepped closer to her and said softly, "Your gown is beautiful."

"Thank you," said Mistrae, dipping her head slightly. "I had it made especially for today."

It was a light blue, floor-length dress, very full below the waist and somewhat tighter above, though the shoulders and elbows puffed out in loose folds. The whole thing was made of heavy velvet or something similar, but it must not have been uncomfortably warm because Mistrae seemed perfectly at ease in it.

"Is it a Distrellian or a Prastorian design?" Uhura asked.

Mistrae looked at her with a puzzled expression, and Uhura knew she had made her first mistake.

"Or do both planets have the same styles?" she amended quickly.

Mistrae said, "Aside from the color differences, you mean? I suppose there are a few variations in the way things fit, but you get used to them so quickly you don't even notice after the first few days. There's so much else to think about."

"I see," said Uhura, not at all sure that she did. "Which planet are you from?"

Again Mistrae gave her that look. "Originally, you mean? I started out on Prastor, but I'm a Distrellian now. I have been for nine years. I was only twelve when soldiers from Distrel attacked my home and killed my entire family, so most of my adult years have been spent here."

The woman spoke so matter-of-factly that Uhura didn't know how to respond. Sympathy seemed out of place, so she asked, "Were you kidnapped?"

"I fought honorably," Mistrae said, her words cold and precise. "As did the soldiers who attacked us. There were no captives."

Uhura lowered her head. "Excuse me if I have given offense. I just didn't understand why you came to Distrel after Distrellian soldiers killed your family."

"I had no choice," Mistrae said, as if explaining to a child why people breathe.

It still made no sense to Uhura. Mistrae wasn't kidnapped, yet she had no choice but to come here. Was there an economic reason? Some deep-seated custom? Or had she infiltrated the enemy's seat of government as a spy? Uhura wished she could ask, but she had already pushed too far for a casual conversation at a social gathering. One more mistake could cause a bigger scene than the one between the captain and Harry Mudd.

"You mentioned color differences between planetary clothing styles," Uhura said, hoping that would be safer ground. "Could you tell me more about how that works?"

Mistrae seemed relieved to get to a safer topic as well. She nodded and said, "Oh, it's quite simple, really. Prastorians wear red, orange, or brown, and Distrellians wear blue, yellow, or green. That makes it much easier to tell who you're shooting at in battle."

Wonderful, thought Uhura. They couldn't agree on what part of the Palko to eat, but they could agree on which colors to wear so they would make better targets. These people might appear human on the outside, but inside they were pure alien.

This wasn't quite the party Chekov had envisioned. Not at the moment, anyway. The Nevisians had apparently been enjoying themselves quite handily before the *Enterprise* crew showed up, but this business with Harry Mudd had derailed things. Chekov considered it his duty to get the festivities back on the right track, but he wasn't yet sure how to accomplish that. In some cultures one simply challenged someone else to a drinking match or started throwing food, but in others one had to proceed a bit more carefully.

And judging from Uhura's and Mistrae's conversation, this was one of those places where it was better to err on the side of caution. He felt bad for Uhura, whose every move seemed to drag her deeper into trouble, but he doubted if he would have fared much better. They may have learned the Nevisians' language, but they had definitely not learned their customs. Mistrae's take on things seemed nearly unpredictable. But Chekov thought he might have discovered the key to understanding her unusual attitude, so when Uhura paused to gather her wits after Mistrae's latest surprise, Chekov stepped forward and said, "Excuse me, but I couldn't help overhearing your conversation. After all these millennia of war, you must have many glorious tales of battle."

Talking with aliens about war was one of the first things a cadet was warned against in the academy. Uhura gave Chekov a look of alarm, but that quickly melted to gratitude when Mistrae nodded and said, "Oh yes, of course."

"Do you have a favorite?" Chekov asked. "One of your own, perhaps?"

Mistrae blushed prettily and said, "No, my little skirmish was nothing spectacular. My family was caught completely by surprise, and we barely had time to defend ourselves before we were . . . overwhelmed. I fought hard enough to win my passage to Distral, but I didn't kill even one of our attackers. Not like Ginn Donan."

Taking his cue from the tone of reverence in her voice, Chekov said, "Ginn Donan. Now that sounds like a heroic name."

Mistrae nodded eagerly. "His full name was Ginn Donan Garreft Hap Elod Griff Ab Iandor."

A bit hesitantly, Uhura asked, "Did he win all those names for heroism in battle?"

"Three of them," Mistrae said. "The most anyone has ever earned. The first, Ginn, he received when he defeated seven trained Prastorian warriors who made a suicide raid against the Grand General of Distrel." She smiled toward the planetary leader and said, "This was a different Grand General, many thousands of years ago. Ginn was only eleven at the time, a ceremonial honor guard in training, but he kept his sword sharp and he used it when it was needed. When the official guards all fell to the Prastorians, he stood atop their bodies so he would be tall enough to fight and he killed them one by one as they tried to gain entry to the Grand General's audience chamber."

"Impressive," Chekov said, wondering how much of it was true.

"Indeed," said Mistrae. "The name Donan he earned a year later, as personal bodyguard to the Grand General, when he learned that one of the General's concubines was a Prastorian spy." Warming to her subject, she spoke louder and waved her arms for emphasis as she said, "The woman knew her secret had been discovered, so she went to the General before Donan could warn him and attempted to murder him in his sleep, but Donan burst in on them both and slew her just as she drew her scarf around the Grand General's neck to strangle him."

Uhura said, "So the General gave him another name for saving his life again."

"Not that time," said Mistrae. "The General was furious at Ginn for killing his favorite concubine, even if she was a spy, and embarrassed at being caught in so vulnerable a position, so he had Ginn beheaded the following day."

Chekov shook his head sadly. "Too many loyal soldiers earn their medals posthumously. But if he won two more names, then the people must have protested the way Ginn Donan was treated and forced the Grand General to honor him, yes?"

"No, no," said Mistrae. "This is the best part. Ginn won his names himself. He returned with a Prastorian army, stormed the castle, and killed the Grand General in hand-to-hand combat. Then he declared himself the new Grand General and ruled Distrel wisely for twenty years before he was in turn betrayed by a spy and went to his just reward in Arnhall."

That would be kind of hard for a beheaded man to do, thought Chekov, but he merely said, "That is quite a story. It reminds me of the way an ancestor of mine, the Czar Romanov, returned to Russia after long exile to lead his people away from socialism. Everyone had thought he was dead, too, but it had all been cleverly faked, so when he returned under the name of Gorbachev and—"

A loud *clang* from just a few feet away stopped Chekov in midtale. He turned to see what had happened, his hand dropping instinctively to his side for his phaser, but he was not armed. The two men who had startled him certainly were; they faced each other with their half-meter ceremonial swords drawn. One wore a bright blue shirt, the other bright orange. Apparently the friction between Distrellians and Prastorians wasn't entirely over yet. They didn't cross blades again, though, merely held their position while the one in blue said, "We need room," and the people nearest them backed away.

The Grand General stepped forward instead. "Here, here," he said jovially, "what's this all about? We're at peace now."

The Prastorian said, "This man insulted Ginn Donan."

"In what way?"

"I called him an opportunistic traitor," said the Distrellian. "He abused his knowledge of the Grand General's palace to stage an assassination and take power for himself. That is not the act of a hero."

The two men continued to hold their swords ready, but Chekov relaxed. Everyone else seemed interested but hardly excited about the situation; evidently this was some ritual way of settling arguments here in the Nevis system.

But moments later he realized how wrong he had read the situation. The Grand General said, "You are of course entitled to your opinion, and it looks like you're prepared to defend it with honor. I approve your duel, but please, move a bit farther from the table. We don't want blood on the roast smeerp."

The men obligingly stepped away from the table, moving together as precisely as a drill team at a parade. Their swords never wavered while they moved, nor when they froze into position again.

"Padishah," said the Prastorian. "I would be honored if you would give the signal."

"General?" asked the Padishah, deferring to his host.

"Certainly," said the Grand General, stepping aside.

The Padishah stepped forward—but not too close, Chekov noted—and said, "I charge you to fight for honor . . . for glory . . . for Ginn Donan—or not, as the case may be. Begin."

With a sudden clang of swords, the men immediately sprang into battle.

Dr. McCoy fought down his revulsion as he readied his medical kit. Somebody was going to need help soon, though by the looks of it the loser would need nothing more than a burial plot. This was no ritual staged for entertainment; these men were serious.

Actually, they were both hardly more than boys. Barely twenty, if human developmental standards applied here.

Neither one was very good with a sword. McCoy had seen some true masters in his travels, people who could slice the clothing off their opponent without touching the skin, but these two merely hacked away at one another like jungle guides clearing a path.

Sparks flew from their blades when they blocked each other, and blood welled from cuts when they didn't.

The people watching them didn't seem to care if they were masters or amateurs. They cheered at every stroke no matter which man made the attack. The issue they fought for seemed forgotten; only the fight mattered now.

After the first few opening jabs and parries, the Prastorian got in a lucky slice across the Distrellian's chest, opening his blue shirt and cutting deep into his pectoral muscles just below his collarbones. The Distrellian cried out in pain and lunged forward to counterattack, but his injury made him slow to raise his sword and the Prastorian easily blocked it. Blocked and then counterattacked; his sword bit deep into the Distrellian's side. The Distrellian fell to his knees, bright red blood leaving purple streaks on his shirt. He tried to rise again and continue to fight, but he couldn't get his feet under him, and a moment later he toppled to his side. His sword clattered to the floor.

The Prastorian raised his sword in victory—or so it seemed for a second, but then McCoy saw the muscles in his arms tensing and realized he was about to administer the coup de grâce.

"Hold it!" The words burst forth before McCoy had a chance to think about it. He rushed forward and caught the surprised Prastorian's arm. "You don't have to kill him," McCoy told him roughly. "You've won your battle already. Now let me save his life."

Without waiting for a response, he bent down to examine the injured boy. Multiple lacerations, two major veins severed, muscles and tendons irreparably damaged—and lifeblood gushing out of every wound. McCoy removed the portable protoplaser from his medical kit and trained it on the largest bleeders first, force-healing the blood vessels and staunching the flow.

The Distrellian had been in shock; now with returning strength came sensation. The pain must have been tremendous. "No . . . let me die," the boy said weakly, trying to push McCoy away.

"Nonsense," McCoy said, brushing his hand aside. "You aren't going to die. I've healed worse injuries than this." That was true enough, but it hadn't been on a banquet-hall floor with portable instruments. Fortunately the injured boy was young and resilient. Young and foolish as well, but the operative word was "young." He could take a lot of punishment and still have strength left to heal. McCoy continued passing the protoplaser over his wounds for a few more seconds; then, when he had stabilized his condition at least momentarily, he took his hypospray from the medical kit and gave him a shot for the pain.

"Why are you doing this to me?" the boy asked, his tone of voice clearly accusing McCoy of violating his person.

McCoy didn't let it faze him. "Because I can't stand to see people die for nothing," he said. He heard a gasp of indrawn breath, looked up and saw the crowd gathered around them, and said, "Stand back. Give him some breathing air here." To Kirk he said, "Jim, I need to get him back to the ship to do a proper job. He'll be a mess of scars if I don't use better equipment to close these wounds."

"Right," said Kirk. He took his communicator

from his belt and flipped it open, but the Grand General put a hand on his arm.

"No," he said. "You've done enough damage. At least leave him his scars to prove that he fought bravely for his honor."

McCoy looked from the Grand General to the boy, who nodded and whispered, "Please."

"That's ridiculous," McCoy said. "You don't have to walk around with a road map across your chest. There are better ways to prove your worth."

"Yes," said the Distrellian boy. "I could have died and been halfway to Arnhall by now if you hadn't interfered."

McCoy looked up at the crowd again. Everyone but the *Enterprise* crew wore hostile expressions. These Nevisians were worse than Klingons.

But they had made the first step away from all that, hadn't they?

"Look," McCoy said, standing, "I know it's a stretch after twelve thousand years of war, but you're going to have to learn to live without violence now. And the first concept you need to understand is reverence for life. You can't just go around killing people because they insulted somebody, and you can't throw your life away for nothing anymore. There are more important things than—"

"That is enough," said the Grand General. His voice echoed in the immense hall. "We do not criticize your . . . your *Federation* behavior; kindly show us the same courtesy."

"Don't everybody thank me at once," McCoy muttered. He looked down at the boy, who had at least quit bleeding, and slowly put away his protoplaser

45

and hypospray. "All right, you can have your scars if you want 'em. If you change your mind, you know where to find me." He looked over at the other swordsman, who backed warily away even though he still bled from his wounds. "I guess it would be a waste of time to even ask if you wanted any help."

Harry Mudd was shaking his head and making cluck-cluck noises with his tongue. "Doctor," he said gravely, "I'm surprised at your callous disregard for local customs." However, his expression was anything but grave. He looked smug as a cat with a mouse by the tail as he turned to Kirk and said, "And you, Captain. If you can't control your officers, I'm afraid I have no recourse but to ask you to leave."

Chapter Five

KIRK FELT the fleeting wish that he and Mudd were both Nevisians. He would love to challenge this overblown, self-aggrandizing *irritant* to a duel, slice him to ribbons, and then see what he thought of McCoy's "callous disregard for local customs." But even though Kirk could outfight him with one hand tied to his opposite foot, Mudd had the advantage here and Kirk knew it. And even if they had been Nevisians, Mudd would no doubt find a way to weasel out of a duel—and somehow make Kirk look bad in the process. He was the slipperiest con artist Kirk had ever met. He'd even managed to somehow foist his android chaperone off on the Grand General, further ingratiating the planetary leader to him in the bargain.

So Kirk swallowed his indignation and—ignoring Mudd—said to the Grand General, "Dr. McCoy didn't mean to offend anyone. He's trained to save people's lives, no matter who or where."

The Grand General wasn't mollified. "That may be fine where you come from, but here in the Nevis system people die with honor."

McCoy opened his mouth to protest, but Kirk waved him to silence. They'd gotten into enough trouble here. "We die with honor too," Kirk said, "when the time is right. Apparently we disagree on when it's appropriate, but with only one life to give we don't want to throw it away lightly."

"Perhaps if you had Arnhall to look forward to, you wouldn't be so choosy," said the Grand General.

That sounded like a religious reference to Kirk. If he'd learned anything in his years in Starfleet, it was never to get into a religious discussion with an alien, so he simply said, "Maybe so. In any case, we didn't mean to put a damper on your celebration. Please accept our—"

"Careful, Kirk," interrupted Mudd. "If you were about to say 'apology,' you should know a few more things about the local customs." Tucking his thumbs into his wide black belt, he puffed out his ample stomach even farther than usual and said, "An apology is an admission of wrongdoing, which requires automatic punishment." He paused dramatically before saying, "And the sentence is, of course, death. So think it over, Captain. Still feel like apologizing?"

Mudd had to be kidding. A society where nobody could apologize? Why, every little mishap could lead to a fight, and every fight to a feud. Global war could erupt over something as silly as . . . as which half of a Palko to eat. And it could last for twelve thousand years.

But something like that would have been in the first-contact files, wouldn't it? In big, bold type: **Never apologize to a Nevisian.** It should have been, but it wasn't. Kirk could imagine half a dozen reasons why not, ranging from inadequate research to lack of survivors to report it.

"No," he said quietly. "Under the circumstances, I don't think an apology is called for."

Mudd nodded. "I thought you might see it that way. You owe me one, Kirk."

Much as it galled him to admit it, Kirk supposed he did. But Mudd wasted no time in evening the score. He turned to the Grand General and said, "For their own good, I think we ought to send them back to their ship before they get into more serious trouble."

"I agree," said the Grand General, obviously still stinging from the perceived insult. He said to Kirk, "Captain, please remove yourself and your people. If you and Harcourt wish to continue your visit, you can do so on board your ship."

Kirk laughed out loud at the thought. "No, thanks," he said. "If I have anything more to say to *Harry,* I'll send him a letter. By smoke signal." He turned to his crew. "Come on. The party's over."

Ensign Lebrun knew something was wrong the moment her new husband entered their quarters after his shift. She had beat him home by a few minutes after her own day in security was over, and had been waiting with the lights turned down low.

"What's the matter, lover?" she asked, rising from her chair by the viewport, where she'd been watching the planet spin below. She held out her arms for him, eager to welcome him home. It was still so new to have him actually living with her; she'd been day-dreaming about how it would be when he arrived, how she would rub the stiffness from his muscles and how they would relax together before dinner, maybe have a drink and talk about their day or maybe just stare into each other's eyes for a while.

But the fantasy started to crumble as soon as she saw his tired expression, and it fell apart even more when he avoided her arms and gave her a quick peck on the cheek, then slumped down heavily into the chair she had just vacated.

"What is it?" she asked, a little less compassionately than before.

"Oh, nothing," he said. "Mr. Scott got back early from that party down below, and he caught me reprogramming the warp panel to flash like it was about to blow up on him next time he asked the computer for a routine systems check."

"You *what*?" asked Lebrun. "Simon, that's *dangerous.*"

"That's what Scotty said, too. Among other things." He sighed heavily.

"What did you do such a dumb thing like that for, anyway?" she asked him.

He looked up at her and grinned weakly. "To get back at him for that ridiculous stunt he pulled with your ring. I couldn't let him get away with that, now, could I?"

She shook her head. "Well, no, but reprogramming the warp panel isn't the way to do it. What if we'd had a genuine emergency? We could have all been—"

"Whose side are you on, anyway?" he asked petulantly.

"Whose side are *you* on?" she demanded right back. "You could have blown us all up over a stupid practical joke."

"For crying out loud, I wouldn't have blown anything up." He got up from his chair and stomped into the kitchen. Lebrun heard him dialing for something to drink, and he came back out with a tumbler of something thick and purple.

"Is that Cetian laliska again?" she asked, though she knew already that it was. Its pungent odor, like garlic and vinegar, was impossible to miss. "You know I don't like the way that makes your breath smell."

"So don't sit close," he told her, settling pointedly into the farthest chair from her at the dining table. Even though there was a coaster right there in front of him, he set the glass directly on the tabletop, leaving a ring from the condensation that ran down its side.

Her fantasy was irreparably shattered. No quiet evening staring fondly into his eyes, no backrubs turning slowly into quiet lovemaking—just this tired irritability and spiteful reaction to everything she said. She stood before him with her hands on her hips, breathing hard and trying not to let herself explode when he took another long drink of his laliska.

"Simon Nordell," she said at last, "is this the way you really want it to be?"

"Me?" He looked at her indignantly. "Why is it always my fault? You're the one who started in with the questions the moment I came through the door."

"All I asked was what was wrong."

"And I told you. Now could I relax for a minute without the security debriefing?"

Security. Every time she tried to be assertive, he blamed it on her job. As if she couldn't show any personal strength on her own.

"Fine," she said, suddenly making up her mind. She stepped into their bedroom and tugged the top cover off the bed, then went back out and flung it onto the couch. "Relax all you want, but you can do it right there, because that's where you're spending the night." She went back into the bedroom, punched the privacy button, and as the door slid shut between them shouted, "And you'd better not try coming in here without an apology."

Whatever he said in reply didn't make it through the room's soundproofing.

She sat on the edge of the bed, suddenly conscious of just how small a starship bedroom was, even in a two-person cabin. And it was a long time until bedtime.

As her breathing slowed, she wondered: Would he come knock on the door? He had *better*. Otherwise it was going to be a lonely night for both of them.

Spock settled into his chair at the bridge's science station, ready for a long evening of data analysis. The Nevis system was astronomically unusual enough that a few hours of observations would no doubt reveal a great deal about the ability of double star systems to support life-bearing planets, and Prastor and Distrel were also interesting in their own right. Two inhabited planets in the same system would provide a wonderful laboratory to study the parallel evolution of both geographic and biological aspects of living worlds. Yet the earlier contact teams had made only the most rudimentary of sensor sweeps. The computer records contained only low-resolution surface maps, and demographic information was even sketchier.

Spock had already made some interesting discoveries. For instance, there was a very good sensor web around both planets, and even scattered through interplanetary space between them. It was apparently a sophisticated information-gathering system, a spy network that, judging from the sensor capability, could track every living being on either planet or in transit between the two. It was no doubt the result of escalating defense technology, but the duration of the conflict in this system bore testimony to its ineffectiveness in preventing attack.

Even so, its very existence underscored the value of a careful survey. The sensor web bespoke a high level of technology, high enough to affect other cultures now that the Nevisians had begun trading. Whether or not they ever planned on joining the Federation—a prospect that seemed somewhat dimmer after the unfortunate first meeting in the Distrellian leader's banquet hall—it never hurt to gain as much information as possible about an alien race's planetary resources or technological and economic capabilities. It might even help the next people who dealt with them to avoid some of the mistakes that the *Enterprise* crew had made.

Spock wondered how much of the trouble they had encountered could have been avoided had they gone down to the surface with better information. Perhaps some of it, but with Harry Mudd complicating the issue something would undoubtedly have happened sooner or later no matter how well briefed they had been. Mudd had almost certainly been waiting for his chance to get back at Kirk and Spock for thwarting his earlier schemes and leaving him a prisoner of the androids; he would have engineered an excuse to throw them off the planet if one hadn't arisen naturally.

Of course that couldn't have been his original intention when he had come to the Nevis system. Mudd couldn't have known that the *Enterprise* would be sent to investigate the results of his trade agreement. He had undoubtedly come here primarily to establish himself as the middleman and skim off half the profit from the sale of Palko fruit, and he had merely taken advantage of the opportunity to settle the score with his old antagonists when it had been presented to him.

That still left the question of the Stella android. What was she doing here? Watching over Mudd, of course, but the androids could have done that just as well on their home planet. They would never have let him go even with a chaperone unless they had a good reason to do so.

Unless he had reformed, Spock admitted. That *was* the sole condition of his release. Logic demanded that Spock at least consider the possibility. But not even logic could make him believe it. It would be easier to believe that the stars could spontaneously rearrange themselves to spell out messages in Klingon.

Mudd could, however, have convinced the androids that he had reformed. This might be a supervised test on their part, to see how he behaved in galactic society before they released him completely. That would be easy enough to check; Spock activated his communicator and hailed the Distrellian Grand General's palace.

"This is science officer Spock aboard the *Enter-*

prise," he told the woman who answered. "I wish to speak with Stella Mudd."

"One moment please." The woman consulted a monitor outside of camera range, then looked back up at Spock. "I'm sorry, sir, but she is in private conference with the Grand General. Would you like to leave a message?"

Did he? Spock considered the implications. If Mudd discovered that Spock wished to speak with his chaperone before the android did, then Harry could order it to answer untruthfully. He did, after all, have limited control over it, even though it wouldn't let him go free. No, it would defeat the purpose of asking the android for information if Mudd had time to prepare it for questioning.

"No, thank you," said Spock. "I will try again later."

He broke the connection and leaned back in his chair. He supposed he could send a message to the androids' home planet, but at this distance it would take even longer to get a reply than simply waiting for the local Stella to become available.

Private conference with the Grand General? It was late evening at the palace. What sort of conference would the Distrellian leader need with a Stella android at that hour?

Unless of course he wasn't aware she was an android. He *had* seemed quite interested in her at the party. Perhaps he was trying to initiate a dalliance with her, or even steal her away from Harry.

From what Spock had seen of her behavior and attitudes, that would be an . . . interesting prospect. He nearly smiled at the thought.

Chapter Six

HARRY WASN'T SMILING. He mopped the sweat from his forehead with his silk handkerchief, then peered cautiously around the corner and down the dimly lit stone hallway. Nobody there, though by now he would be hard pressed to say where *there* was. The Grand General's palace was a veritable honeycomb of corridors and levels, leading deep underground and far past the outer walls of the compound on the surface. Mudd had spent the last half hour exploring ever farther downward, looking for secret passageways or locked rooms that might indicate hidden treasure beyond, but he had found everything here depressingly open and mundane. Storage rooms filled with old tax records, ancient furniture stacked haphazardly to the ceilings, dusty paintings of rulers deceased for millennia, but not a hint of anything more exotic.

What was it with these Nevisians? Had they no

imagination? These were the cellars of the Grand Palace; surely there must be some planetary secrets stowed here.

If so, they were well disguised. And the one secret that Mudd most wanted to find seemed best hidden of all. He had found absolutely no clue that it even existed, much less where it might be, and he had already spent far too much time searching for it. Fortune had smiled on him in making the android Stella resemble the Grand General's first concubine, killed years ago in one of this hellish planet's incessant battles, but even the Grand General's infatuation with her could only distract her for so long. She would eventually come to check on Harry, and he didn't want her to find him here.

It would be embarrassing enough if someone from the palace found him. Fortunately the vault was on the ground floor where the Grand General could show off his riches to visitors without inconveniencing them on stairs, so nobody could accuse Mudd of going after the family jewels. Also, the party upstairs was winding down and most of the Prastorians had gone home, so the staff was busy cleaning up the detritus of the week-long bacchanalia, but there might still be guards protecting whatever was stored down here. And Mudd had trespassed far beyond the point where he could reasonably claim to have just taken a wrong turn on the way to the bathroom. He would have to feign drunkenness, or even total dementia, if he were accosted now.

And all for what? Tax records and a few antique chairs? This was ridiculous. Worse than that; it was downright insulting. He hadn't stopped a war and set up an interplanetary distribution system just to start a fruit-sales network. He was after much bigger game here.

He'd had plenty of time to study the androids' records during his incarceration with them. They had been in this sector of the galaxy for over a million years; even though they weren't programmed to explore on their own, they had amassed considerable information about people who had visited *them*. And one of the most intriguing records concerned a group of Nevisians who had visited the androids over thirteen thousand years ago. A thousand years *before* they had gone to war with each other. They had been a younger, more exuberant race then, swaggering out into the local region of space with every expectation of founding a galactic empire. They were proud, cocky, ambitious—and unfortunately undergunned. The androids had no record of who finally chased them back to their home system, but the Nevisians had quickly become minor players in local interstellar politics, then no players at all. They had pulled home their explorers, withdrawn their ambassadors, and dropped out of sight. Some time later, probably for something to do, they had begun to fight among themselves.

The kicker was, they had done all this without starships. According to the androids, they had simply *beamed* themselves where they wanted to go, even across interstellar distances. That was a trick nobody in the Federation knew how to do, and Mudd figured he could name his own price for it if he came up with the technology.

The trouble was, the Nevisians had apparently forgotten it. They still had fairly respectable transporter capability—they beamed back and forth between Prastor and Distrel as easily as most people beamed from starship to surface—but Mudd had seen no sign of interstellar travel in the entire time he'd been here. He had already examined the transporters in the palace, and even bribed one of the operators into selling him the schematics for them, but they were obviously not what he was looking for. Now he was reduced to skulking about in the shadowy catacombs in search of ancient clues. It was enough to make an entrepreneur weep.

Worse, now that Kirk was here with the *Enterprise*, Mudd had to move fast. It wouldn't take that pointy-eared pet Vulcan of his very long to grow curious about the level of technology here, and if he discovered the long-range transporter before Mudd did, Mudd could kiss his profit on it goodbye. The Federation might not mind if he sold exotic fruit to the rest of the galaxy, but technology like that would be confiscated "for galactic security" or some such excuse within a heartbeat. Mudd's only chance was to make a swift escape with it and sell it to as many races as possible before anyone could hoard it for themselves.

Provided he could make an escape at all. By pretending to take an interest in interstellar politics and proposing to stop the Nevisians' twelve-millennium war, he had managed to win his release from the android planet and reduce his number of keepers to one of the Stella harpies. He had assumed that she would be easy enough to shake when the time came, but now he wasn't so sure. Without a working interstellar transporter he would have to leave by ship, but hers and the *Enterprise* were the only ones available. Mudd was certain she had disabled hers just to thwart him should he try to liberate it, and while he was sure he could eventually find whatever she had done and repair it—he was good at bypassing lock-outs and the like—he suspected she wouldn't allow him the time. The *Enterprise* would be even harder to hijack, though Mudd wouldn't rule out the possibility. The larger the ship, the larger the crew, and the more weak links for a sufficiently gifted operator to exploit.

However, all that would have to wait until the time was ripe, and unfortunately it was nowhere near that stage yet. In fact, it was time to retrace his steps and put in another appearance upstairs before bedtime, lest his disappearance arouse suspicion in that infernal mechanical Stella.

A noise from below made him pause just as he was about to step into the stairwell and begin the tedious ascent. It had been a high-pitched whine, followed by a whoosh of displaced air. Almost certainly a transporter. Could he have finally stumbled upon his quarry? He took a cautious step forward and peered down to the next floor, but he couldn't see anything from that angle and he didn't want to reveal himself by openly descending the stairs.

Another transporter sounded, then another and another. And now Mudd heard voices whispering softly. That answered one question: someone had beamed *in* rather than out. And from the sounds of it they had materialized in the open corridor directly below him. That seemed an odd place for someone to arrive, unless they were interested in the same thing Mudd was.

Could it be Kirk already? Damn the man for meddling—he always managed to arrive at the most inconvenient moment. It had taken all Mudd's self-control to smile and welcome him to the peace celebration, and it had been a stroke of sheer luck that an opportunity had arisen to kick him back off the planet before he could do any more damage than he had. Mudd suspected he wouldn't be so lucky a second time.

But on the other hand, maybe he had just been handed Kirk's head on a platter, for if it *was* Kirk and his crew sneaking into the Grand Palace to steal the silverware, Mudd just might be able to get them kicked right on out of the Nevis system.

Taking from his pocket the miniature tricorder that he had intended to use to probe the secrets of the interstellar transporter, he knelt down, supressing a grunt, and peered around the edge of the stairwell. All he needed was one clear scan of them that he could show the Grand General, and the game would be up.

But what he saw instead made him nearly drop the tricorder. They were Prastorians. Dozens of them in deep red battle armor, armed with disruptors, gathering for a sneak attack on the palace.

Mudd had seen disruptors in action when he first arrived here. They were directed energy weapons, something like phasers, but considerably messier. They had no niceties like a "stun" setting; they were for killing, nothing else. And they had a very, very long range.

Not even waiting to scan the Prastorians with his tricorder, Mudd crept slowly backward, stood up, and turned to go. He had to get upstairs and spread the alarm. But as he started upward with exaggerated caution to avoid making any noise, he momentarily lost his balance, and when he reached out to steady himself against the banister his tricorder clicked against the wood and the sound echoed in the stair-well.

He immediately heard a shout from below, and the footsteps of many people running toward him. Mudd glanced down the corridor, looking for cover, but it was too far to the nearest doorway. His only chance lay in outrunning the soldiers on the steps, or at least keeping one flight between them so they couldn't get a clear shot at him.

He took the first few steps two at a time, heedless now of the noise he made, but he only made one flight before he had to slow to one step at a time. It was no contest and he knew it. Of his many skills, running was probably his least impressive.

There was no reason now to remain silent. It was highly unlikely that anyone in the palace could hear him, but it was even less likely that he could outrun trained soldiers, so Mudd shouted at the top of his lungs "Help! Attack! Help!" as he ran. The footsteps below paused, and voices hurriedly conferred in whispers, but that only gained Mudd a few seconds before they were after him again.

The fact that they paused at all, however, gave him another idea. As he rounded the corner and began to ascend yet another flight, he slapped the walls repeatedly with his hands, hoping it would sound like more footsteps, and he shouted, "Thank God you've come! They're right behind me! Prastorian soldiers. Get ready to shoot!"

"How many of them?" he asked in a deeper voice, then answered in his own, "Only ten or twenty—you can take them easily."

He continued to stagger up the stairs, panting now

from the exertion, but his fake dialogue had earned him a reprieve. He made it up two more flights before he heard pursuit behind him again. As soon as he was sure they were gaining on him he resumed screaming "Help! Attack!" and he made two more flights before he slipped on a step and fell heavily to his knees. He was only three or four flights from the ground floor, but that was as far as he was going to make it; his left knee could barely hold him when he stood up. Running on it was out of the question.

So he shouted upward one last time, "We're under attack!" Then he turned and stood on the landing, arms at his sides, to await his doom.

But just as the Prastorians burst into view, he heard a door slam open above him, and a familiar voice screeched, "Harcourt? Harcourt Fenton Mudd, what are you up to now!"

Oh joy, Mudd thought Of all the people who could have come, it had to be her. "Now we're in trouble," he said to the surprised Prastorians.

Spock's call caught Kirk in the shower. Could Admiral Tyers have responded already? She'd been out of her office when he'd filed his report; he didn't expect to hear back from her until tomorrow. He switched off the ultrasonic beamer, stepped out of the cubicle, and padded across the soft carpet to the intercom. "Kirk here," he said.

It was impossible to detect emotion in his first officer's voice, but Kirk had known Spock long enough to hear the urgency there as he said, "Captain, I am detecting widespread disruptor fire on the surface of Distrel."

Kirk felt his heart skip a beat. This was worse than a call from Starfleet, and he'd expected that to be bad. "How widespread?" he asked.

"There is significant activity in all inhabited areas of the planet."

"Who's doing the shooting?"

"Both sides are fighting heavily now, but it appears to have been initiated by Prastor."

Kirk looked out his window at the planet below. By naked eye, it looked as peaceful as ever. No flashes of weapons fire, nor even spaceships, could be seen on this scale.

But the *Enterprise* had better sensors than eyesight. "Why didn't we see them coming?" he asked.

Spock said, "I detected a large number of focused tachyon transmissions only moments before the disruptor fire broke out. I can only assume that the Prastorians beamed directly to their Distrellian targets from their own planet."

"Planet-to-planet transporters?" Kirk asked.

"That is correct. I have raised our shields to block any attempt to beam aboard the *Enterprise,* but the Prastorians have so far shown no interest in us."

"That could change without warning. Go to yellow alert; I'll be right up." Kirk switched off the intercom, donned a regular duty uniform from his closet, and as the alert klaxon began to sound throughout the ship, he headed for the turbolift. On the ride up to the bridge he pondered his options. The *Enterprise* couldn't intervene directly because of the Prime Directive, and if the battle was being fought hand-to-hand all over the planet there was very little a starship could do to prevent it anyway. A Federation starship carried enough weaponry to sterilize the entire world, but it was powerless to stop a surface war without destroying that surface and everyone on it as well.

What had triggered this, anyway? Kirk wondered if his and Mudd's altercation at the Grand Palace had struck more sparks than had been apparent at the time. It seemed unlikely, but he supposed it was possible. It was far more probable that the Prastorians had simply used the peace treaty as an opportunity to prepare for a full-scale assault and catch the Distrellians with their defenses down.

The turbolift doors opened onto the bridge. It had been staffed at minimum, since it was evening and the ship was in orbit around a friendly planet, but the yellow alert had already brought Sulu to the helm and Lieutenant Uhura to communications. Spock was at his science console. Kirk strode across the bridge to his side and asked, "Situation?"

"Unchanged, Captain," Spock said. "Fighting continues all over Distrel. Interplanetary transporter activity is still high, and beams are traveling in both directions, but so far fighting has not broken out on Prastor."

Kirk turned to Uhura. "See if you can reach the Padishah. I want to ask him what he's trying to pull here."

Uhura turned to her communications console, but after several attempts to hail the Prastorian leadership she shook her head and said, "No response, Captain."

"Try the Grand General, then."

"Yes, sir." She was more successful in that; a moment later she said, "On screen."

Kirk turned to face the main viewer, from which a harried Grand General peered out. His hair, normally standing straight out, was matted on one side, and his clothing was rumpled. He looked to be in a private sitting room or library, and in the background, slightly out of focus, Kirk saw at least four armed bodyguards.

"Grand General," Kirk said. "We're monitoring intense combat on Distrel. What is your situation?"

"Under control, for the moment," said the Grand General. "We had a tricky moment with a squadron that attacked the palace before we got our shields up, but we won't get caught unguarded again."

"I meant the planet as a whole. Can you repel this invasion?"

"Repel it?" asked the Grand General, as if that was a completely foreign concept. "Whatever for?"

"What for?" Kirk asked, equally incredulous. "To stop them from killing your people."

"Ah, yes, the way your doctor did with my footman. No, thank you, that won't be necessary."

"But—" Kirk stopped himself. Much as he hated the situation, the Prime Directive prevented him from arguing. "What caused this?" he asked instead.

"Prastor attacked us, of course," said the Grand General in the tone of voice reserved for answering dumb questions. "Why should you care, anyway?"

"Because if our presence here contributed to the situation in any way, we have a moral obligation to help set things right again."

The Grand General shook his head. "Things *are* right again. Now if you will excuse me, I have a traitor to execute." He reached forward as if to switch off his communicator, but Kirk stopped him.

"Wait. Who is the traitor, and what did he do?"

The Distrellian leader peered at Kirk for a long few seconds before he said, "Harry Mudd, of course. As for what he did, he lured us away from the teachings of our ancestors, just as you are trying to do. Would you care to come down and join him in the firing squad?"

Chapter Seven

SULU KNEW he was in for a long night. He could sense it coming with the inevitability of a derelict freighter closing on a space station. He'd missed out on the banquet, and after Chekov had returned and told him how it had gone he'd been glad to have avoided it, but he had the sneaking suspicion that the next trip to the surface would be even worse, and this time he would be along for the ride.

Sure enough, at the Grand General's latest statement, the captain said, "I'll come down all right, but it'll be to negotiate for his release." Never mind that interplanetary war was crackling all around the palace; Kirk had a job to do and he was going to go do it.

That clearly wasn't what the Grand General had expected him to say. "Whatever for?" he asked. "I got the distinct impression that you and he were not the old friends he said you were."

"We're not," Kirk said with a wry smile, "but he's a

citizen of the Federation, and as such it's my duty to protect him."

"Why bother?" asked the Grand General. "An execution won't send him to Arnhall, but another run through the proving ground could only improve his perspective on life. Even you would have to agree with that."

Oh, great, thought Sulu. They're religious fanatics. Or at least they believe in reincarnation. Chekov hadn't mentioned that little detail.

Kirk said, "Harry is a bit rough around the edges, but we prefer rehabilitation to execution. Would you agree to turn him over to us for safekeeping? I can promise he wouldn't trouble you any further."

The Grand General ran a hand through his hair, restoring the matted patch to its former prominence. "I don't know, Captain. We caught him emerging from the catacombs with a squad of Prastorian soldiers. Leading the enemy against his own people is a pretty severe breach of military etiquette. Our law is very clear on such matters."

Kirk laughed. "Leading an army is the last thing Harry Mudd would do. He was probably running away."

The Grand General hesitated. "Possibly. But if that's the case, then what was he doing in the catacombs in the first place?"

"Harry Mudd?" asked Kirk, laughing even harder. "Check his pockets. And count your spoons. But don't execute him for treason. He hasn't got a treasonous bone in his body."

Again the Grand General hesitated, and Kirk jumped into the breach before he could recover his sense of purpose. "Let me come down and help you get to the truth of the matter," he said. "Then we can decide what to do with him."

Obviously reluctant, the Grand General nevertheless said, "Very well, Captain."

"We'll be right there. Kirk out." He turned to Lieutenant Uhura and said, "Keep an eye on the situation down below. I want you to let me know at the first sign of trouble. Keep a fix on us and be ready to beam us out if that shield around the palace goes down. If it does, the place will probably be filled with Prastorians in no time."

"Yes, sir," she said.

Here it comes, thought Sulu.

But Kirk turned to him and said, "Mr. Sulu, you have the conn. If the *Enterprise* comes under attack, take her out of range and give the conn to Mr. Scott."

"Aye, sir," Sulu said, trying to hide his surprise.

"Spock, you come with me." Kirk turned to go, then paused. "I forgot to ask if Harry was injured. Uhura, call Dr. McCoy and have him meet us in transporter room one. And tell security I want two people to accompany us, just in case." He turned back to Spock and said, "All right, let's go see if we can't save at least one life down there."

As the two of them left the bridge, Sulu tried to get a handle on his emotions. Why did he feel so let down all of a sudden? Had he actually wanted to beam down with the captain? Apparently so. "Let's go save a life" was a powerful motivator. The landing party might be risking their own lives among hostile aliens light-years away from home, but they were doing it for a higher cause.

Well, all right, this time it was for Harry Mudd, but it was the principle of the thing that mattered.

And the strange thing about it: despite the hollow feeling in the pit of his stomach when he'd thought he would be chosen to go along, and despite the immense responsibility he had been given instead, going on another dangerous mission was the part of his job that Sulu liked best.

Twice in one day. That was really too much. Dr. McCoy hated transporters anyway—the very idea of taking a body apart atom by atom and squirting it across space gave him the jitters—but to suffer the indignity just to beam down into the middle of a war was asking too much of a man.

Of course doctors always wound up visiting battlefields, so he couldn't say this came as a surprise. The moment he had heard that fighting had broken out again he had packed his medikit and prepared for the call. Nevisian courtiers at a royal party might prefer death to rehabilitation, but McCoy was willing to bet there were plenty of people in the general populace who felt differently.

The whole situation frustrated McCoy to no end. Soldiers marched out with higher and higher technology to kill each other over squabbles that shouldn't ever have escalated into violence in the first place, while doctors crept around beneath the fusillade with higher and higher technology trying to save the wounded. And people who just wanted to live their lives in peace wound up caught in the middle of it all, funding both the warriors and the doctors with their taxes. It seemed to be the nature of life itself, that endless struggle between violence and compassion.

There had to be a better way. Countless societies had tried to find it, and some had arguably succeeded,

71

but at what price? The Federation with its military might, promoting peace but ready to stamp out with violence anyone who threatened that peace too aggressively? The Vulcans with their iron-willed self-supression that left them no emotions at all? The Klingons and Romulans had gone the other route, glorifying violence and embracing it openly as a way of life, but were they any better off? McCoy didn't think so.

Then there were the Nevisians. Fighting an interplanetary war longer than humanity had even been civilized, and all over nothing. According to the Grand General they had tried to make peace many times, but it had never lasted. McCoy could have told him why not: because they hadn't changed the basic nature of the Nevisian people. Deep down they had the same violent instincts as everyone else, and those instincts needed an outlet.

The solution was beyond McCoy, but as he crossed from sickbay to the transporters, he devoutly wished someone would come up with one. He was getting tired of patching up the wounded.

The transporter-room door swished open before him. Vagle, the transporter tech, was already there, along with two people from security. McCoy recognized Ensign Lebrun and Lieutenant Gorden. Lebrun looked a bit red around the eyes; McCoy almost offered her something to soothe the irritation, but then he remembered that she had just gotten married and reconsidered. That was another incomprehensible social situation, as far as he was concerned, almost as baffling as warfare.

Gorden looked a bit nervous as he checked the

charge on his phaser. He was young and eager to make a name for himself. McCoy made a mental note to watch out for him—he could get himself hurt if he wasn't careful.

The door opened again and Captain Kirk entered, with Spock close behind.

"All here, I see," said Kirk. "Good. Let's go."

As they took up positions on the transporter platform, McCoy looked over to Spock. "Can you believe we're going down there to rescue Harry Mudd of all people?"

Spock nodded solemnly. "Since that is in fact our mission, I have no difficulty encompassing the concept."

Should have known he would say something like that, McCoy thought. A perfectly reasonable response to the question, except for the undeniable derogatory implications.

"Hah," he said. "The vaunted Vulcan reserve isn't much of a solution, either, is it?"

"I beg your pardon?" asked Spock, puzzled at the apparent non sequitur.

"As well you should," McCoy told him. "I was trying to be civil."

"As was I, Doctor, but apparently you were prepared to take offense all the same."

Was that really how Spock saw the situation? If so, then it was worse than McCoy thought. If two people who were trying to be civil could still wind up angry at each other, how could anyone truly make peace? He wanted to ask Spock about it, maybe draw him out into a real conversation for once, but there was no time for it now. Kirk chose that moment to say,

"Energize." Vagle slid the activation controls forward, and the ship grew indistinct around them.

They appeared in a stone cubicle barely big enough to hold all five of them. Lebrun immediately turned around to take in the entire situation. There were no windows, no furnishings other than a single flat panel of light overhead, and only one door, a heavy metal one, which was closed and had no knob on the inside. Circles in all four walls looked ominously like the barrels of disruptors aimed straight at them. Strategically, this situation stank.

"What the—did Vagle miss his mark?" Dr. McCoy asked.

"I believe these are the coordinates we were given," said Spock. "The structure we are in is hardly surprising if considered logically. Since the Nevisians possess transporter technology, this is apparently a foyer where visitors can be examined before being allowed through the shielded walls into the interior of the palace. I suspect this is a common practice on both planets of this system."

That made sense, all right. Lebrun wasn't any happier about it, but it made sense. And the beam-out stations would be similarly designed, but shielded from arrivals so they couldn't be sabotaged from outside.

"Then why were we able to beam directly inside before?" McCoy asked.

Kirk said, "Because the shields were down. I bet they won't make that mistake again soon." He rapped on the door with his knuckles. "Open up. We're friends."

The solid thunk of a heavy bolt being withdrawn

echoed in the tiny cubicle, then the door swung inward toward them. It couldn't be forced open easily, swinging that direction. And those disruptors insured that an enemy wouldn't have long to try blasting through, either.

Four armed guards stood just beyond the door. Two male and two female; apparently these people weren't hung up about gender in the military. Of course if the Nevisians had been at war as long as they said they had, then everyone was probably in the military. The guards eyed Lebrun and Gorden carefully, obviously wondering if they should try to confiscate their phasers. Lebrun gave them her best steely-eyed stare, trying not to laugh at the startled appearance their straight-out hair gave them, and after a moment they said, "This way, please." Two of them led the *Enterprise* landing party into the palace, while the other two stayed behind to guard the entry.

The Grand General was waiting for them in his audience chamber, an ostentatiously large room hung with tapestries and paintings and sporting only one chair—the oversized throne on a two-foot dais on which the Grand General himself sat, flanked by six more guards. The fat man off to the side, looking forlorn with his hands and feet in manacles, had to be Harry Mudd. He was bruised and cut up a little on his left side where his shirt had been ripped open, but otherwise he looked uninjured. A red-haired human woman stood beside him, disapproval written all over her features. A Nevisian in red battle armor, also manacled, stood on the other side of him. The Nevisian was in much worse shape than Harry; he bled from half a dozen wounds and wisps of smoke still rose from the singed chestplate of his armor.

"So, Captain," the Grand General said, leaning forward in his chair. "What do you offer me for this scum of a traitor?"

"Are you sure he's a traitor?" Kirk asked.

"He was surprised in the company of several Prastorians as they emerged from the catacombs in a sneak attack."

"I was taken prisoner by them," Mudd said indignantly.

"Hardly an honorable defense." The Grand General sniffed disdainfully. "Even so, he was heard to shout, 'Attack!' That seems rather unlike a prisoner, does it not?"

"I was shouting 'Help, we're *being* attacked.' I was trying to warn you."

"You were either spying out a remote beam-in site for the Prastorians, or you were spying on your own. Either action is a reprehensible repayment of our trust in you."

"Nonsense." Mudd puffed out his chest and said, "I had overheard a whispered conversation between the Padishah and one of his footmen earlier in the day. Not enough to be sure of anything, and I didn't want to threaten the fragile peace with a baseless rumor, so I took it upon myself to investigate, and that's how I wound up—"

"I don't believe you," said the Grand General.

"You," Kirk said to the smoking Prastorian soldier. "What's the truth here?"

The man looked at Kirk with eyes full of hatred. Lebrun reached instinctively for her phaser, but stopped short of pulling it from her belt.

"The truth?" asked the man. "The truth is, we don't need your kind here, nor his. We were doing fine before he arrived, and the Prastorian army is merely setting things back to the way they should be. *Without* his assistance."

"The words of an assassin and a coward." The Grand General slapped the arms of his throne for emphasis.

"History will judge me a hero," the soldier said defiantly.

"Perhaps, but what will the Gods of Fate judge you? That's the more immediate question. Execution following capture during a sneak attack is hardly a ticket to Arnhall. You'll be cycling through this life for generations at this rate."

"I would have fought to the death had not this— this alien—knocked me unconscious." The Prastorian soldier glared at the red-haired woman.

Apparently these people believed very strongly in reincarnation and an eventual afterlife as a reward for the righteous, thought Lebrun. Strongly enough to die willingly to get there. Not a good sign.

"Stella saved you?" McCoy asked incredulously of Mudd.

His nod was nearly imperceptible. "There appear to be advantages to having a . . . determined companion," he said.

She shook her forefinger at him. "As I've told you all along, you worthless, womanizing, sorry excuse for a husband. But do you listen? Oh no, you're too high and mighty to listen to your wife. Well, let me tell you—"

"Oh, do be quiet," Mudd said in a soft voice. "My ears hurt enough as it is."

Surprisingly, the woman shut up. Lebrun looked at her with disbelief. This shrew was that poor man's *wife?* How could he tolerate such a creature? She must have some redeeming quality that Harry found desirable—or had when he proposed to her—but what that could be Lebrun was hard put to guess. She shuddered at the thought that she and Simon could ever become like them; then she reddened with the realization that they had already taken the first step. When the yellow alert had sounded and she had received the call to return to duty, she had put on her uniform again and opened the bedroom door to find Simon working on his third Cetian laliska. She had left without a word of explanation, and he had offered no apology in parting.

When I get back, she vowed, I'll apologize for both of us.

The Grand General apparently liked this woman. Laughing, he said, "Such spirit. You'd make a good Nevisian, Stella! You should consider it."

"I have my duty to Harry," she said simply.

"And you have my permission to abrogate at any time," Mudd muttered.

Now Kirk laughed, which Lebrun thought was very insensitive of him, even under the circumstances. He said, "I think we've established that the Prastorians attacked on their own. And whatever Harry was doing in the cellar had no effect on you—except possibly to warn you of the invasion. So it looks to me as if you owe him a favor."

"We owe him nothing," insisted the Grand General. "He is a meddlesome alien who has disturbed our way of life beyond measure. And he lulled me into dropping my guard."

"Then let us take him away from here and get him out of your hair completely."

Lebrun thought that was an unfortunate choice of words, given the Nevisians' electric-shock coiffure, but if the Grand General took offense he showed no sign of it. "We could teach him a few things about honor if he stayed among us," he said.

"Do you really want his influence to spread?" Kirk asked.

The Grand General thought that over for a moment, then laughed uproariously. "Well argued! Indeed, we do not. Take him then. Take him away." He looked over at Stella. "But you, my dear, must do us the courtesy of remaining at least through the day. Give me that much time to convince you to stay."

"I cannot leave Harry," said Stella.

Mudd had perked up considerably in the last few minutes. "Give him his day, Stella," he told his wife. "I'll hardly be going anywhere aboard the *Enterprise,* and I could use the rest from your endless . . . advice."

She considered his statement, then nodded slowly. "Very well," she said, "but I will not be swayed from my duty."

Duty, thought Lebrun. She apparently wouldn't rest until she'd reformed the man to her own image. Was that what marriage was all about? She certainly hoped not. Yet wasn't that what she had been trying to do with Simon this evening? When she got home, they would definitely have to talk.

Chapter Eight

MUDD COULD HARDLY believe his luck. Finally separated from the last of these infernal androids! Not by nearly enough distance, but the *Enterprise* was the best shot at a permanent escape he was likely to get. Maybe he could convince Kirk to warp out of the system before she could catch up again. It would mean leaving behind the secret of the interstellar transporter, but that was a small price to pay for freedom. There were plenty of other opportunities in the galaxy for a man of sufficient ambition.

"Thank you, Kirk," he said, meaning it. "Consider your debt to me paid in full." He held out his manacled hands to one of the guards flanking the Grand General, and after receiving a silent nod from his leader the guard produced a key and unlocked them.

"The feet, too, please," said Mudd. "We don't want

to make Kirk carry me to the beam-out point, now, do we? I'd owe *him* a favor if we did that."

He might have to be carried even so—his left knee still hurt where he had twisted it in falling on the stairs, but it held his weight now, although shooting pain ran all the way down to his foot when he stood on it. He would try, at least, to walk out of here on his own.

He shook the circulation back into his extremities, then tucked his ripped shirt back into his belt as best he could. His side hurt where he had hit the stone floor when the Stella android had shoved him out of the way during the heat of battle, but it wasn't bad enough to require immediate attention. He wanted nothing to slow down their departure from this place.

"Shall we be off?" he asked Kirk. "I know you're a busy man, worlds to save and all that; I'd hate to cause you any unnecessary delay."

Shaking his head in his sardonic, holier-than-thou fashion, Kirk said, "Harry, you really take the cake."

Mudd replied as he always did to a snide remark. "Why, thank you, Captain." And then, purely for the sake of playing with Kirk's head, he turned to the android, took its right hand in his own, and said, "My dear, I shall count the hours." And the days, and the weeks, and the months, he thought, but he prudently left that unsaid.

He considered a parting remark to the Grand General, but decided that discretion was the better part of valor in this instance as well. You don't insult a man in his own castle, and Mudd could think of nothing to say that couldn't be taken as an insult if the General chose to take it that way. So he merely led the way out of the throne room and began the long trek down the hallway to the outer wall and the fortified transporter points, trying not to limp. The others followed, and the two palace guards who had brought them in accompanied them back out.

Dr. McCoy walked alongside Mudd, waving a diagnostic scanner at his side. Its irritating whistle cut straight to the inner ear. And no telling how deep its scanning beam penetrated.

"So what's your verdict, Doctor?" Mudd asked him. "Will I live to see another sunset?"

"Probably," McCoy said. "But I'd suggest staying clear of white Palko fruit for at least a month. You've got enough of the purple toxin in your system to trigger a deadly reaction just breathing the fumes from a white slice. What were you doing, living on the stuff?"

The news was slightly alarming, but a man of Mudd's girth grows used to the notion that food can be as harmful as it is pleasant. He laughed and said, "I make it a point not to turn down a delicacy, Doctor. You never know when the next opportunity will arise."

"Well, Harry," said Kirk, "You'll be dining on simpler fare where you're go—" His communicator bleeped for attention, and he immediately snatched it from his belt and flipped it open. "Kirk here."

Lieutenant Uhura said, "Captain, we're picking up increased transporter activity outside the palace. It looks like Prastor is beaming another attack force just beyond the walls."

"Understood. Get a lock on us. As soon as we're past the shield, or if the shield goes down, beam us away immediately. Kirk out." He closed his communicator and returned it to his belt. "You heard her," he said. "Let's get to the beam-out point before all hell breaks loose."

Mudd wholeheartedly agreed, but they had hardly made half the distance to the outer wall before they heard a tremendous explosion and the entire palace shook with the blast. A bright flash lit up the far end of the corridor, and another explosion sent dust and smoke rolling toward them.

"I believe they have breached the walls," Spock said with his characteristic understatement.

All of the *Enterprise* crew, and the two Distrellian guards who accompanied them, had drawn their weapons. The *Enterprise* crew stood their ground, but the Distrellians rushed off toward the source of the explosion without a backward glance. Typical, thought Mudd. Headlong into glory. It was hard to comprehend how an otherwise sane people could embrace violence so completely.

"Harry," Kirk said, "do you know another way out of here?"

"Indeed I do," said Mudd, thinking furiously. There were dozens of transporter stations around the perimeter of the palace, but all of them would be guarded. And if Mudd and the others showed up without their Distrellian escorts, they would probably be denied access beyond the shields.

But what if they went to an outbound transporter station? Those were less heavily guarded, because they were normally shielded except when the transporter was in use to beam someone away from the palace.

And Mudd knew one of the operators. He had bought the schematics to the transporter from him.

Even if his post was guarded now, he would vouch for Mudd—he would have to, for fear that Mudd would betray him if he didn't. Yes, that would work, and it proved once again what Mudd had always maintained: It definitely paid to have contacts in as many places as possible.

Now, which way was that transporter station? Mudd turned once around, looking for clues. The palace was laid out like a wheel with corridors radiating outward like spokes from the center, so it was easy to navigate from the Grand General's residence in the hub, but the farther out you got along one spoke the harder it was to go anywhere else. They'd been going north, and the station he wanted was in the library wing on the west side, so they needed to turn left. Mudd had picked the transporter operator in the library to approach, figuring that in a military society his station would be seldom used, and that he would be bored and glad to have someone to converse with. His reasoning had paid off at the time, but now it meant circling a quarter of the way around the palace.

The *zip-crack* of disruptor fire echoed up the hallway, and a few bright blue energy beams lanced past the T-intersection at the end where the two guards had taken up positions to shoot from cover.

"Harry, do you know another way out or not?" Kirk demanded.

"I said I did, Captain, and I do. I was just getting my bearings. This way." Mudd led off through an archway into a curving side corridor. It wasn't one of the main routes around the center, but right now that might be just as well. And if Mudd remembered correctly, a northward jog a little ways ahead would take them past the one room he hadn't been able to search before: the vault where they stored the palace jewels. Though no doubt considerable wealth was stored there, Mudd had considered it a low priority compared with the interstellar transporter, but now under the confusion of the Prastorian attack he might as well at least see if he could pick up a memento of his stay here.

And maybe, just maybe, he could use it to pay for one final favor from the transporter operator. If Mudd could get him to activate just one segment of the outgoing beam a moment before the *Enterprise* activated *their* transporter, he could make his escape right here and now. He would still have to beam aboard the *Enterprise,* since it was the only interstellar ship besides the android's available, but he could aim for a cargo bay somewhere and hide out until the ship was safely out of the Nevis system. Mudd hadn't liked the tone of Kirk's voice when he'd made that crack about "simpler fare"; it would be better to take his chances as a stowaway than accept whatever Kirk had planned for him. Kirk wouldn't think to look for him on board; he would assume Mudd had escaped to somewhere else on Distrel, so Mudd could hide his time until the *Enterprise* called at some more desirable port.

Spock would probably calculate his chance of success at about 1.63 percent, but Mudd could think of no better option at the moment. Sometimes you just had to trust in your own ingenuity.

The hallway they were in ended at a wide meeting room. The walls were covered with paintings of former Grand Generals, and shelves and pedestals around the perimeter held busts and medals and other bric-a-brac. Mudd led the way across it, aiming for the rightmost of the triple doors on the opposite side, but a gleaming silver dagger with a jeweled hilt hanging on the wall just to the left of the doors caught his attention and he steered closer to it. It was impossible to tell at a glance if the jewels were real, but they were certainly impressive. A dagger like that could fetch a fine price with some collectors Mudd knew. So he stumbled just as he reached the doorway, reached out as if to catch himself against the wall, and smoothly lifted the dagger from its support as he passed on through the doorway.

An alarm instantly began clanging overhead. Well, that answered the question of its value.

"Drat the luck," Mudd said quickly, not even breaking stride. "The door must have been wired."

"The knife you were attempting to steal was more probably the cause of the alarm," said Spock dryly.

Confound the Vulcan; he *would* notice. Putting a wounded tone in his voice, Mudd said, "Certainly you don't expect me to proceed into a conflict unarmed when there are weapons to be had? A dagger is a poor substitute for a phaser, I admit, but it's better than nothing. Unless of course you'd like to trade me."

"That would be illogical," said Spock. "Though we have not tested your skills as a marksman, there is a high probability that I am a better shot than you; therefore the phaser would be more valuable in my hands."

"There you go," said Mudd, as if that closed the argument.

Another loud bang echoed down the main corridor they had left only moments before. Shouts of alarm and the *zip-crack* of more disruptor fire followed close behind. It sounded as if the fighting was closer now; the Prastorians had evidently made it through the gap they'd blown in the wall. At least nobody was likely to come investigate an alarm with that going on so near.

Kirk apparently thought otherwise. "Hurry it up, Harry," he urged.

"I'm limping as fast as I can," Mudd snapped back at him. "It's not much farther." They came to another cross-corridor, and Mudd paused to peer around the corner. Yes, he had guessed right; two soldiers stood outside a heavy door about twenty feet away, both looking anxiously down the hallway in the other direction, from which even more battle noise sounded.

Mudd backed up and held out a hand to stop the others and whispered, "Wait here. I'm going to have to talk our way past these guards."

"Are you sure that's smart?" Kirk asked him. "What if they've already heard about you?"

"They haven't," Mudd told him, earnestly hoping that was true. If it wasn't, well, Kirk and the others had phasers; they could probably get him out of trouble if he couldn't talk himself out of it. And nothing ventured, nothing gained, Mudd had always believed, so before Kirk could protest any further, he stepped out into the hallway and walked toward the guards.

"What's your status here?" he asked as he drew closer, tucking his dagger prominently into his belt. "Do you need reinforcements?" It was always best to take the initiative in situations like this.

"No, sir," one of the guards said.

"Good," said Mudd. "As you can no doubt hear for yourselves, things aren't going as well elsewhere in the palace. The Grand General has sent me to ensure that the most valuable items here don't fall into enemy hands."

The guards exchanged a puzzled glance, then one of them asked, "In what way?"

"I have been instructed to prepare what I can for relocation if that should become necessary."

"Relocation!" the other guard said. "Is it that bad?"

"An attack force came up through the catacombs before we got the shields up," Mudd replied, neglecting to mention that they had been nullified already. "The Prastorians are already inside the walls." That much was true; he could hear them uncomfortably well.

Even so, the first guard said, "We'd have to have word directly from the Grand General before we could let you remove anything, sir."

Mudd nodded. "Of course, of course. But you understand why he couldn't speak to you himself; he's a bit busy at the moment." Another barrage of disruptor fire echoed down the long corridor, lending credibility to his remark. Mudd said, "He told me to leave it to your discretion when to move; I am merely supposed to prepare the . . . ah . . . items for transport. You may accompany me inside and assist if you wish." That should mollify them, and if he couldn't palm a few precious trinkets under the noses of two soldiers, his name wasn't Harry Mudd.

They were nervous about the situation, he could tell, but the increasing clamor of battle helped them make up their minds. "All right," the first guard said to the second, "you go give him a hand, and I'll keep watch. But we're not moving anything until we're absolutely sure we have to."

"Oh, you'll know when the time comes," Harry told him. "Don't worry about that." That was true enough as well. As he waited for them to open the door for him, Mudd told himself that he was probably doing them a favor. The way things sounded near the outer wall, they very probably *would* have to flee with whatever they could carry before this battle was over. Of course Harry planned to be long gone with the best of the treasure by that point, but he could certainly fill a sack with his leavings for them, and the Grand General would probably be grateful to have that much rescued from the invaders.

Provided he survived the attack, that is.

Mudd knew it probably only took a few seconds, but the combination lock seemed to take forever to open. At last the guard spun the lock wheel and pulled the massive steel door outward, and as the interior lights flickered on, Mudd nearly gasped with delight. Oh, yes, this was a *vault*. No piddly little collection of insignificant sentimental artifacts; this place held real wealth. He stepped inside and turned once around, taking it all in. Shelves along all four walls held silver and gold artifacts of all description: figurines, chalices, jewelry boxes, and more. Cloth sacks and wooden chests on the floor spilled over with coins and jewels. One corner of the vault was stacked high with bars of what appeared to be platinum, and atop the pile, as if tossed there casually by the last person to need them, rested a gold crown, a jeweled scepter, and a richly brocaded mantle fit for a king. Distrellian blue, of course.

"Ginn Donan's?" Mudd asked the guard who had

accompanied him. He had heard the tales of the Nevisians' biggest hero—over and over again in speech after speech as he had negotiated for peace.

"That's right," said the guard.

"Those were on the list," Mudd told him. "Find something to hold everything in while I look for the other items we're supposed to save." Nice as they were, Mudd had no need for royal finery—he needed something a bit more portable and concealable—but that should keep the guard busy while he took inventory.

No doubt Kirk and his cronies were growing ever more fidgety out there in the hallway, but Mudd didn't particularly care about that. They wouldn't leave without him for the simple reason that only he knew where they were going. When Mudd was good and ready to go he would entrust the guards with the sack of swag he had chosen for them to "preserve," and he would walk out with his own treasure safely stowed away and they wouldn't suspect a thing.

Diversion, that was the key to this sort of operation. He found a suitably impressive diamond necklace and palmed it while he selected an even larger ruby brooch to hand to the guard, and a moment later he added two rings and a bracelet to his own stash while asking the guard if the jeweled tiara in his other hand was the genuine article or just a clever duplicate for show.

When the guard assured him it was real, he gave it to him to add to the scepter and crown, then hitched up his pants and slipped the necklace, rings, and bracelet into a pocket as he turned to look for more.

A soft whirr and a thump from out in the hallway drew his attention, and he stuck his head out the door far enough to see the guard out there slumped on the floor. A moment later the security officer who had accompanied Kirk came into view, holding out her phaser. The *Enterprise* crew had apparently lost their patience.

Mudd sighed in exasperation. Kirk always had to spoil things just when they were starting to pay off. Well, there was no sense getting into a firefight over it, so Mudd said to the remaining guard, "Here, help me with this, will you?" and bent down as if to scoot a jewel-filled chest near the door out of the way. That put the guard with his back to the door, and the moment he bent over, the security officer stunned him as well.

Mudd snatched up a double handful of gemstones and poured them into his pockets, added a bar of platinum for good measure, then stepped over the unconscious guard and met the woman at the door. Kirk and the others were right behind her. "Have you no discipline?" Mudd asked them. "I told you to wait. I had just earned their confidence and was about to—"

"I don't care what you were about to do, Harry," Kirk said. *"We're* about to be overrun. Now move it." He grabbed Mudd roughly by his collar and pulled him out of the vault, then propelled him down the corridor with a rough shove against his back.

"Really, Kirk," Mudd said as he struggled to keep his footing, "I must protest this treatment! I—"

A steady barrage of disruptor fire swept through the intersection of hallways in which Kirk and the others had been hiding. Where it struck the walls, great sections of stone blew free and tumbled to the floor.

"I see your point," Mudd said, rushing ahead.

But the battle had been working its way inward from the outer walls along both of the main-spoke corridors flanking the treasury. As they reached the next one, more disruptor fire lanced past the junction, and a detonation against a cornerstone sprayed them with rock chips.

Mudd's pockets rattled as he leaped backward, nearly knocking over Kirk in his haste to avoid the battle. A few baubles fell to the floor and rolled away.

"If we get caught up in this because of your little shopping expedition," Kirk growled, "I'll make you wish you were back with the androids."

"Too late," Mudd told him. "I already wish for that. At least they didn't shoot at me."

The security officer brushed past him and stuck her head around the corner, then pulled back fast as more disruptor fire peppered the walls. "They're coming fast," she reported. "If we're going to get across this passage, we've got to do it now." Without waiting for Kirk's order, she stuck her hand around the corner and fired her phaser a few times blindly; then she shouted "Go!" and stood out in the corridor, firing rapidly.

The other security officer leaped across, then Kirk and Spock. McCoy was preparing himself for the jump when a disruptor beam caught the woman solidly in the chest, spinning her around and slamming her up against the corner. McCoy grabbed for her just as two more beams struck her, and this time their combined molecular dispersion charges finished the job the first one had started.

Mudd stared aghast at the spot where she had been. Not even a shoe remained. She had been completely vaporized. This woman had died right before his eyes, and he didn't even know her name.

The other security person fired back down the corridor. "Come on!" shouted Kirk, and Mudd backed up for a running leap across the perilous junction, but when he looked beyond Kirk he stopped cold. A flood of blue-clad Distrellian defenders were retreating toward them from that direction, too, and the fighting looked even more intense there.

"Look out behind!" Mudd yelled. He turned to look behind himself, and winced to see smoke and the flash of disruptor fire there as well. They were trapped.

"The vault," said Spock in a loud voice. "It is the only defensible position."

"We can't let them box us in," Kirk protested. "We've got to get *out* of here."

"On the contrary, Captain," Spock said as he reached out over the security officer's head and contributed his own phaser to the return barrage. "We need only wait for the attackers to knock out the shields, which is undoubtedly their first priority, and then the *Enterprise* can beam us away."

"Spock, you're a genius," Mudd said, meaning every word of it, for the Vulcan's plan meant that he didn't have to cross the gauntlet of disruptor fire.

He backed away to give the others room, and one by one Kirk, the security officer, and Spock leaped across. An energy beam narrowly missed Spock, blasting more rock chips from the corridor, one of which sliced into his cheek. Bright green blood welled out of the cut, but he hardly seemed to notice.

"Into the vault, Harry," Kirk said unnecessarily,

for Mudd was already moving toward it, but he froze when a phalanx of Prastorian soldiers burst into the corridor from the other end. They stared at him for a moment, obviously unsure whether to shoot or not. He and Spock were wearing blue, but the one remaining security officer wore red, and Kirk was in his usual olive green. The vault guard that the security officer had stunned lay sprawled a few feet in front of them, but Mudd couldn't guess how that would affect their decision.

Their hesitation lasted only a few seconds, however, before one of them shouted, "It's the aliens! Get 'em!"

Mudd ran for the doorway, but it was a losing race. Time seemed to telescope for him; he imagined he could actually see the disruptor beams stretch up the corridor toward him. The first of them lanced past on the right, but telescoped or no, he had no time to dodge the next one. It hit him in the right leg, which buckled immediately and pitched him forward. That might have saved his life, for the next beam passed overhead, but as he reached out to catch himself against the wall he leaned directly into the path of the next one, which hit him in the side. The same side that the android had injured, Mudd realized as pain washed over him and he fell back against Dr. McCoy.

They both fell to the floor, McCoy cursing frantically. Mudd heard him as if from a long ways away, and he saw Kirk and Spock and the security officer firing back down the corridor, but his vision was growing indistinct. He dimly felt another shock to his other leg, but everything, even the wound in his side, now seemed filtered through thick haze.

Someone grabbed him by his arms and dragged him

into the vault. His head banged the door sill on the way through, adding insult to what Mudd was just beginning to realize was a serious injury. Whoever had rescued him laid his head on a sack of money, then Mudd heard the whirring of medical instruments.

The vault door boomed shut. The light immediately went out, then a moment later a flashlight beam shot out, wobbled a moment, and shone into his face.

He tried to tell whoever held it to quit blinding him, but he couldn't get his breath. Not at *all*, he realized with growing alarm.

Shadowy forms hovered over him, just outside of the light beam. Through the steadily increasing hum in his ears, Mudd heard Kirk ask, "How is he, Bones?" and he heard McCoy answer, "He's fading fast, Jim. I've got to get him to the *Enterprise.*"

"As soon . . . shields . . . down," Kirk said, his words fading in and out. Mudd heard the chirp of a communicator and Kirk said something else, but his voice sounded like the buzzing of an insect now.

At least the pain was fading as well. Mudd tried to move his arms, his head, tried to blink his eyes, but nothing responded. He could only lie there on the floor with his head on a sack of money and stare into the light.

Someone else turned on another light and swept it around the vault. Jewels glittered in its beam like stars twinkling through an atmosphere. Not a bad last vision, Mudd thought, if it came to that. He had always said he wanted to end his days surrounded by fabulous riches, and here he was.

But where, oh where were the beautiful women that were supposed to go with it?

Chapter Nine

KIRK TRIED to bring his breathing under control. His heart pounded and he felt twitchy as a cat in a kennel. Being shot at always did that to him. Usually afterward, when he had time to think about it, but somehow the reaction always seemed even worse for the delay. Once the fighting was over he had far too much time to reconsider his actions and berate himself for all his bad decisions.

He had plenty of them to think about now. The look of shock on Ensign Lebrun's face when she was hit would haunt him forever. She'd had no time to feel anything before she was hit again; her death had been painless, clean, and sanitary—but she was just as dead.

Kirk would love to blame Harry Mudd for that. Mudd had, after all, delayed their getaway with his greedy side trip to this vault. But he had already paid dearly for his avarice, and in truth the vault had probably saved the rest of their lives. Without it they would have been caught in the crossfire somewhere farther along and not had any place like this to retreat to. Kirk could hear fighting outside even through the massive door. This was no small-scale skirmish; this was an all-out assault on the planetary government. The Prastorians were sweeping through the entire palace.

Besides, if anyone was to blame for her death, it was Kirk. Lebrun had been doing her duty, which was to protect her crewmates—and especially her captain—from harm. If he hadn't brought her here, or if he hadn't come in person to do a job that could probably have been done by communicator if he had insisted on it, she would still be alive.

He knew his reasoning was faulty. Spock had told him so often enough in similar circumstances. If he followed that argument to its logical conclusion, then Admiral Tyers was responsible for ordering them here in the first place, or it was Lebrun's own fault for joining Starfleet before that. But Kirk felt personally responsible even so. Maybe everyone *was* to blame, including himself. There was certainly plenty of guilt to go around.

Mudd groaned feebly, and Kirk looked down at him. His normally round features looked harsh and angular in the flashlight beam, and his eyes had rolled up in their sockets, giving him a blank white stare that sent shivers down Kirk's spine. All the anger he felt for Mudd fled at the sight of him lying there, helpless and dying, at Kirk's feet.

"Can you do anything for him, Bones?" he asked.

McCoy shook his head sadly. "I'm trying to stabilize him, but he's just too badly hurt. Those damned disruptors don't leave a doctor anything to work with. I'll have to put him on full life support within the next couple of minutes or I'm afraid we'll lose him."

Kirk considered ordering the *Enterprise* to target the palace's shield generators so they could beam out immediately. It was only a matter of time before they went down anyway. But it would undoubtedly be considered an act of war, and Starfleet would have his head if he tried it. He couldn't take that kind of action just to save one man.

Now every harsh word he had heaped on Mudd was coming back to haunt him. The man hadn't deserved that kind of treatment. He was a fraud and a charlatan and a con artist to beat all con artists, but he was not a scoundrel. He even had an odd sense of honor about him, as long as you realized that he honored wealth and comfort most of all.

And Kirk could hardly fault him for womanizing, now could he?

In another life, Kirk could easily imagine himself and Mudd hoisting a few frothy mugs of Romulan Ale and arm-wrestling for the right to dance first with the prettiest woman at the party. He even knew how it would turn out: Kirk would win, but Mudd would cut in before the song was half over. And they would both go back to drinking and swapping tall tales afterward. Only chance had thrown them together as adversaries.

He knelt down beside Mudd. "It wasn't supposed to happen this way, Harry," he said sadly.

"I'm losing him, Jim," McCoy warned.

Kirk took a deep breath, then pounded his fist into his palm. "No, dammit! I won't let it end like this." He snatched the communicator from his belt, flipped it open, and said, "Kirk to *Enterprise*. Lock phasers on to the palace shield generator and—"

"Jim!" McCoy shouted.

He looked down to see Mudd shimmering away to nothing.

"Belay that order," Kirk said as Mudd faded away completely. But as seconds passed without beam-out for the rest of them, he said again, *"Enterprise,* what's the holdup?"

"You said to belay the order, Captain," Uhura replied. "We're still waiting for the shields to go down."

"What? They're still up? Then what happened to Harry?"

"I don't know, sir. What did happen?"

"He disappeared, that's what. I thought you'd beamed him aboard. Bones, could the disruptor charges have had some kind of delayed reaction?"

McCoy shook his head. "I suppose it's possible. I don't know that much about these Nevisian weapons. But it looked more like a transporter effect to me."

"Spock?"

"I concur," said the first officer. "However, if the shields are still functional, there are few places he could have gone. He must still be in the palace."

"Then we've got to find him. Uhura, scan the palace for his transporter trace."

"It won't matter, Jim," McCoy said. "He's dead now anyway."

"You don't know that. He was still—"

"No he wasn't. His heart had already stopped and his brain activity was practically gone as well. I couldn't have saved him even if we had got him on board. Wherever he is now, he's dead."

The vault shook, and over a second later a loud rumble came through the walls. Somebody had blown up something big, far enough away that the sound had taken a moment to reach them.

"Shields are down, sir," Uhura said. "Transporting."

And a moment later, the four surviving *Enterprise* crew members stood on the platform back on board the ship. The yellow-alert klaxon was still sounding.

Kirk drew a deep breath. He would have loved to take a minute to calm down, but unfortunately duty called.

"Bones, get ready for casualties," he told McCoy. "Gorden, report back to security and let them know what we're up against if we're attacked. Spock, back to the bridge. Hold the fort until I get there."

If his first officer had been anyone but Spock, he would have gone directly to the bridge himself, but he knew Spock would be able to handle the situation for the few minutes he needed to take care of his other duty.

He went to the intercom on the wall and said, "Computer, locate Lieutenant Nordell."

"Lieutenant Nordell is in his quarters," the computer answered.

Kirk already knew where that was, since he had just been there a few days ago to discuss wedding plans. He still held his communicator open, so instead of using the intercom again he spoke into that as he hurried out of the transporter room and into the turbolift with Spock. "Uhura, keep scanning for Mudd, and transmit a message to the Grand General offering medical assistance." That much they could do without violating the Prime Directive. At least not too badly.

"Yes, sir," Uhura replied.

As he and Spock rode the turbolift upship, Kirk looked over and noticed the cut in Spock's cheek.

"You're hurt," he said.

"Not badly," Spock replied. He wiped the trickle of green blood away with the back of his hand, then cleaned his hand on his pants leg.

"Have Bones look at it anyway when you get a chance," Kirk told him, knowing that Spock wouldn't do it unless ordered to.

The turbolift stopped at deck four and Kirk stepped out to perform the duty every captain hates most.

Simon Nordell knew what had happened the moment he saw the captain at his door. He had stood up from the table as he called out "Open," but even before Kirk spoke, he felt his legs go weak and he had to sit back down.

Kirk stepped into the small living room and said, "I'm sorry."

Nordell tried to speak, but his throat had suddenly constricted. Finally he managed to croak, "How?"

"Protecting everyone else's lives," Kirk said. "We came under heavy attack and had to cross a corridor under fire. She was hit by a disruptor."

Nordell had to struggle to make sense of the captain's words. This wasn't just some random security officer Kirk was talking about; this was Nordell's wife. How could something like this happen to her, so soon after their wedding? He tried to imagine her getting shot, then wished he hadn't. The image chilled him to the core.

"Did she—?" Did she suffer? Did she have any last words? But he couldn't bring himself to ask.

"She died instantly," Kirk said. "She was . . . completely vaporized. There was nothing we could do."

They could have stayed out of danger in the first place, Nordell thought. They could have taken someone else. They would have done just that if she hadn't been available.

But she had. If he hadn't practically driven her out of their quarters, she might still be alive. He looked at the empty laliska glass in front of him, the condensation around its base leaving a ring on the table. He picked it up, hefted it in his hand. The captain watched while he decided whether or not to smash it, but the urge passed and he set it back down.

"We fought," he said, not looking up. "We fought all the time. But I loved her."

"I know," said Kirk. "Sometimes it works that way."

"But you never appreciate what you've got until it's gone, do you?"

The captain shook his head. "No, you never do."

Nordell took a deep breath, let it out slowly. Kirk seemed to be waiting for him to speak, but he had nothing to say.

After a minute, the captain said, "Are you going to be all right? Should I call someone to be with you?"

"No, I'll be fine." Nordell wasn't at all sure if that was true, but if it wasn't then he certainly didn't want someone else around to watch him go to pieces.

"I . . . have to get to the bridge," Kirk said, glancing upward. Nordell realized the yellow-alert siren was still sounding. He had completely blanked it out the moment the captain entered.

"I should be in engineering," he said, standing.

"You don't have to go if you don't want to," Kirk said.

"I want to." If he was at his job, then maybe he could keep his mind off the mess his life had suddenly become.

Kirk nodded, obviously understanding. Nordell got up, steadied himself against the table, then accompanied him out the door, wondering if he would have the courage to come back later tonight.

The turbolift ride to the bridge seemed to take forever, but Kirk knew no amount of time would erase the image of Nordell's face when he learned of his wife's death. He knew, as Nordell did, that only action would keep him from dwelling on it.

There was plenty of that waiting for him on the bridge. Kirk took in the situation at a glance. Chekov had returned to the navigator's station while they were on the planet, and Scotty was manning the engineering station. Uhura and Spock were also at their posts, and everyone looked tense.

"Captain," Sulu said as soon as Kirk stepped out of the turbolift. "We've just tracked a starship leaving the atmosphere."

"Harry's ship?" Kirk asked.

"I'm not sure. It doesn't have a registry beacon, and it doesn't correspond to any known starship type."

Kirk rounded the railing separating the upper workstations from his command chair and looked over Sulu's shoulder at the situation monitor. The ship was a tiny wedge of silver against the blue-green planet. "Put it on screen," he said.

On the main viewer the ship was bigger, but no more recognizable. But then Kirk hadn't expected the androids to build a Starfleet ship. "Any life-form readings?" he asked Spock.

"None, Captain," Spock replied.

"Keep tracking it. Uhura, have you reached the Grand General yet?"

"Yes, sir," she replied. "He rejects our offer of assistance. He says . . . he says we've done enough damage already."

"Maybe he's right," Kirk said, settling into his command chair. "What's the situation on the planet?"

"Still fighting, sir," Sulu said. "There's still an awful lot of transporter activity going on between Distrel and Prastor, too."

"Both ways?" Kirk asked.

"Yes, sir. But so far very little fighting has broken out on Prastor."

"At least none that we can detect at this range," Scotty amended. "I'm workin' on increasing the sensor range, but I think we'd be able to see disruptor fire if it was goin' on over there like it is here."

"That's odd. I wonder why people are beaming over there if not to strike back."

"We cannot be sure the beams are carrying passengers," Spock pointed out.

Sulu checked his monitors again and said, "The starship is headed for Prastor as well."

Something wasn't right here. Lots of transporter activity, but no fighting, and a starship suddenly launched on autopilot.

"It's a bomb!" Kirk announced. "Spock, scan that ship for explosives. Or maybe just a triggering device for whatever they're beaming over."

Spock went to work, but a moment later announced, "They're out of range, Captain."

"Chekov, lay in a course to follow them. Sulu, warp factor two." That was plenty fast within a solar system; in fact if they kept it up for long they would overshoot and find themselves in interstellar space.

The *Enterprise* leaped out of orbit, but the ship on the viewscreen continued to dwindle. "They've gone into warp as well," Sulu said.

"Warp three," Kirk said. At that speed they would catch the ship in seconds—and flash past Prastor only seconds after that.

But the other ship accelerated to warp three as well, then dropped back to normal space the moment it reached the planet.

The *Enterprise* dropped into orbit only a few thousand kilometers behind. "Scanning," Spock said.

"Somebody's beaming down," Scotty announced at the same time.

There was no intercepting the beam. If that was a bomb . . .

"Red alert," Kirk said. "Sulu, get ready to take us out of here. Chekov, target that ship and blow it out of space if it moves another inch closer to the planet. Spock, what beamed down?"

"Materializing now, Captain. Scanning . . ." He paused, narrowed his eyebrows, and said, "It's an android."

"The *Stella* android?" Kirk asked.

"It appears to be."

"Uh-oh," Kirk said. Thinking aloud, he said,

"She's supposed to monitor Harry, and judging by her performance in the cellars she's programmed to protect him as well. But she couldn't find him when the battle broke out because we had left her behind with the Grand General. You don't suppose she's going to try to stop the whole *war*, do you?"

"How could she do that?" Chekov asked.

"I don't know, but I think we'd better stop her from trying. Spock, send those coordinates to transporter room one." Kirk punched the intercom call button on his armrest and said, "Transporter room, lock on to that android and beam her aboard. Inside a confinement field."

"We are unable to do that," Spock announced. "She has entered a shielded area."

"Dammit!" Kirk said. These two planets had more shields than a Roman legion. But he couldn't let the android run amok down there; if it thought Harry was in danger there was no telling what it would do. "All right, then, we'll do this the hard way. Sulu, Chekov, and Scotty, you come with me. Spock, you have the conn."

He rose from his command chair and headed once more for the turbolift, wondering who he would lose this time.

Chapter Ten

CHEKOV HAD BEEN DRINKING when the yellow alert had sounded. Not heavily, but the events of the day had seemed to require some kind of finishing touch, and after watching two men hack away at each other with swords only a few feet away from him, a good stiff drink seemed the most appropriate response.

Technically, since he was off duty and it was only a yellow alert, he was not required to respond. He nearly decided not to—he could feel the effect of the vodka—but he hadn't gotten to be chief navigator by shirking his duty over a technicality. Yellow alerts most often led to red alerts, and his place then was on the bridge unless he was totally incapacitated.

Now as he left his station with the captain, Sulu, and Scotty, he wished he had hit the bottle a bit harder. Not so he would have been left behind, but to knock down the jitters he felt about this whole situation. Besides what he had seen for himself on the monitors, Sulu had given him that "Here we go again look," and Scotty had passed out extra power packs for their phasers; neither act exactly inspired confidence.

Nor did the captain's words on the way down in the turbolift. "Remember, gentlemen, this is an android. Phasers will have little effect on it except at full force, and we can assume that it will defend itself if attacked. Our best bet is to try to reason with it; let it know that Mudd is already dead and that there's no point in continuing on with whatever it intends to do."

"What if it already knows he's dead, and it came here for revenge?" Chekov asked.

"Then we disable it," Kirk said.

Chekov and Sulu exchanged another look. Right. Disable it. Simple.

The captain wasted no time in the transporter room. The moment the turbolift delivered them to deck seven he strode across the hallway and in through the still-widening doorway, said to Ensign Vagle, "The same coordinates we just gave you," and took up his position on the platform. Chekov and the others hurried to take their places as well, and the moment they were on the grid he said, "Energize."

They materialized in a crowded street paved with large flat stones. There were no vehicles in evidence, just red- and orange-clad Prastorians. There were plenty of them to fill the avenue, all pushing past one another and yelling to be heard over the din of their own voices and the loudspeakers on every corner that blared the message, "Citizens in squadrons twelve through nineteen, please report to your duty stations for battle assignments."

Chekov was keenly aware of his own greenish yellow uniform. Wrong color here. Every Prastorian he saw—men and women alike—wore a disruptor pistol, and everyone who saw him reached instinctively for the weapon. They only relaxed when they realized he and the others weren't Distrellian.

Chekov smelled sweat and fear, some of it his. He glanced uneasily around at the buildings. Not a palace in sight, which either meant that the Stella android wasn't going after the Padishah, or that the Padishah didn't live in a palace. Where the android *had* gone was harder to determine, but Scotty solved that by consulting his tricorder.

"There," he said, pointing toward a long, low building across the wide street and down a few hundred feet. "Something with a fusion power pack just passed through here, at any rate, headin' that way."

"That's got to be her," Kirk said. "Come on."

"The building's shielded," said Scotty. "The shield extends right out into the street."

Kirk nodded. "Understood. That's undoubtedly why she beamed down here instead of inside. But that may buy us the time we need to stop her." He led the way through the crush of Prastorians, who parted before them and closed up the gap again behind.

It was nearly impossible to see far through the crowd. The Prastorians averaged a few inches taller than humans, and their stiff hair stuck up even higher. Sulu solved the problem by climbing up on an ornamental planter and peering over their heads. "There she is!" he called out, pointing off to the left of where they had been headed.

He jumped back down and they moved off after

their quarry, bumping their way along and calling out "Make way," and "Excuse me," and occasionally "Move!" when someone blocked their path.

However, the Stella android was much more massive than her pursuers. She merely bowled aside anyone in her way until she reached the doorway in the long, blank wall of the building. They drew close to her while she tried to figure out how to open the door with the control panel on its face, but they were still yards away from her when she gave up with the controls and simply kicked down the door.

A flood of disruptor fire erupted outward through the doorway, narrowly missing the android, which leaped backward. Prastorians screamed as some of their own people were hit, and they backed away, pushing the ones behind them back with them.

The android, realizing her mistake, backed into the crowd as well.

"Now," said Kirk, shoving past the few remaining Prastorians between them and grabbing the android by the arm. She spun around, ready to knock him away, but stopped when she saw who it was.

She looked like she might finish the motion at any time. Chekov prepared to help subdue her if that proved necessary, but she decided to speak instead. "I don't care if you are the captain of a starship," she said in the shrewish screech that had previously been reserved only for Harry Mudd. "You'd better have a darned good reason for accosting a lady in the middle of the street like this."

Chekov nearly laughed out loud. Stella, a lady? But he kept his opinion to himself.

"Unfortunately, I do," said Kirk. "Whatever you're

trying to accomplish here, just wait a minute. Harry's already dead, and you can't bring him back to life, so let's talk it over before you start an interplanetary incident here for nothing."

"Harry is dead?" the android asked, her Stella voice and personality making even that seem like some terrible failing on his part.

No more disruptor fire came from the doorway, but Kirk pulled her deeper into the crowd anyway. "I saw him die. We were ambushed in the palace on Distrel before we even made it to the *Enterprise.*"

"That . . . cannot . . . be." Her voice slowed and grew monotonous. Apparently all her computing power was going into changing her mental map of the situation.

"It's true. We tried our best to save him, but he'd been hit too many times. He's dead."

One of the Prastorian women nearby had overheard him. "You were in the Distrellian royal palace just now?"

"Yes, I was," Kirk said brusquely. "And I lost a good friend there because of this ridiculous war of yours."

"That's unfortunate," the man next to her said, not sounding very sincere. "But think of the tales you'll have to tell each other when you're reunited in Arnhall."

"Yeah, right," Chekov said, sarcasm oozing from his voice.

"Ah, a skeptic." The Prastorian man turned to look at him more closely. "I have always wanted to meet one." He smiled wide while reaching to his waist, and his expression distracted Chekov just long enough that he didn't see the disruptor until the Prastorian had fired it at him, point blank, right into his chest.

It hurt like hell, but just for an instant.

Sulu had been watching the Stella android, which seemed to have seized up at the news of Mudd's death, when he heard the snarl of unleashed energy and Chekov's scream. Chekov fell to the paving stones, his chest smoking from the fist-sized hole blown into it. He had the most surprised expression on his face that Sulu had ever seen.

Sulu reacted without conscious thought. Some part of him must have known he couldn't draw his own weapon and fire quickly enough, so he chopped downward with his right hand and knocked the disruptor pistol from the Prastorian's grip, then grabbed that same arm with his left hand and spun the man around, bringing the arm up behind his back until it nearly touched the back of his head.

"Ow!" the man shouted. "What did you do that for? Let me go!"

Sulu didn't trust himself to speak. He grabbed the man's free arm and pinned that one behind his back too. Holding both arms in one hand, he pulled himself close to the Prastorian to use him as a shield in case the others tried to shoot.

They didn't seem inclined to do so. Most of them simply stared at him as if he'd lost his mind. A few even laughed.

"You—" Sulu tried to speak, but his tongue got all tangled up in his mouth. "You—" he tried again. "You killed Chekov!"

Indignantly, the man said, "Well, yes, but it was a practical joke, nothing more."

"A practical *joke!*" Sulu screamed. "I'll show you a

practical joke." He yanked upward on the man's arm, but Kirk stopped him short of breaking it.

"Don't," Kirk said, pushing down on Sulu's hand. Sulu didn't lower it, but he didn't push upward any higher.

"But—but he—" Sulu couldn't say it again. Not Chekov! Killed in cold blood over some stupid mistake that he didn't even know he'd made, a mistake that Sulu still didn't understand, would probably never understand.

Kirk was having trouble finding his voice as well, but he swallowed hard and said, "It's too late for him. Don't get the rest of us killed too."

The man he was holding tried standing on his toes to relieve the pressure on his arms. "Oh, come now. Surely you can't *all* be skeptics. I didn't think there were that many on the planet."

"We're not from around here," Kirk snarled at him. "In case you hadn't noticed. Bring him along, Mr. Sulu. He can stand trial for murder on the ship. Mr. Scott, bring Chekov." He glared at the Prastorians who surrounded them, and slowly, deliberately, drew his phaser. "Now, let us pass and nobody else will get hurt."

But the Prastorians merely laughed. The woman who had first spoken to them said, "Look, now, he was just making a point. Your friend is probably—"

Whatever else she said was drowned out in a roar of voices and screams from across the street. The *zzzt* of disruptor fire carried through the screams, and someone nearby shouted, "Incoming!"

The woman who had been arguing with Kirk turned without another word and ran off toward the commo-

113

tion, drawing her disruptor as she ran. She didn't get twenty feet, though, before an energy beam caught her in the shoulder and she staggered backward and fell to the ground.

"Distrellians!" someone else yelled, and through the gaps in the milling crowd Sulu could see people wearing dark blue uniforms pop into existence and begin firing their weapons at whoever stood in front of them.

The *Enterprise* crew stood in the worst possible place. The blank white wall of the building behind them stretched away for a hundred feet in either direction, putting them on display like targets in a shooting gallery, and its energy shield extended out into the street, preventing beam-out. Their best hope of survival was to fight their way directly across, *toward* the attacking Distrellians, and get out from under the shield so the *Enterprise* could pull them to safety.

Fortunately, that was the direction most of the Prastorians were going. Obviously welcoming their chance to die gloriously for the cause, they rushed ahead with disruptors blazing, shooting down the invaders the moment they appeared. Not without taking heavy casualties themselves, but that didn't slow them for a second. They attacked like wasps, more and more of them piling into the melee in a seemingly endless supply until their victims were hidden behind the crush of bodies.

Sulu shoved his captive along ahead of him, happy to use him for a shield. Scotty followed close behind, Chekov's body slung over his shoulder in a fireman's carry; and Kirk brought up the rear, tugging the Stella android, which had still not recovered from the news of Mudd's death. She tottered along precariously, not resisting but not helping at all, only taking a step when Kirk's forward motion overbalanced her and she was forced to move in order to stay upright.

The noise and confusion worked to their advantage at first—nobody paid much attention to the aliens in their midst when they had deadly enemies to kill—but the closer they drew to the line of fire, the less that mattered. Disruptor fire ripped past on either side, some of it coming from behind as overeager Prastorians tried to get in lucky shots from cover. Sulu kept his head down and bulled on through, his skin crawling in anticipation of that one fatal shot that would find *him* amid all the others.

What he felt first, however, was the fiery heat and jolt of impact as his prisoner took an energy beam in the stomach. The Prastorian doubled over and fell to the pavement, exposing Sulu to more fire, but Scotty's surprised yell made him ignore his own danger and whirl around to help his crewmate.

Scotty seemed uninjured, but his eyes were wild and white all the way around. It took Sulu a moment to realize he wasn't carrying Chekov anymore. He looked down, expecting to see his friend's body on the paving stones, but Chekov wasn't there, either.

"He vanished," Scotty said, shouting to be heard over the cries of battle all around them. "Just . . . vanished."

"Are we out from under the shield yet?" Kirk demanded. "Maybe the *Enterprise* beamed him aboard."

Scotty glanced at his tricorder, left activated on his

belt. "Not yet. We've still got fifteen feet to go." He looked up, his eyes widened, and he shouted, "Look out!"

He grabbed for Sulu's arm and tugged him to the side, but he wasn't quick enough. Sulu felt the searing fire of a disruptor charge rip through his right side. His breath left him in a convulsive scream, and when he tried to breathe in again he found that he could not. Either his diaphragm was paralyzed or his lungs had collapsed, he didn't know which.

He did know that he had maybe twenty seconds of consciousness left before he became another dead weight for Scotty to carry, so he did the only thing he could think of to help save his own life: He drew his phaser—awkwardly with his left hand when his right refused to cooperate—set it to maximum stun, and fired ahead to clear a path for him to run across the street.

He could hardly walk, much less run. He staggered ahead, his entire right side in agony, stumbling over the bodies of the dead and the people he had merely stunned.

But he had drawn too much attention to himself. Distrellians and Prastorians alike turned to see who was this new enemy in their midst, and he couldn't shoot fast enough to take them all down. He saw ten, twenty arms raise in unison, and from the disruptor pistol in each of them, white hot death shot forth and blasted him into oblivion.

Chapter Eleven

WHEN THE WEIGHT fell away from his shoulders, Scotty at first thought he had dropped Chekov, but it became instantly apparent that that wasn't the case the moment he turned to pick him up again. Chekov was gone, his body simply spirited away without a glimmer or a sound.

Scotty wondered if the *Enterprise* could have locked on to him and taken him on board, but he knew as soon as he thought of it that that wasn't the explanation. This was like no transporter beam Scotty had ever heard of. He had felt no confinement beam stiffen the body first, no residual heat from the scan, had seen and heard none of the flickering light or humming sound that normally accompanied a transport. Something else had happened to Chekov, and he had no idea what it was.

Sulu heard him cry out, and when he turned to see

what was the matter, Scotty explained as best he could amid the din. "He vanished."

Kirk asked the same question Scotty had first asked himself, and just to make sure, he checked his tricorder, but they were still under the shield. He looked up again just in time to see a Distrellian woman firing her disruptor methodically in an arc from left to right in a path that would hit Sulu's exposed back with the next shot.

He shouted a warning, grabbed Sulu's arm, and pulled as hard as he could, but it wasn't enough. The beam caught Sulu in the side, its molecular dispersion charge blasting away his uniform as if it weren't even there and charring his ribs and arm black.

Sulu reacted instantly, whirling around and firing back at the woman who had shot him. But no, that wasn't it—he kept firing, mowing down Distrellians and Prastorians alike like grass under a scythe, and Scotty realized he was trying to clear a path. He was using the last of his strength to give Scotty and Kirk a chance to escape, even though it would cost him certain death.

"Don't do it, lad!" Scotty yelled, but it was too late. At least a dozen disruptor beams converged on Sulu, the first ones blasting him backward and knocking Scotty, Kirk, and the Stella android down like dominoes before the combined charges completely vaporized him.

Could they have done that? Even as he struggled to rise, Scotty looked for the telltale signs that should have been there. A boot, a ring, a lock of hair—*something* should have been blown free after a blast like the one Sulu had taken. He had seen nothing like that. Just the scintillating brilliance of the energy discharge, then nothing. Gone without a trace, just like Chekov.

He didn't get a chance to search for clues. The captain pulled him back down before he had managed to do more than lift his head, and said in Scotty's ear, "Stay down. Our only chance now is to play dead until they forget about us."

Scotty saw the wisdom in that. Sulu's frontal assault hadn't lasted more than a second.

He felt a hollow, numb feeling wash over him as it finally sank in that Sulu was gone, Sulu and Chekov both, snatched away in the prime of life like pawns on a chessboard struck by an angry, capricious hand. As Scotty waited for the tide of battle to sweep past, he knew he would be a long time overcoming their loss.

If he got the chance. The battle wasn't over yet. They had another fifteen feet to go before they were out from under the shield, and it was the worst fifteen feet yet. People were dying right and left, and more people pushed their way forward to take their turn on the front line. They should have been stacked dozens deep by now, but as Scotty watched sideways with his head on the ground, his arms protecting him from being trampled, he saw body after body flicker away just as Chekov and Sulu had done. A momentary hope rushed through him as he thought that maybe some kind of emergency medical system was in operation here, beaming away the critically wounded before they died, but he knew even as he thought it that that wasn't the case. Chekov had died on Scotty's back—Scotty had felt him shudder and go limp— and Sulu had taken enough hits to blow up a shuttle- craft. No amount of medical intervention could bring him back. And Scotty saw a clear pattern among the bodies around him: those with any sign of life remained untouched. Only the unmistakably dead were removed.

He realized with disgust that this wasn't an emergency medical system he was seeing, only a sanitary way of dealing with the corpses.

The battlefront wasn't going to move on. Nor did it seem likely to stop any time soon. The individual fighters seemed to have forgotten the aliens in their midst, at least as long as they remained on the ground, but even so, Scotty knew another run for the far side of the street would just be suicide. And waiting where they were would be little better; one of those wild disruptor beams was bound to hit them sooner or later.

"Captain," he said, turning his head toward Kirk. "We've got to fall back."

"We can't go back, Scotty," Kirk said. "We've got to get out from under this shield."

An energy bolt sliced past overhead, spearing a man just behind them. Scotty turned away and said, "Aye, that's true enough, but we aren't going to make it this way."

"Have you got a better suggestion?" Kirk asked. He wasn't being sarcastic; Scotty could hear the hope in his voice.

That was the problem with pulling their fat out of the fire so many times before, Scotty thought. People started counting on you to do it again. But maybe, just maybe he *could* do something here. It would certainly be worth a try. He rolled over a bit so he could free his tricorder, then used it to scan for the shield's energy pattern. Some of the readings had seemed unusual to him when he'd scanned it after they first arrived, but he had chalked it up to alien technology and not given it another thought. Now he wondered. . . .

The shield, like many energy barriers, was essentially a series of polarized waves. The generator sent focused pulses outward thousands of times per second, their high energy and high frequency supersaturating the target space at the quantum level so that incoming energy beams were reflected back to their source. But this shield pulsed more slowly than most that Scotty had seen, and that suggested a weakness.

"What I'm thinkin,'" he told the captain, wincing from a close disruptor detonation beside his leg, "is that if we can't get out from under the shield, maybe we can move the shield off from over us."

"How?" Kirk asked.

"Well, if I use my tricorder to monitor the shield pulse rate, and connect it to my phaser so it'll modulate the energy output slightly out of phase with the shield, I might be able to set up a feedback loop that could overload the shield in an area big enough to beam us up through."

"You *might* be able to?" Kirk asked.

Scotty nodded. "It depends on how strong the shield generator is."

"And what happens if it's too strong?"

Scotty shrugged. "It'll overload the phaser instead."

"I see." Someone tripped over the android, caught his balance by stepping squarely on Kirk's left leg, and leaped over Scotty—straight into the path of a disruptor beam. As he toppled to the ground, Kirk said, "How good are the odds?"

"Do I look like Spock, Captain?" Scotty asked. "I

haven't got a clue. From what I see here, I'd guess a phaser with two power packs linked in parallel would be able to overload it, but I can make no guarantees."

Another energy beam lanced past just over their heads.

Kirk said, "It looks like we'll have to take that chance, Scotty. Back to the wall." He scooted around on his side and began to do an infantry crawl, tugging the compliant Stella android along beside him. She seemed to be recovering somewhat; at least she kept crawling on her own once Kirk got her started.

There was a gap of maybe twenty feet now between the crowd and the wall. A few Prastorians ran back and forth in the open space, trying to find a better vantage from which to fire at the Distrellians, but they gave little heed to the three figures who emerged from the crowd and took what cover they could behind a stone planter barely big enough to hide one of them.

Scotty immediately got to work. Exposing the phaser's klystron modulator was the easy part; connecting it to his tricorder was a bit trickier, since he didn't have any patch cords with him, but he solved that easily enough by stripping a pair of leads from the unneeded data-storage lines and patching them into the output bus, then running those over to the phaser. The extra battery pack proved the hardest connection to make, simply because of the amount of power that had to flow through the leads. Scotty settled for holding it in his hand and pressing the contacts into the charging port for the other pack, knowing that it would overheat and probably burn his fingers, but he couldn't think of a better way. If it worked, Dr. McCoy could regenerate his hand.

And if it didn't, he wouldn't be needing the hand much longer anyway.

Kirk had taken out his communicator and was filling in the *Enterprise* on their situation while he worked. He heard Spock say, "Has Mr. Scott taken into account the secondary harmonic vibrations that will undoubtedly be set up by his actions? There is a thirty-five-percent probability that the phaser will overload when they begin."

"Aye," Scotty said loudly toward the captain's communicator. "A fat lot o' difference it'll make knowing about it, 'cause there's nothing I can do about it with this setup, but if you get us out of here quick enough we'll be long gone before it gets out o' hand."

"What about innocent bystanders?" Spock asked.

What indeed? Scotty hadn't even considered that until now, but Spock's words cut him to the core. How quickly a person could forget the niceties of civilized behavior when his own life was on the line. But Spock was right; they couldn't endanger anyone else with this, even if they were all busy killing themselves off just across the street. He said, "We're maybe twenty feet away from the nearest one and behind a heavy stone planter. And by the time it blows, there won't be very much energy left in the power packs. I'll drop the whole works the moment we've broken through, and when you beam us aboard it'll blow up back here where it won't hurt anybody. Who knows, maybe it'll even distract 'em from killin' each other for a few seconds."

Another disruptor bolt slashed through the crowd and blew rock chips off the wall overhead.

"And maybe it won't," Scotty muttered, shoving the phaser's intensity setting all the way up to *Kill*. "I'm ready, Captain."

"All right, do it. Stand by, Spock."

"Ready here," Spock said.

Scotty aimed both tricorder and phaser upward. When the tricorder locked on to the energy barrier's modulation signature and began outputting a counterwave into the phaser, he pulled the trigger. A bright but noticeably flickering beam shot upward, and where it struck the shield, a circle began to glow.

"It's working," Scotty said, but the moment he said that he realized he'd spoken too soon. The energy readings began to fluctuate, and the phaser grew uncomfortably hot.

Not the power pack, but the phaser itself.

"The shield frequency is changing," Spock said through the intercom. "Can you compensate?"

"I'm trying," Scotty said, adjusting the tricorder sensitivity with the side of his thumb. He needed a third hand here, but it was too late to ask for help. In fact, Scotty watched with mounting horror as the fluctuations grew even more intense, and before he could counteract it the tricorder's energy reading went off the scale.

He let off the phaser's trigger, but it had already gone critical. Its emergency overload beeper went off, the piercing tone warning of imminent explosion. And he knew from experience that there was no stopping an overloaded phaser.

"Get back, Captain!" he cried out. "She's gonna blow!"

"Get rid of it!" Kirk yelled, and Scotty looked for someplace to throw it, but there were people everywhere. The beeper rose in pitch, keeping time with the angry whine that now issued from the phaser. Scotty whirled around with the fiery hot weapon in his hand, rejecting target after target. Not *in* anything; the containment would just magnify the blast. Not over their heads, for he couldn't know just when the phaser would blow, and if he misjudged it would fall right into their midst. Not behind the planter, for the captain and the android were still there. There was no place, no place, no—

No time. Scotty felt the phaser begin to melt and knew he had less than a second left. He couldn't have thrown it away now if he had wanted to; the molten polymer had fused with his hand. He had just one option left: he could save the captain's life, and he did it without hesitation. He jumped away from Kirk and curled himself around the phaser so his body would absorb the blast.

The roof, he thought suddenly, knowing that his last inspired moment had come an eternity too late. I should have thrown it on the roof.

Chapter Twelve

"No!" KIRK SCREAMED, reaching out toward Scotty just as the phaser blew. The entire power pack discharged through the weapon at once with a detonation that shook the ground and tumbled Kirk backward over the android.

He struggled to his feet again, pain and anger burning through every fiber of his body, but when he saw the foot-deep, five-foot-wide crater in the ground where Scotty had been, that heat turned to the icy, ultra-calm rage of a man pushed beyond his limit of endurance. He had watched Chekov, then Sulu, and now Scotty die within the space of a few minutes. And for what? To prevent this mechanical monstrosity—this . . . this caricature of a human being—from stopping the war that had killed them. He should have let her do it. Hell, he should have *helped* her do it. He should have done it himself from orbit, raining hellfire and destruction down on these insane creatures until they understood what *war* was.

He should have . . . what? Where in the long chain of regrets that led to this moment did he really have a choice? Like every great failure in history, each of his actions had seemed like a good idea at the time.

Now he had only one last person to save: himself. It hardly seemed worth the effort, but Scotty had given his own life to protect Kirk's; if nothing else, Kirk owed it to him to make sure he didn't die for nothing.

"All right," Kirk said to no one in particular. "Let's try this one more time."

His voice seemed flat, and he realized that he could hardly hear the crowd around him now. Everything not conducted through bone to his inner ear had to compete with the ringing from the blast.

He looked up to judge what he was up against, and realized that he had an audience. The explosion had drawn the attention of Prastorians and Distrellians alike, and for a moment, anyway, they had paused from their killing spree to see what he would do next.

What *could* he do next? He had a few seconds at most before they started shooting at one another again . . . unless he could keep them distracted somehow without antagonizing them. But how could he do that? He had exactly two things to work with: a phaser and an android woman in the electronic equivalent of shock. He didn't even have his communicator anymore; that had been torn from his grasp in the explosion and was nowhere to be seen.

Drawing the phaser would be suicide; Sulu had already proved that. That left the android. But how could he use her to get out of here?

He had no idea, but he had to do something and he

had to do it now. So he cleared his throat and spoke loudly to the Nevisian people around him: "Now that I've got your attention, there's something I think you should know."

What? What could he tell them that would make any difference? Kirk had never thought so fast in his life. To buy some time, he bent down and helped the Stella android to her feet. She stood beside him, blinking and turning her head from side to side. Her clothing was ripped, her nearly indestructible "skin" was smudged and scraped, and half of her red hair had pulled free of its bun and had fallen into her eyes. She looked as bad as Kirk felt, but she actually seemed more responsive than before.

Her disheveled appearance gave him an idea, though. He said to the crowd, "You fight for honor, but there's no honor in hitting a lady." The idea of calling Stella Mudd a lady nearly made him laugh. It would never have occurred to him if she hadn't called herself that when he'd first grabbed her. If the real Stella was anything like the replica that Harry had made then she was anything but, and right now the android looked more like a homeless waif than a genteel woman, but that was exactly the image Kirk needed.

The Nevisians didn't seem to care much about the difference between men and women, at least not in battle, so Kirk said, "There's no honor in attacking anyone who isn't part of your fight." Punctuating his sentences with short pauses to let his words sink in, he said, "This woman came here, unarmed, to help you, and how do you repay her? With confusion and mayhem. And when she tried to leave,

you callously—and completely without honor—
prevented her from going. You killed her bodyguards
and you nearly killed her as well. Is this what passes
for honor around here?"

He didn't wait for response. "If it is, then I spit on
your honor." That caused a stir. Kirk wondered if he
had gone too far, but he knew he couldn't back down.
To apologize to a crowd was to invite attack. It would
be better to challenge them than to appear weak—
especially if what Mudd had said about apologies
around here was true.

And with that thought, Kirk realized he had his
weapon. He had had it all along. Puffing out his chest
to look as belligerent as possible, he said, "I spit on
your honor and I demand an apology. You have
offended—worse, you have *insulted*—an innocent
bystander with your petty conflict, and as her protec-
tor I demand an apology from each and every one of
you."

Silence filled the street for a heartbeat, two heart-
beats; then one of the Prastorians holstered his disruptor and began to clap. For a few seconds only he
applauded, but he kept it up and pretty soon his
neighbors holstered their weapons and joined him.
The applause spread outward like ripples on a pond
until everyone was doing it, and the street that only a
minute earlier had echoed with the clash of battle now
roared with their approval.

At least that's what Kirk assumed it was. He
noticed that no apology had been offered yet, but if
they kept clapping long enough for him and the
android to cross the street and get out from under the
energy shield he really didn't care.

"Come on," he said. He took Stella's arm and led her into the press of people. They parted for him, then closed up behind, still applauding.

Two more Distrellians shimmered into existence just as Kirk and Stella reached the far side of the street. They appeared with weapons drawn and ready to fire, but the applause stayed their hands. They both leaned close to another Distrellian who had already been there, no doubt asking what was going on, and when she told them they nodded and joined in as well.

Kirk breathed a sigh of relief as he and Stella neared the site where the Distrellians had arrived. This had to be the edge of the shield. The *Enterprise* would beam them up any moment now, and they would be out of this insane mess. Without Chekov, Sulu, or Scotty, but it was too late to do anything for them.

Kirk turned around after he had passed through the entire crowd. He nodded sternly at the people in front, accepting their gesture without approving of it, expecting at any moment to find himself back on board the ship.

But without his communicator to lock on to, the *Enterprise* must have been having difficulty zeroing in on him, because he and the android remained on the street long enough for the applause to die down and an embarrassed silence to descend.

"Thank you," Kirk said, thinking that might trigger another round of applause, but it didn't.

One of the Distrellians in the front of the crowd shouted loudly, "Let's send him to Arnhall!"

"Yes, Arnhall!" a Prastorian answered, and then more voices took up the cry. "Arnhall, Arnhall!"

And everyone drew their disruptors.

Kirk didn't like the looks of that. "Hurry up, Spock," he muttered.

But he didn't beam out. He watched, horrified, as everyone in the crowd—at least all those with a clear shot—leveled their disruptors at him . . . and fired.

Spock, in the transporter room now, worked furiously to lock on to the captain, but with hundreds of others in the Prastorian street below, singling out one man was nearly impossible. It would have been simple if he still carried his communicator, but Spock had wasted precious moments zeroing in on its signal only to discover that no one nearby matched the captain's transporter trace. Now he had set the computer to scan through the entire crowd, but it was having difficulty keeping track of everyone. Individual traces moved back and forth, and others beamed in or away, complicating the scene almost beyond even the computer's ability to sort through it.

At least the disruptor fire had stopped. The energy fluctuations from the battle had made scanning unreliable at best. Spock assumed that the captain had had something to do with its halt, but he would have to wait until the captain was on board to learn what he had done.

Whatever it was, it was a short-lived phenomenon. Just as the computer announced in its quiet female voice, "Matching signal discovered outside shield perimeter—initiating transporter sequence," a concentrated burst of disruptor fire swept through the target area and the computer said, "Signal lost."

Spock felt a brief surge of telepathic anguish. He turned toward Ensign Vagle, the transporter operator, and said, "Do not despair, Ensign. We found him once; we will find him again."

"Yes, sir," Vagle said. He seemed surprised at Spock's statement. Spock wondered if he had misjudged the man's emotional state, and would have asked him if that was the case if the moment were not filled with other pressing business.

"Computer, scan the captain's last known position."

"Scanning," the computer replied. "No matching trace found."

Either the disruptor fire was still interfering, or the captain had moved. "Search for the android," Spock said. To Vagle he added, "The android is a much more unique target, and therefore theoretically easier to locate. And the probability is high that if we find the android, the captain will not be far away."

The computer immediately said, "Matching signal discovered. Initiating transporter sequence."

Spock considered ordering it to wait until they found the captain, but he realized there was no reason for that. In fact, it was better this way. They knew where the android had been, and if it was still functional they could simply *ask* it where Kirk was.

The black-clad, red-haired form of Stella Mudd shimmered into existence on the forward transporter plate. She staggered sideways when the confinement beam released her, and Spock immediately rushed to assist her down from the platform.

"Where is Captain Kirk?" he asked her.

She looked at him with a face devoid of expression, blank as only an android could manage. Her voice was equally toneless as she said, "Dead. Dead . . . dead . . . dead."

She was clearly damaged. But was she talking about Harry Mudd or Captain Kirk? And could Spock trust her assessment in any case?

"Where was he standing in relation to you?" he asked.

She blinked, then jerked her head to the right in a motion too fast and too extreme for a human to survive. "He . . . was . . . here," she said, raising her right arm to indicate the space just beside her.

"Ensign, scan that region."

"Scanning," Vagle replied. "No one there. Sir, that spot was the focus of the disruptor burst we just saw."

Spock didn't like the sound of that. He asked the android, "Was the captain shot? Is he injured?"

"Dead," the android replied again. Then she seemed to recognize Spock for the first time and her face took on some animation. "Spock," she said, her voice lowering at least an octave and taking on a male timbre. In fact, it was the captain's voice. Mimicking it almost perfectly, the android said, "Tell Spock . . . he has the helm. Godspeed."

It was eerie to hear the captain's voice issue from a woman's throat. Even Spock felt a shiver run down his spine at the sound of it, and the content of the message didn't help, either. That sounded like the last words of a dying man.

"Ignore life signs and search for a body," Spock ordered the ensign. They might still be able to revive him if they could get him to sickbay soon enough. Dr. McCoy was standing by to treat anyone who was injured.

"I can't find anything there," Vagle answered.

Spock left the android to stand on her own and

rushed back to the control console to try the search himself, but he was no more successful than Vagle.

"He . . . vanished," said the android. "They shot him . . . he fell . . . he said, 'Spock. Tell Spock . . . he has the helm. Godspeed.' Then he vanished." Again, her eerie mimicry left no doubt that she was talking about Kirk.

And the telepathic burst that Spock had felt—that must have been Kirk's death cry.

Spock felt a surge of remorse wash through him. The human part of him was reacting to the situation in its usual emotional fashion, but he also felt a different kind of remorse, a more sinister kind, that came from his Vulcan heritage. He clamped down on both of them and concentrated on the business at hand.

"What about the others?" he asked. He already knew Chekov's and Sulu's fate, and he could guess Mr. Scott's as well, but he needed confirmation before he abandoned the search for their bodies.

"Dead. All of them . . . dead. Even my . . . beloved Harry. What am I . . . to do?"

"I do not know," Spock said. What indeed? He faced a similar question himself. Even though Starfleet procedures were quite explicit in such cases—the first officer was to assume command of the *Enterprise,* report the situation to Starfleet Command, and await further orders—Spock felt that more was required of him. But he couldn't recover the bodies if they had all been vaporized, and nothing he could say to the Nevisians would change anything either.

Ensign Vagle's stunned expression reminded him that the crew would need time to grieve. Humans required a long period of adjustment before they could accept tragic news. And they often needed someone to blame for it. Even a scapegoat would do, if the actual guilty party was not available. He suspected that in this case he would fill that need for them, and unpleasant as he found the prospect, he vowed to perform the duty to the best of his ability.

And Stella? Perhaps she could serve in that same capacity. As an android she would excel at it, for even more than a Vulcan, she had no feelings of her own to interfere with the process.

There was no need for her to remain damaged no matter what function she served. Spock went to the intercom and said, "Security to transporter room one."

"What are . . . you doing?" she asked as she took a hesitant step forward.

He held out his hand to help stabilize her. "Calling you an escort to engineering," he said. "They will repair your damage, and then we will see what you are best suited for now that your guardian duties are over."

"Over," Stella echoed. "Dead."

When the two security officers arrived, she let them lead her away without protest. Spock looked at Vagle and said, "There seems little point in continuing to scan for survivors, but you may do so if you wish."

"Yes, sir," Vagle said, and from the tone in his voice Spock knew that he would be at it for hours. He made a mental note to order the man to cease and go to bed if he was still there by ship's midnight.

He left the transporter room, but was immediately faced with a choice. Should he take the turbolift back to the bridge and announce the captain's and the others' deaths to the entire crew, or should he take the few steps across the hallway into sickbay and deal with Dr. McCoy's inevitable wrath?

Do the toughest job first, he decided, turning toward sickbay. And besides, as illogical as it seemed, he discovered that he needed the doctor's presence in his own hour of grief.

Chapter Thirteen

"WHAT DO YOU MEAN you can't locate the bodies?"

McCoy stood in the middle of his emergency room, where he had been preparing his diagnostic equipment and biobeds for incoming wounded, and glowered at Spock. First he had the temerity to march in here and announce in his matter-of-fact fashion that Jim was dead, and now this.

"I mean just that," Spock said, standing as stiff-backed and poker-faced as ever. "They appear to have been vaporized by disruptor fire, except in the case of Mr. Scott, who was vaporized by phaser overload while attempting to counteract the energy barrier that prevented us from beaming them to safety."

His emotionless tone of voice while delivering such news was more than McCoy could bear. "Dammit, Spock," he said, "don't you *care*? Doesn't *anything* crack that Vulcan calm of yours? We've lost four of our finest officers, including the best friend either of us has ever had, and you stand there and talk about it like it was some kind of simulation that we all failed."

Spock's face grew a shade greener than usual, but that was his only visible reaction to McCoy's words. When he spoke, however, his voice was even softer than normal, and his words shocked McCoy to the core.

"It is a myth, Doctor, that a Vulcan feels nothing. Even were I not half human, I would sense a deep and powerful anger building in me as well. An anger that, if left unchecked, would lead me to pursue the captain's killers and remove them from the universe. Not only the killers themselves, but their offspring and all their relations until I had eradicated their very genetic code. Without the iron self-control that we Vulcans have developed to keep this type of rage in check, I could easily become an avenging monster capable of sterilizing both of the planets in this star system in retaliation for my captain's—my *friend's*—death. Would you prefer that to my . . . inhumanly calm reaction?"

McCoy shivered despite himself. "No," he said quietly. "No, that wouldn't help anything."

"I agree. Unfortunately, Vulcans have no middle ground to occupy in such conditions as these. We either accept what has happened and go on with our lives, or we allow our emotions to overwhelm us completely. History has proved the latter option to be unacceptable."

McCoy nodded, grudgingly accepting Spock's statement at face value. "All right, I can understand that, but speaking as a doctor, that's not healthy. Your human half, at least, needs to go through some distinct stages before you can integrate what's happened into your life."

"And what phases are those?" Spock asked.

"Shock. Denial. Anger. Bargaining. Depression. And finally, only after you've worked through everything else, acceptance."

"I see." Spock sat down on the end of one of the biobeds. "Since I cannot allow that to happen, especially now that I am captain of the *Enterprise,* what repercussions can I expect?"

He was serious. He really had no intention of allowing the grief process to proceed normally. Lots of people tried to deny it, but it nearly always happened to them anyway. Spock, on the other hand, would probably succeed in suppressing it—but there would indeed be a cost. "Physically, you'll probably lose stamina," McCoy told him. "Your immune system will become depressed—no pun intended—so you'll probably catch just about any cold or flu that's going around. And you won't sleep normally, which will in turn make you lose stamina and depress your immune system even more."

"And mentally?" asked Spock.

"Your judgment will suffer. A human would get irritable. During the denial phase, you could become delusional. You'll probably—" The silliness of what he was saying suddenly struck him. "Dammit, Spock, this is ridiculous. You've got to grieve properly or before long you'll be unfit for duty."

"I see." Spock stood again, still rigid as a post, and said, "I will take your thoughts under advisement." He took a few steps toward the door, then turned back to McCoy. "What of you?" he asked. "Will you be proceeding through the same phases you outlined for me?"

McCoy felt a flash of unreasonable fury at the mocking tone in Spock's voice, but a second later it faded as he realized the Vulcan had meant no mockery. He really didn't understand human nature.

McCoy's reaction to his innocent question was answer enough. That and the almost crippling regret he felt over all his angry outbursts at Kirk over the years. He knew it was irrational—they had been close friends—but right now the harsh words they had exchanged were all McCoy could remember. "Yes," he said to Spock. "And you'd better get used to it. Everybody on board but you is going to go through the same process."

"I suspected as much." Spock nodded, as if confirming an earlier decision. "Thank you, Doctor. I must go now and make the shipwide announcement. Please take whatever precautionary measures you believe necessary."

He turned away and walked out of sickbay, leaving McCoy standing there in the middle of his emergency room, wondering what precautions he could take. How do you prepare a body for the news that its head has just been cut off?

The bridge seemed like an alien place to Uhura. She had sat in this same chair before the same control board for her entire tour as communications officer, but now with Spock in command and new faces at the navigation, helm, and science stations, the place seemed utterly foreign. She was still reeling from the news that Spock had just broadcast on the intercom, even though she had already known her friends were dead. She had monitored their signals from the moment they beamed down to the moment they had died, wincing as each communicator's homing signal—and each person carrying it—winked out in turn.

Now another signal from the planet caught her attention. A cluster of signals, actually. Tight-beam radio transmissions between moving targets. She wouldn't normally have detected them, but the scanners were still set on maximum sensitivity after their search for the captain. Uhura tuned to the signals' frequency and heard a voice saying, "—two big cylinders in back are probably the engines; orange squadron aim for those. If you can't destroy the engines directly, try to cut them loose—those supports look like a weak point. Yellow squadron, aim for the center of the disk, try to open it to space, and red squad, take the lower cylinder. Watch out for—"

They were talking about the *Enterprise!*

Uhura swiveled around in her chair and said, "Ca—Spock—I mean, Captain, we're under attack!"

"Shields up," Spock ordered immediately. "Red alert. Lieutenant, visual on screen."

Ensigns Stanley and Brady, the new navigator and helmsman, weren't as fast as Chekov and Sulu, but they got the shields up within moments of Spock's order. Since she hadn't been monitoring on visual to begin with, Uhura took a bit longer to focus on the source of the transmissions and put the image on the viewscreen, but within a few seconds she had that as well.

Something was rising from the planet. Lots of somethings. Small, fast, wedge-shaped ground-to-orbit fighters, by the looks of them. As they drew closer, the ones in the lead began to fire at the warp engine nacelles, then more and more of them arrived and swarmed like angry wasps around the entire ship, firing at every section of it. The deck rocked under the blows.

"Damage report?" Spock asked, his voice as even as if he were asking for the time.

Uhura listened to the intraship channel, where reports were already coming in.

"Minor damage on decks seventeen and twenty," she said.

"Shield integrity deteriorating," Lieutenant Wolfe, the new science officer, said. "Down to eighty-five percent."

"Should we return fire?" Stanley asked, not taking his eyes off the viewscreen.

The tendons in Spock's neck stood out for a moment, as if he were clenching his jaw tightly to keep from speaking. Was he actually thinking about it? Uhura would never know, for a moment later he unclenched his jaw and said, "Negative. It would serve no useful purpose. Helm, take us out of orbit. Warp one. Put some distance between us and the warships."

"Yes, sir."

The *Enterprise* streaked away from Prastor, leaving the fighters far behind. When the planet was merely a bright disk among the stars, Spock said, "Full stop. Lieutenant, scan for pursuit."

Uhura did so, but after circling around the spot where the *Enterprise* had been for a few minutes, the warships shot away around the planet. Uhura saw the energy discharge of more disruptor fire, but she couldn't tell what they were shooting at. Whatever it was, it didn't fight back, and soon enough the fighters returned to the ground. "They've gone home," she reported.

Spock nodded. "Stand down to yellow alert. Lower shields. Lieutenant, prepare to send a message to Starfleet Command, code level forty-seven. I will prepare the message in the briefing room."

"Yes, sir." Code 47 was the highest level of encryption, used only for extremely sensitive and urgent communications. Spock was undoubtedly going to make his report on the captain's death, and didn't want the information to get into the wrong hands. Captain Kirk had been a major presence in the Quadrant for so long that news of his passing could destabilize the entire region if it were announced by the wrong people.

Uhura took some pride in that knowledge, but it was small comfort compared with the loss of the captain. And of Chekov and Sulu and Scotty.

She had never told them how much they meant to her. They would have all been embarrassed if she had, but just the same, she regretted never saying anything. She was the communications officer; she could have come up with some way to get the message across if she had tried.

Why did people always wait until it was too late to say the important things?

Simon Nordell removed the android's belly plate and set it carefully beside her on the workbench. It unnerved him to see winking lights and circuit boards inside a woman's body. Women had always seemed mysterious to him, and this only added to the impression.

He had left her clothing in place, not wishing for any more distraction than he already had. Besides, the android had been reluctant to allow even this minor violation of her personal space; Nordell wasn't sure she would allow access to other areas anyway. It had been all he could do to get her to lie down and let him work on her at all. Fortunately her main processing center was in her abdomen, rather than in her head.

He hoped the problem would be something simple to fix. He didn't have high hopes—this was, after all, an alien device—but he figured he could at least look for the obvious. Burned-out circuits or tripped breakers would probably be apparent no matter who had built them. Or it might even fix itself if he gave it enough time. The android's speech had improved considerably just in the last few minutes.

This was the first time he had worked on a machine that could tell him where it hurt. Not directly—her diagnostic and repair circuitry had apparently gone down when she'd overloaded—but she could at least report the results of his actions. It was simultaneously fascinating and terrifying, working on a sentient machine.

He didn't have to do this. Less than two hours after he had learned of his wife's death, no one would have faulted him for staying home and letting someone else cover for him. But the whole engineering department was still reeling from the news of Scotty's death, and besides, Nordell couldn't stand the thought of sitting in his and Leslie's quarters and listening to the silence. He kept replaying their last moments together and wishing he could change them. She had been angry when she left, and rightfully so. He had been a complete ass, sitting there at the table drinking his laliska when he should have been with her in the bedroom, down on his knees apologizing to her. But he had been too proud to apologize, and now he would forever wonder: Had her anger had anything to do with her death?

He needed to keep the android talking so he could tell if his adjustments did any good. And he needed to talk himself, to keep the question from burning up his own mind. So as he used his multiphase tricorder to analyze the circuitry he could reach from the access panel, he said, "So what's it like being an android, anyway?"

Potentials shifted along hundreds of data lines. Nordell watched, fascinated, as his tricorder traced a visual image of her thought processes.

Her answer surprised him, with both its speed and its forcefulness. And her voice took on a much more human—although irritating—timbre. "I am Stella Mudd. Harcourt's wife."

Her programming evidently ran deep. He didn't want to argue with her and throw her into another feedback loop, so he kept a straight face and said, "Yes, of course. How long have you been married?"

"Seven years, eight months, and six days, Terran standard."

Hardly any mental activity required for that one. She must keep a running tally, like some of the people Nordell knew who marked off on a calendar how much longer they had until shore leave. "Is it that bad?" he asked.

"Harcourt is a scoundrel," she answered, her voice taking on even more animation. "He drinks, he chases other women, he keeps unsavory business associates, and worst of all, he doesn't listen to me when I try to correct his behavior."

That struck a bit close to home. And it didn't seem to take any more effort than the previous question. Nordell decided to give her a tougher one, something that would exercise her brain but—he hoped—wouldn't overload anything. "Do you love him?"

Energy danced along the web of her electronic neurons. It took her a few seconds to respond. "I . . . of course I do. That's why I try to improve him. Or tried to."

Two data lines went into wild oscillation as she said those last three words. Nordell adjusted his tricorder to dampen the traffic along those lines, then said, "Why didn't you just learn to accept him for what he was?" He watched those two data lines closely to see if his use of the past tense would affect her.

"I . . . that's not what marriage is for," Stella replied. "Marriage is when two people who don't get along try for the rest of their lives to change each other's behavior."

God, I hope not, thought Nordell. He wondered how much the suppression of those two information pathways had affected her cognitive ability. But that statement had sounded pretty lucid to him. Scary, but lucid.

"What about companionship?" he asked. "I always thought marriage was when two people decided to live together because they liked each other."

Stella raised her head and speared him with an eagle-eyed gaze. "What planet do you come from?"

"Mars," Nordell replied. "But that's not why I think that. My wife, Leslie, was from Venus, and she felt the same way. At least I thought she did, despite our last conversation." He added quietly, "I guess I'll never know for sure."

Stella's features softened—at least as much as they could on a face set in a perpetual scowl. "Why? Did she leave you, like that good-for-nothing Harry left me?"

Nordell shook his head. "No, she was killed on Distrel, trying to rescue your good-for-nothing Harry from execution."

The potential in the two data lines tried to rise again, but he kept them suppressed. Stella laid her head back down and said, her voice heavy with exasperation, "I always said he would come to a bad end. If he had listened to me, he—"

Nordell looked at his tricorder. The android appeared to have locked up, but data was flowing at a tremendous rate on every line. He reached for the adjustment on his tricorder to dampen them out, but before he could complete the motion Stella's right hand came up with lightning speed and snatched the tricorder away.

"Hey, what are you doing?" he shouted, startled.

"I must go back to Prastor," she replied. She sat up, took the belly panel from the table beside her, and fitted it into place, hiding the circuitry behind realistic skin and an equally realistic belly button.

"You can't go back there," Nordell said. "The war is still going on."

"All the more reason," Stella told him. "I tracked him there; he may still be—that's strange." She turned her head from side to side, then slid off the table and turned all the way around. "I can't locate him now."

She must have planted a homing device in him, Nordell realized. Apparently powered by his metabolism, if she couldn't pick up its signal now. "You can't locate him because he's dead," he told her. "I suppressed your memory of it, but it's true."

"I'll be the judge of that." She pushed past him toward the door. "That good-for-nothing con man has faked death to get away from me before." Thanks to his suppression of the data lines that led her to believe in his death, her Stella personality was in full control now, and in complete denial.

Nordell grabbed her arm and tried to stop her, but she shrugged him off without even turning around. He watched her stride out the door and turn toward the turbolifts.

He reached out to the intercom and punched the shipwide call. "Security," he called. "Security to engineering." Then the significance of his words struck home and he felt the weight of the entire universe come down on him. Security. Leslie would be answering that call if she were still alive.

Chapter Fourteen

HARRY HAD DIED and gone to Heaven. He was sure of it. He remembered dying clearly enough, although the last few moments of it were mercifully elusive from recollection, and this place where he found himself now was certainly Heaven. If it wasn't, he didn't care; it was good enough for him.

He had awakened in a pool of warm water. Rather hot water, in fact. The heat had concerned him for a few seconds until he realized that the temperature was just right for relaxing in, and that the jets of bubbles that shot out from the sides were already beginning to soothe the aches and pains from his recent exertion. Then when he looked up and saw the two Nevisian women standing at the foot of his bath, wearing only their smiles, he knew for certain he had gone to the right place.

Especially when the one on the left, light-haired and

humanoid in all the right places, said, "Welcome to your new life. I am Aludra."

"And I am Cipriana," said her dark-haired companion.

"And I'm enchanted," Mudd said, sitting up and looking around.

Heaven appeared to be a large building filled with row upon row of tiled pools like the one he rested in. There were no windows, but skylights all along the ceiling let out steam and let in sunlight, which illuminated a multicolored tile mosaic landscape on the walls. There wasn't a stitch of clothing among the hundreds of people he saw soaking in the pools or standing beside them—a delightful sight even for a veteran spacehand who had seen similar situations many times before.

The only disconcerting sight was that everyone here was Nevisian. Their hair had the same hemispherical static-charge look common to Prastorians and Distrellians alike, and though the dampness had taken much of the stiffness out and made everyone appear a great deal more human at the moment, it was obvious that they weren't. And the tiled room echoed with the voices of people conversing in the Nevisian language.

As he watched, two more very surprised-looking people—both Nevisian—materialized in pools down the row from him, and attendants moved to welcome them.

Mudd had never been particularly religious. And it did seem a bit odd that everyone in Heaven spoke Nevisian. But then, he reasoned, he had died in the Nevis system, and the operative word was "died." This was *somebody's* afterlife, no matter what they called it. He was just glad it existed at all. If he wanted to find the human area he would probably have to take a celestial shuttle of some sort.

All in due time. He was in no hurry to go anywhere. Especially when the dark-haired woman at the foot of his pool, Cipriana, said, "We're here to give you a hero's welcome to your new home. Would you like us to bathe you?"

A hero's welcome, eh? Where he came from, that meant considerably more than just a bath, but he had to admit that would certainly make a good start. He lay back in the pool and smiled wide. "My dears, that would be divine."

They both bent down and slipped into the pool with him. From an alcove above his head they took thick padded mitts and drew them onto their hands, then began rubbing his chest and back and sides with the scratchy fabric.

"Oh yes," Mudd sighed, closing his eyes and letting them work their magic. "For this, I would die again and again."

The blond woman, Aludra, giggled. "Silly. If you die a second heroic death, you'll go straight to Arnhall; you know that."

"No, actually, I didn't," said Mudd. "Where's Arnhall? And do they have women as beautiful as you there?"

They both smiled, and Cipriana said, "When we finish our own heroic doublets they will."

"Ah, certainly." Mudd turned to put an itchy shoulder blade under Aludra's mitt. "How do you know I died heroically, anyway? I could have tripped on a stairway, couldn't I, and wound up here just the same?"

Aludra laughed, a high-pitched, musical sound that echoed on the tile walls. "It would have to be a pretty spectacular fall. Only heroes appear in the baths. Accident victims generally get a second chance on their homeworld. And of course cowards are dumped on the street."

"Of course," said Mudd.

She looked at him quizzically, then said, "You really didn't know, did you?"

"No," Mudd admitted.

"That's two of them," Cipriana said to Aludra. "I thought we might have this sort of problem when we started allowing aliens to join us." She said to Mudd, "Do you know Leslie Lebrun Ensign Three Two Seven Five Six Oh?"

"No," said Mudd. "At least I don't think so. Why?"

"Because she arrived just a few minutes ago, and she didn't know where she was, either." Cipriana pointed to Mudd's left. "She's right down there." Aside to Aludra she whispered, "So many names! She must have incredible stories to tell!"

Mudd squinted through the steam. He saw a few heads bobbing above the water, and attendants, both male and female, scrubbing away on their bodies.

And about five pools away he saw a woman with hair hanging down into eyes that were much deeper in their sockets than everyone else's here. Her face was much wider than usual and her ears were rounded on the edges rather than made of overlapping petals. She was, in short, human. Mudd recognized her as the security officer who had accompanied Kirk—and who had been vaporized in the crossfire only a minute or two before Mudd himself had been hit.

That clinched it. If she was here, then this was indeed the afterlife, for he had watched her die.

She didn't seem nearly as happy as he was about winding up here. She held her arms around her knees and her head bowed. Rather than bathing her, her attendants—a muscular young man and an older, motherly woman—sat on the edge of her pool with their feet dangling into the water and simply talked with her.

"Leslie?" Mudd said. "Miss Lebrun?"

She looked up, and her eyes lit with recognition. "Harry Mudd!" Then her brows furrowed and she said, "You didn't make it either."

"No," Mudd told her, "but I believe your sacrifice did save the lives of your crewmates." He couldn't know that for certain, but their absence from the baths seemed fair evidence. Kirk would, of course, go straight to Hell for his crimes, but certainly McCoy wouldn't, nor Spock or the other young security officer.

"I guess that's some consolation." She unwrapped her arms from her knees. "Could I . . . join you over there? No offense," she said to her attendants, "but I could use the human contact right now."

"Certainly, my dear," Mudd said. "I would be delighted."

The older woman said, "Of course you may. That's why people who fought together arrive here together, so you can talk about what happened before you go on to start life anew. Here." She and the man helped Lebrun out of her pool and over to Mudd's. Harry moved aside to give her room on the underwater bench, surprised to realize he was averting his eyes to protect her modesty. Death had apparently affected him as well, or perhaps it was merely the plethora of other delights to occupy his attention, but whatever the cause, she seemed too innocent and upset for him to add to her troubles by ogling her naked body.

Her attendants helped her into the pool, then left to help another person who materialized in a pool nearby. Cipriana and Aludra stayed in the water, though four bodies nearly made it overflow.

When Lebrun had slipped into the water and the jets once again veiled her in bubbles, Mudd smiled at her and said, "I must thank you for your bravery and courage in attempting to rescue me—and I fear I must apologize as well for delaying our departure. I allowed my . . . ah . . . my natural attraction for precious treasures to cloud my judgment."

"Your greed, you mean?" Lebrun said, a trace of a smile on her lips.

Mudd laughed. "You and your captain were cut from the same mold. He always preferred such terms as well. But really, I believe life is what you make of it, and what you call a thing says a great deal about your attitude toward it."

"Life. Right. And what do you call this?" Lebrun held her arms out to include the whole building, and by implication the whole situation that had brought them here.

"An opportunity," said Mudd. "For one, I have escaped that damnable android chaperone of mine. For another, we do seem to have physical bodies again, which is more than I was led to expect. We might even be able to contact our former companions in life and continue our business as usual if we wished, though—"

"No communication is permitted with those you left behind," said Cipriana. "You must leave your former life in the past."

"As I was saying," Mudd finished, "given the circumstances, I for one am glad to be quit of it. A fresh start, that's what I call this."

"I was married the day before yesterday," Lebrun said quietly. "I'm not quite so eager to give that up."

Mudd snorted. "Believe me, if your marriage was anything like mine, another day or two would have been all it would take to change your opinion."

Aludra looked puzzled. "What is marriage?"

"It's when two people agree to share everything, and spend the rest of their lives together," said Lebrun.

"In theory," Mudd corrected. "In practice, it's when two people agree to make life miserable for each other."

Cipriana frowned. "How could you agree to spend your lives together?" she asked Lebrun. "You know you'll be separated the first time one of you is killed."

"I . . . I didn't expect to be . . . killed," Lebrun said. She sniffed, and wiped at her eyes with a wet hand. Cipriana wrung out her bath mitt and handed it to her to dry her eyes with.

"Nobody does, the first time," Aludra said. "But it eventually happens to all of us. It can be very difficult if you've formed strong attachments, but you always have a happy reunion in Arnhall to look forward to."

"That's the second time I've heard you mention—" Mudd began, but a sudden commotion far down toward the other end of the building stopped him in mid question. It sounded as if someone was banging on a door. Banging *hard*. Had they locked an avenging angel out by mistake?

Perhaps they had, for a second later a bright rectangle of light appeared in the wall as the door burst inward. People shouted in alarm, and the blue bolts of disruptor fire speared outward through the sudden gap.

Disruptors in Heaven? That shocked Mudd more than anything he had seen or heard so far.

The shooting died down, and a babble of voices rose to replace its noise. It was difficult to see clearly through the steam, but Mudd thought he could see five or six clothed people near the door—all wearing red.

An ugly suspicion rose in his mind. "Just a minute," he said, turning to Aludra. "Where are we, exactly?"

"Exactly?" Aludra asked, reluctantly looking away from the commotion. "We're in pool seventy-three in hero's reception hall nine, in the city of Novanar, on the southern continent of Kelso. On Prastor," she added helpfully.

"On Prastor," Mudd repeated. He could actually feel his worldview reorient itself to accommodate the news that he hadn't gone to Heaven. It felt a bit like going into warp drive with a badly tuned engine.

Somehow he was still alive, miraculously healed of his disruptor wounds—and back in the same universe he had thought was safely behind him. "Dammit," he said, then, embarrassed at having sworn in the presence of three ladies, he said, "Pardon my Klingon, but I believe our troubles are not over after all."

"Are you kidding?" Lebrun said excitedly. "If this

is Prastor, then we can get back in touch with the *Enterprise.* And I can join my husband again."

"That's precisely what I was talking about," Mudd said. He leaned back in the water and let the jets work the renewed tension from his muscles. He had the unpleasant suspicion that he would need all the relaxation he could store up to get through the days ahead.

Chapter Fifteen

KIRK FLINCHED HARD at the touch of hot water, splashing gallons of it out over the rim of the tub to wash down the tiled walkway and lap at the ankles of the dozens of nude people who stood before the other tubs. He looked down, and when he couldn't see beneath the swirling bubbles he felt with his hands and discovered that he was naked as well.

And whole. He should have been a cloud of ions after taking that many disruptor hits all at once. But he couldn't remember actually being shot. Just the entire crowd of people, Distrellians and Prastorians alike, aiming at him.

Two nude women noticed him and walked up to the foot of the tub. One was young, tall, and thin; the other was shorter and closer to Kirk's age. "Hello," they said, smiling. "Wel—"

"Where am I?" Kirk asked.

"—come to Distrel," the tall one finished.

"Distrel?" Kirk turned once around in his tub, but the interior of the bathhouse gave no clue to his location. The women looked Distrellian enough, with their narrow faces and wide eyes and stand-up hair—but they looked human enough in other ways to make that an uncertain conclusion.

"How did I get here?" he asked.

The older woman said, "You must have been killed in battle. Weren't you?"

Kirk shrugged. "I was certainly in the right place for it. I thought I'd talked my way out of trouble, but right at the last there, somebody shouted, 'Let's send him to Arnhall!' and they all pulled their guns on me."

"Ah!" said the same woman, smiling brightly. "They gave you a hero's send-off. Whatever you said must have been very impressive. But this must be your first death."

"I—" At her words, all the close calls in his life flashed through his mind. The space battles, the hand-to-hand fights, the hostile aliens—the myriad ways an explorer endangered his life every day. But none of them had actually managed to do him in. And the fact that he was here, apparently on Distrel again, convinced him he wasn't dead this time either. Apparently the *Enterprise* had managed to beam him away just in the nick of time, but he hadn't gone back to the ship. "There must have been a transporter accident," he said.

"No," the woman replied. "If this is your first time, you're in the right place. In fact, I believe these other gentlemen must be friends of yours." She nodded toward Kirk's right.

He looked in that direction, but the steam obscured

his vision. Sound traveled quite well through it, though, and just at that moment Kirk heard a voice with a distinctly Russian accent say, "Yes, up just a bit . . . now over to the left . . . there. Ah, yes, now keep doing that for the rest of the week."

Could it be? "Chekov?" Kirk called out, hardly daring to hope.

He heard a splash and a female voice squeal in surprise, then, "Captain?"

"Captain Kirk?" asked another voice with a Scottish burr.

"Scotty! And Sulu?"

"Here, Captain!"

This was flat-out impossible, but at the moment Kirk didn't care. Something had rolled back the clock to a moment before they had died and whisked them here to this Roman-style bath, and he wasn't going to question it. He climbed out of his pool, thanked the two women who had greeted him, and walked through the mist until he saw his three officers. Scotty and Sulu were standing waist-deep in the water at the edge of their pools, looking excitedly toward Kirk, but Chekov, in the farthest of the three pools, lay back in the water while two attractive young women rubbed him down with stiff sponges.

He did at least wave when he saw Kirk approach, and he said, "Captain, come on in. The water's fine!"

"I can see that, Ensign." Kirk knelt down at the edge of the water so they wouldn't have to crane their necks to talk with him, then in a what-the-hell mood slid on in and sat on the underwater shelf at Chekov's feet. The place was apparently safe for the moment, and he could certainly use the relaxation.

Sulu and Scotty each had a pair of female attendants as well, who resumed scrubbing their backs with sponges. One of Chekov's delightful pair asked Kirk, "Would you like a pool and assistants of your own? We can find four baths side by side."

"No, thanks," Kirk said. The hot water was pleasure enough, and tempting as it might be, he didn't need the distraction. He needed to figure out what to do next.

"If you prefer men, that's no problem," the woman said.

Sulu snorted, and Kirk laughed. "No, that won't be necessary. I'm quite comfortable as it is. But if someone could bring me a communicator, I'd like to send a message to my ship."

"Your ship?" the woman asked.

"Starship," Kirk said. "The *Enterprise.* We're from the United Federation of Planets. We came to talk with the Grand General when we learned that you and Prastor had stopped fighting. But unfortunately, we were caught up in the hostilities when war broke out again."

The woman's brow furrowed. "Wait, let me get this straight. You were here, on Distrel, when you died? If that's so, then you should have been sent to Prastor. Or Arnhall if it was your second death. Unless it was a coward's death, in which case you should have gone to Prastor as well, but straight back into battle to try it again."

Kirk shook his head, trying just as hard as her to make sense of things. "No," he said, "we were on Prastor at the time. It's a long story. But we were all . . . Dammit, how could we have been revived after what happened to us there? Chekov, maybe—he wasn't hit that badly—but not Sulu or me. And

Scotty; I saw Scotty blown to bits by an overloaded phaser. Nothing could rejuvenate a man after that."

"The Gods can," the woman said simply. "They do it all the time." She pointed toward an empty pool in the next row over, and after only a few seconds a woman materialized in the water. She looked startled for a moment, then tilted back her head and laughed. "Oh, wow," she said. "That was wild."

Kirk bet it was, if her experience had been anything like his. There was obviously some kind of resurrection legend at work here—only this one was apparently based on a real phenomenon. Well, they would soon get to the bottom of it. He turned back to Chekov's attendant and said, "Whatever happened to us, we need to get back to our ship."

Her face took on a horrified expression, as if he had just suggested they kill someone as a practical joke. "No, that's—you can't do that," she stammered. "Nobody is allowed to contact anyone from their former life. You're Distrellians now. You live here, and work here, and you fight for Distrel next time you go to war."

That explained the bathhouse. In a society where a person's home planet determined what colors they wore, someone who arrived without clothing would start right off with one fewer tie to home. And if they were unarmed they couldn't cause much trouble even if they did still think of themselves as enemies. But from what Kirk saw around him, these people had been conditioned to abandon everything when they "died," to accept their new home enthusiastically as a step on the way to an even better life.

"And when we die a second time we go to Arnhall,"

he said, the picture finally coming clear for him. "I'm afraid that's not an acceptable choice."

"It's the only choice you've got."

Kirk found it a bit distracting to argue with a nude woman, especially one he didn't know, but the seriousness of the situation helped him concentrate. "Look," he said, "we're not Nevisian. We got caught up in this whole affair by accident. We don't belong here. Let us contact our ship and we'll go on about our business, and leave you to continue yours."

"There aren't any exceptions," the woman said. "The rules are very strict about that. If you try to contact your ship, you'll be put in jail."

Kirk sat back to think it over. This seemed like a simple misunderstanding, but his experience with other aliens led him to think it probably wasn't. Most isolated races were surprisingly intolerant of alternative customs, insisting that visitors live—and apparently die—according to local ways.

Scotty had been listening patiently to the entire exchange between Kirk and the woman, but now that Kirk had fallen silent he said, "There's just a wee problem with all o' that. The people on board the *Enterprise* don't know we're still alive. They'll search for our bodies, but they'll be searchin' the wrong planet. Eventually they'll give up and go on about their duty, and we'll be stranded here. No reunion in Arnhall for us."

The woman shrugged. "Loss is part of war. That's what the system is designed to teach us."

"What about *their* loss?" Sulu asked. "They'll mourn our deaths, never knowing we actually survived. That's worse than anything you people have to endure."

"Hmm," said the woman. She thought about that a moment, but before she could reply one of Sulu's own attendants said, "But it's not more than your people are used to enduring, is it?"

"What do you mean by that?" he asked her.

"I mean if your people don't normally have an afterlife, then their reaction to your deaths will be just what it would normally have been whether you were resurrected here or not. Nothing has really changed for them. And for you, it's a second chance. A fresh start."

"We were doing quite well the first time around," Kirk told her.

"And you will undoubtedly do well again," she replied.

Kirk could see she just didn't understand what the fuss was about. None of the Nevisians did. These people didn't see the problem because to them death was no big deal. Like some of the religious fanatics back on Earth in earlier centuries, they were so sure they would be rewarded in the afterlife that they didn't care about this one.

Whatever the truth, one thing was certain: arguing about it with the Valkyries wasn't going to get them anywhere. They needed to buck their way up the chain of command a ways—or slip out from under it entirely.

"All right," Kirk said, holding out his hands as if giving in. "We'll do it your way. But we're not getting anywhere by soaking in hot water all day so—"

"Oh, I wouldn't say that," murmured Chekov.

"—so let's get on with it," Kirk continued, ignoring him. "What comes next? Orientation? Debriefing? Or do you just give us a set of clothes and a disruptor and send us back to the front lines?"

The women all seemed surprised that he would want to cut short his time in the baths, but they had obviously been trained to accede to newcomers' requests, so long as they weren't too outlandish. And Kirk suspected they would be glad to foist these troublesome aliens off on someone else.

"Very well," said the woman he'd been arguing with. "The next step is clothing, followed by aptitude testing and job placement. You're not sent into battle for at least ten years, but of course the battle might come to you sooner. If you're ready, I'll take you to the fitting room and we can get started."

Kirk found the idea of an aptitude test amusing, in a wry sort of way. He wondered what they would find for a starship captain to do.

Spock recognized Lieutenant Nordell's voice calling for security. He punched the intercom button in the armrest of the command chair—he had to look for it, since he didn't yet have the captain's almost instinctive familiarity with the controls—and said, "Spock to engineering. What has happened?"

"It's the android, sir," Nordell replied. "She just suddenly got up and left. I couldn't stop her."

"In what direction was she headed?"

"For the turbolifts, but the last thing she said before she left was 'I've got to go back to Prastor.' I was suppressing data transfer on the lines that carried her knowledge of Harry Mudd's death, so I think she believes he's still alive and somehow on Prastor."

"Security to transporter rooms," Spock said. They

could catch her there. She wouldn't be able to beam away from this distance.

A beep from the science station drew his attention, but that was no longer his duty. Lieutenant Wolfe could take care of the situation there while he was engaged in recapturing the android. But a moment later the new navigator, Stanley, got something on his board as well.

"Report, Ensign," Spock said.

"Something just appeared on my scanner, sir. Extremely short-range. It's—oh, it's going *away*. It's a shuttlecraft!"

That was undoubtedly what the science station had detected: the shuttlebay doors opening. The android had known they were out of transporter range and had gone straight for a shuttle. Spock had underestimated its resourcefulness.

"Get a tractor beam on it," he ordered, and the new crew members moved to comply, but before they could focus the beam on the departing shuttle, it had slipped out of range.

"Follow it!" Spock said, putting more urgency in his voice. Humans often needed that extra urging to perform at their peak.

But it didn't matter. Not even Chekov and Sulu could have caught the shuttle before it reached Prastor. At this close a proximity, human reaction time was the limiting factor. The *Enterprise* streaked after it only a few seconds behind, but by then the shuttle had entered the atmosphere, leaving a glowing ion trail behind it as the android piloted it at top speed to the surface. She was headed straight for a city—the same city she had beamed to before from her own ship.

The bilge crew tried again to snare it in the tractor beam, but the ion trail and the atmosphere interfered too much for a steady hold, and the shuttle began to veer wildly as the android fought to escape.

"Stop the tractor beam," Spock ordered. If they kept it up, she would crash into a building and probably kill people on the ground. For the same reason, they couldn't just shoot the shuttle down. "Transporter room," Spock said, "can you lock on to the shuttle and beam the android out of it as soon as she lands?"

"I'll try . . . No, sir. It's entered a shielded area. The same one as before."

That left only one choice. "Security," Spock said, knowing at least two officers would be in the transporter room by now, "beam a safe distance from those coordinates. Set phasers on maximum. Fire the moment you spot the android, and make sure you've disabled it, but do not enter the shielded area. Stay in direct communicator contact, and transporter room, stand by to beam them back at the first sign of trouble."

He heard a chorus of "Yes, sir"s over the intercom. He hoped he wasn't sending more crew members to their deaths, but they couldn't allow the android to cause any more trouble down there either. This time, though, they wouldn't waste time trying to apprehend it. They would merely stop it and let the Prastorians clean up the mess.

Chapter Sixteen

LESLIE LEBRUN was surprised to learn that she qualified for a number of jobs. After she and Harry had begun to wrinkle like prunes in the hot water they had been given bright red clothing to identify them as new Prastorians and were sent on to the employment office for evaluation, where she discovered that her experience in starship security made her a shoe-in for a guard job on Prastor. Or, she had always liked to draw, and a quick sketch of the interviewer had delighted him with her unconventional use of line width and shading, enough so that he assured her she could easily support herself by selling portraits if nothing else. But according to his tests she also had the technical skills to assemble electronic equipment if she wished. Or—Lebrun blushed when he mentioned it—she could be a receptionist in a bathhouse.

"I mean it," he said when he realized the significance of her color change. "You look enough like us to be quite appealing, and just different enough to be exotic. Exotic is good in a welcoming agent."

"I'm sure it is," Lebrun said, looking away at the walls of the small office in which she and Harry and the interviewer sat. "But I don't think it's the job for me."

"Of course it is. You'd be wonderful at it," Mudd urged her, showing the first sign of animation he had expressed since learning that he was qualified to be a store clerk, a farmworker, a waiter, or a tax collector.

"And I'd be naked most of the time," she said to him in English. The words sounded odd to her after speaking Nevisian for the last few hours, but she didn't want the interviewer to understand her. "I need clothing for what I have planned."

"And what is that, my dear?" Mudd asked, also in English.

"Escape."

"What are you saying?" the interviewer asked.

"I was just reminding Harry why I couldn't take that job," she replied in Nevisian. "Religious reasons," she added when he started to ask. She turned back to Harry and said in English, "What do you say? Do you want to come with me?"

Harry sighed. "Considering my exciting opportunities for meaningful employment here, and the rather restrictive rules governing travel and communication, I believe I may be better off taking my chances on the *Enterprise* after all."

Lebrun had horrified their hosts by asking to be returned to the *Enterprise,* and they had both endured a lengthy lecture on the reasons why she couldn't, all of which had boiled down to "That's not allowed." So she had pleaded ignorance and promised to adopt a new life as she was supposed to, figuring she could make a break for it as soon as she had a chance. All she had to do was find a radio—or even make a simple spark-gap transmitter out of a battery and a wire—and send an SOS. The emergency monitors on the ship would instantly pinpoint her location, and a sensor scan would tell them who was calling for help.

But she would have to do it quickly, before the *Enterprise* left the system, or she would be stuck here forever.

"I believe my religion would allow me to work with electronics," she said to the interviewer. That should put her in contact with the equipment she would need.

"An excellent choice," he said. "And you, sir?"

"Could I try my hand at it as well?" Mudd asked.

The interviewer shook his head. "No, I'm afraid not. You wouldn't be allowed to work together anyway, you understand. The rules demand that you be separated after your orientation so you can pursue new lives."

That could complicate things. If they separated her and Mudd, she would have to contact the ship on her own. That probably wouldn't be any more difficult than having his help, and in fact it might be easier without having to look out for him, but on the other hand he did have experience living on the fringes of society, and that could come in handy if they needed to hole up for a while.

She looked around the room again. A tiny, nondescript office, fairly well soundproofed from the others, no guards at the door. . . . This was probably the best opportunity she could ask for. In one smooth motion she stood up, reached across the desk, and yanked the interviewer forward by his hair, grabbing his throat in her other hand and squeezing to prevent him from screaming. Mudd actually screamed louder than the interviewer, but it was just a startled squeak.

Lebrun let go of the man's hair and grabbed one forearm. "Get his other one," she hissed at Mudd.

It took him a second to understand, and even longer to catch the flailing limb, but Lebrun kept her grip on the man's throat so it didn't really matter. His legs were pinned by his own weight now that she had him bent over the desk, and although he could no doubt work one free and start kicking the wall with it if he thought about it, he was in no position to do much thinking. His air and blood flow had been cut off; Lebrun only had to hold tight for a few more seconds before he collapsed onto the desktop.

"Was that really necessary?" asked Mudd when the man went limp. "Now we're fugitives already."

"You want to try getting by here on your own?" Lebrun asked. She tore off the man's sleeves and pant legs and began tying him up with the cloth—a trick she had learned in security training.

"I have done quite well on my own in the past," Mudd said proudly, but then he said, "But you're right, we must stick together."

After they tied up the interviewer, Lebrun went through his desk drawers and found a disruptor and a set of knobby metal tubes on a ring that had to be keys, which she pocketed even though she had no idea what they went to. At least she would have them if it turned out they needed them later.

"All right," she said to Mudd. "Now we go out the door like we just got the jobs of our dreams, and walk straight out of the building. Ready?"

He was panting a bit already just from the exertion of tying up the interviewer, but he wiped the sweat from his forehead and nodded. "If we must."

"We must," she said, mimicking his precise enunciation. She grasped the door by its shiny glass knob—all the doors she had seen here were manually operated—and pulled it open. "Stay close," she said, and set off down the hallway.

Spaceship mechanic! Scotty rubbed his hands together like a land speculator about to close a deal on a whole planet. Perfect. He hadn't even realized that the Nevisians had spacecraft. They were apparently tiny little interplanetary things with no warp capability at all; designed, of course, for combat and nothing more, but they were spaceships nonetheless. The moment the Distrellians let him get his hands on one, he was as good as free.

Unfortunately, their inadvertent generosity didn't extend to the other *Enterprise* crew members. Chekov and Sulu had been given work in cartography and heavy equipment operation, respectively, while Captain Kirk had been offered only desk jobs. Management, to be sure, one of them coordinating battle plans, but it was hard to see how that would help them get back to the ship.

And they had to do that soon, before the *Enterprise* was sent on another mission somewhere else. Spock would no doubt have reported their deaths already, which meant that he was now awaiting orders, and at this distance from Starfleet those could come in less than a day.

They were in the final briefing room before being

released. It was a small amphitheater, with seats for themselves and about fifty others, and walls covered with painted cloth murals that depicted presumably local scenes while cutting down on echoes. A no-nonsense drill-sergeant-type immigration official stood up front and explained what came next. They would be sent to temporary housing first—spread out all over the planet so there would be no more contact with people from their former lives—and given a day to explore their new homes before being shown to their jobs. That would be too late for Scotty and the others. Without a warp drive those fighter ships would do them no good at all if the *Enterprise* was already gone.

The pep talk was full of buzzwords about duty and honor and bravery and so forth. And one piece of fatherly advice that galvanized all four Starfleet officers:

"And I know some of you weren't ready to leave Prastor yet, but don't think you can just sneak off and kill yourselves to get back. You'll go back, all right—the Gods keep track of where you came from and who you associate with—but it'll be in the middle of the closest battle with someone you know in it, and your own people will blow you right back here. The same goes if you're killed trying any other method of escape, or killed while committing a crime."

Kirk leaned over to Scotty and whispered, "That may be our fast ticket out of here."

"How's that, sir?" Scotty asked.

"If one of us were to . . . well, you know . . . he'd wind up on Prastor. In the middle of a fight, sure, but *outside* a shielded area. If the *Enterprise* is still looking for us, then they'll beam me up, and then we could come here to Distrel and pick up the rest of you."

Even though he'd noted that Kirk had said "me," Scotty felt the hair rise on the back of his neck. Commit suicide just to cross from planet to planet? "I don't like it," he whispered back. "We have no idea how this resurrection business works. We seem to have come through it all right this time, but until we know what makes it tick I don't think we'd be smart to try it again. I'd rather steal a ship and go back that way."

"Yes, but can we do that quickly enough?" Kirk asked. "We might only have a few hours left."

"We know they have spaceships here; you just get me close to one and I'll handle the rest."

Kirk nodded and resumed listening to the pep talk, or appeared to at least. But he was no doubt planning their escape, as was Scotty. The way he figured it, they would have to make a break for it before they were split up, then head for the spaceport, sneak in, and steal a ship.

And if that didn't work . . . well, the odds of someone getting killed between here and there were fairly high. They might just have a chance to try Kirk's other idea as well.

Kirk was evidently thinking along the same lines. He leaned back over to Scotty and whispered, "When I give the signal, we take out the drill sergeant, get his disruptor, and head for the spaceport."

"Aye, sir," Scotty said. Kirk leaned the other way and whispered the same to Sulu, who in turn passed the message to Chekov.

A few minutes later the briefing was over, and

people got up and began moving out the door toward the transporters, where they would be sent off to their new homes. The immigration instructor stood by the doorway, wishing everyone well. The *Enterprise* crew hung back so they would be the last ones out, and when they drew abreast of him, Kirk held out his hand. The instructor gripped his forearm in the Nevisian lodge-brother style of greeting, and Kirk gripped his in return.

"Good luck, and welcome to Distrel," the instructor said.

"Now," Kirk replied.

Chapter Seventeen

THE BUILDING COVERED a city block. Mudd was sure they had walked at least that far, probably more, all at a breakneck pace. He was as eager as Lebrun to get away from the scene of the crime, but there were limits.

"Slow down," he gasped as he puffed his way down the hallway behind her. "We don't . . . look nearly . . . nonchalant enough at this pace."

"Sorry," she said, not slowing any that Mudd could detect. They were approaching a cross-corridor that looked as if there were a strong light source off to the left, and sure enough, as they turned into it they saw a door with a frosted window, illuminated unmistakably by bright sunlight.

"All right, look happy," Lebrun said, pushing open the door.

"I'm afraid 'worn out' is the . . . best I can manage at this point," Mudd gasped. He clutched the doorframe for support while he paused on the threshold to catch his breath and look at their surroundings. The rushing, banging, *active* sounds of a busy city grew apparent when his heartbeat slowed enough to allow him to hear it. They seemed to be in the back of the building, apparently at an employees' entrance. Just a few yards from the door stood a little kiosk that looked at first like a bus station, except there was no street or even a landing pad for a bus to arrive on. A stone path linked it to the building, and other paths fanned out from it to buildings across the commons. It must be a transporter station, Mudd thought, and he nearly went over to investigate it, but Lebrun set off across the commons toward one of the other buildings and he had to hurry to keep up with her.

Lollipop-shaped trees alongside the paths provided shade for the few pedestrians who used them. Nobody paid any attention to Mudd or Lebrun; everyone else seemed to be hurrying just as fast, and all of them were looking nervously off to the left. Mudd glanced over to see what they were worried about, and nearly tripped when he saw bright lances of disruptor fire spear out from around the corner of the building. People were fighting right out in front.

A man and a woman appeared in the transporter station and ran off toward the battle, drawing their own weapons from shoulder holsters as they ran. Mudd watched with horrified fascination as they reached the corner, took immediate aim at something out of sight, and fired five or six shots each. Return fire suddenly speared past them and one bolt hit the man, who fell backward, twitched once, and vanished. The woman yelled something unintelligible and leaped forward out of sight, firing her disruptor as she went.

"That way," Mudd said, pointing off in the other direction.

"Right," said Lebrun. They rushed off across the grass to the right of where they had been heading, intending now to put another building between them and the battle, but a loud roar split the air from above and they stopped again, looking up to see what had caused it.

A Federation shuttlecraft was landing just a few hundred feet away, between them and the battle.

"All right!" Lebrun shouted. "They came for us!" She ran toward the shuttlecraft, and Mudd took a few steps after her, but when the door slid open and he saw who stood there, he skidded to a stop. His feet slipped on the soft fern and he landed on his butt, no doubt getting an embarrassing grass stain in the process, but that was the least of his worries.

"Harcourt!" the Stella android shouted. "Harcourt Fenton Mudd, you come here this instant!"

Mudd hesitated. Much as he hated returning to her clutches, for once he believed he might be better off following her advice. He stood up, brushed off his pants, and took a few steps toward the shuttle, but the sight of dozens of blue-clad Distrellians running around the corner of the building brought him to a halt again.

Lebrun didn't see them; she was close enough to the shuttle that its bulk hid them from sight. And Stella didn't see them, since the door opened on the wrong side of the shuttle for that. Harry made a split-second guess whether he could beat the Distrellians to the shuttle, and realized that he could not. And to them, he was no doubt a blazing red beacon of a Prastorian target.

He turned toward the transporter station. Maybe he could beam away, if he could figure out how to operate it before the Distrellians caught up with him. Or failing that, maybe he could make it back inside the building.

He ran as hard as his feet would carry him. From behind he heard the shouts of his pursuers, and Stella screeching, "Harcourt, come back here! You can't get away from me that easily."

The ground vibrated with the sound of something massive pounding after him, undoubtedly the android.

Dear God, let the Distrellians get me first, Mudd thought.

The gods—or perhaps just random chance—obliged him. Mudd felt the white-hot pain of a disruptor blast strike him square between the shoulder blades, and he pitched forward into darkness.

"Dammit, I was *kidding!*" he shouted as he fell.

The immigration instructor was no match for four Starfleet officers. The moment Kirk grabbed his right arm, Scotty took his left, Sulu slipped behind him and locked a forearm around his windpipe so he couldn't cry out, and Chekov snatched his disruptor from its holster. Kirk yanked his shirt up over his face so he couldn't see, then tore one of the wall hangings into strips to tie him up and gag him with. Within three minutes he was an immobile bundle hidden between two rows of seats, and Kirk was leading the way out the door.

He could hear voices off to the right, so he turned left. A short hallway led to a set of wide double doors, which let them out into a drizzly wet afternoon rain shower. Kirk wasn't too excited about walking in the rain, but he wanted to get a little distance from the immigration building.

Maybe they could do even better than that. Walkways converged on a small, hexagonal glass and stone building that had to be a public transporter station. It was open on three of its six sides; Kirk crossed over to it and stepped in through one of the open archways.

Then again, maybe it was just a shelter from the rain. Or a receiving station only. There was a hexagonal grid on the floor and ceiling, but no controls that Kirk could detect. "Scotty," he said, "see if you can figure out how this thing works."

"Aye, Captain," Scotty replied.

There were, at least, maps of the city on the three walls. While Scotty examined the hardware, Kirk stepped up to one of the maps to see if he could spot the spaceport. All the labels looked like little squiggly lines to him, but there was one boxed-in area near the center of the map that had to be YOU ARE HERE.

There were no main streets. In fact, there were very few streets at all, by the looks of it. Just buildings and parks and lakes and so forth, if he was interpreting the symbols right. Apparently most traffic was carried by transporter. Or maybe hovercraft, though the sky seemed pretty free of anything but rain at the moment. Kirk looked on the map for an open area big enough to land a spaceship in. It would probably be on the edge of the city, since people wouldn't want to live too close to a military target—though that might not be true of Nevisians, he realized.

Sulu and Chekov had come up on either side of him. "Do you see anything that looks like a space-port?" he asked them.

"Hmm . . ." said Chekov, leaning closer to the map.

"Captain," said Scotty, "it's a transporter all right, but I'll be blessed if I can see any activation mechanism for it. People must carry some kind of personal control device, as near as I can figure."

"Which we didn't stick around to be issued," Kirk said. It looked like they might have to walk the whole way, or rob an innocent bystander of his bus pass—but that wouldn't help a bit if they couldn't figure out which direction to go.

"What about this?" Sulu asked, tapping at the map. Kirk looked to see what he had found, but a sudden change in the lighting made him flinch back and look out.

They had moved. They were now in one of a long row of transporter stations on the edge of a wide stone courtyard. Across the way were hundreds of stores, and thousands of people carrying packages under their arms or in wheeled carts. It wasn't raining here, and though the sky was still cloudy it was much brighter.

"You touch the map!" Scotty exclaimed. "Brilliant!"

"This isn't a spaceport," Sulu pointed out.

"No, but it's a good start," said Kirk. "Excuse me." He leaned out of the transporter station and called to an older woman walking past. "We're trying to reach the spaceport, but we've gotten a bit lost. Could you show us where it is?"

She looked him over carefully, then nodded. "You look like the type, all right. It's up here." She stepped up to the edge of the station and pointed high up on the map. "That green spot there."

"Ah, thank you," Kirk said.

"Any time."

He waited for her to back away from the door, then reached up and tapped the spot, just as Chekov asked, "I wonder what green means?"

The light changed again. Kirk looked outside and saw row upon row of wedge-shaped fighter craft, painted black and streamlined for atmospheric flight. "Jackpot," he said. "Come on."

But the moment he stepped out of the transport station, a jangling alarm went off.

"That's what green meant," he said, stepping back up. "We evidently need security clearance to get through. Quick, get us out of here."

Sulu thumped the map at random, but nothing happened. Kirk pressed his finger more deliberately against the spot that had taken them to the shopping center, but that did nothing either.

"Control lockout," Scotty said. "We're trapped."

"Not yet we aren't," Kirk said, pulling from his waistband the disruptor that Chekov had appropriated from the immigration instructor and charging out across the pavement toward the closest row of ships. He didn't see any fences or forcefields; if they could make it across the first fifty yards or so of open space it looked like they could hide among the ships themselves.

He heard shouts from off to the right and turned his

head to see soldiers pouring out of a guard shack a few dozen yards away. The guards didn't fire immediately, perhaps reluctant to shoot someone wearing their own colors, and by the time they decided to, Kirk and the others were too far away to present good targets. Disruptor bolts zipped past and blew chips of rock out of the pavement, and one struck a wingtip that jutted out toward them.

"Chekov, Sulu," Kirk said as all four of them raced into cover behind the first fighter ship, "you and I will draw off the pursuit. Scotty, you hot-wire one of the ships and beat it for the *Enterprise*. We'll try to hide out here at the spaceport until you can beam us aboard, but if we're not here you'll just have to scan for us wherever they send us."

"Aye, Captain," Scotty said grimly, acknowledging the unspoken thought that they might be back on Prastor by then if what they had been told about the rules of war around here was true.

Kirk led the way farther down the line of fighters, dodging out into the open a couple of times to make sure the guards saw him. Disruptor bolts lanced out at him each time he did, one of them singeing off most of his hair on the right side of his head. Too close, he thought, ducking back into cover and firing a few shots back at their pursuers to slow them down.

He was just turning to put some more distance between them when he saw someone else materialize out in the open only a few yards back the way he had come. Someone wearing Prastorian red and flailing wildly for balance.

"—was kidding!" the man shouted, and Kirk recognized the voice and his ample outline at the same moment.

"Harry," he shouted, "take cover!" He fired past Mudd at the spaceport guards and sent them skittering for cover themselves, but the blue energy bolts whizzing past made Mudd freeze rather than jump behind one of the ships. That split-second hesitation cost him; one of the guards hit him in the left leg with a lucky shot and Mudd fell, howling, to the pavement.

Kirk fired a couple more times at the guards, then tossed the disruptor to Sulu. "Cover me," he said, then jumped out and raced toward Mudd. Disruptor bolts zipped past all around him, but Kirk ran straight for Mudd, grabbed an arm, and strained to drag him behind one of the fighter ships' landing skids.

"Ow, my shoulder!" Mudd yelled. Then, when he saw who had grabbed him, he said, "What are you doing here?"

"Saving your worthless hide," Kirk told him as he heaved Mudd's massive bulk closer to safety. Just one more tug would do it. "For the second time. You owe me one, Har—" Kirk said, but he never finished the sentence. The disruptor bolt must have caught him in the head; he never even felt this one.

Chapter Eighteen

LEBRUN TURNED at the door of the shuttlecraft to see how Mudd was doing, and was horrified to see him running the other way. "No, Harry, this way!" she shouted, adding her voice to Stella's. What devotion, she thought. Stella had flown right into the middle of a battle to save her husband.

Suddenly she was shoved aside, and Stella took off at a dead run straight for Harry. She seemed impossibly fast, and her feet ripped up foot-sized divots of lawn with every step, but she couldn't outrun disruptor bolts. Half a dozen beams shot past the shuttle, one striking Stella square in the back and two more hitting Harry.

Stella didn't even slow down. Harry, on the other hand, pitched forward, dematerializing on the way.

That did for Stella what the disruptor bolt in the back didn't. She stopped, tilted her head left and right as if listening or looking for something just out of sight; then she turned around as if to run back to the shuttle, but before she could move, two bright red phaser beams lanced out from the tree-lined path off to the side and speared her in the side and chest.

Phaser beams, not disruptors, Lebrun realized. She looked to the left and saw two *Enterprise* security officers—she recognized Smith and Rusch—firing steadily at Stella.

"No, she's one of ours!" Lebrun shouted, but it was too late.

Or maybe not. Incredibly, Stella turned toward the source of the beams, and even took a few steps toward them. Then a disruptor bolt hit her left arm and blew it away at the elbow, and Lebrun realized why she was able to withstand so much fire. Circuitry dangled from the wound, and sparks shot out from the bare wires.

Stella turned again, and the phasers followed her. The spot where they hit glowed cherry red, then white, but still she didn't go down. She was definitely damaged, though. She took a few more stumbling steps toward the shuttle, then fell to her knees. Another disruptor bolt hit her in the shoulder and her head slumped to the side, but she stood up again and took a few more steps before something inside finally overloaded and she froze up. She fell like a tree, face first, and the ground shook when she hit.

Lebrun looked over toward Smith and Rusch just as they shimmered away in a transporter beam. She waited a couple of seconds to see if the *Enterprise* would beam her away as well, but when nothing happened she stepped back up into the shuttle door way. She could hear heavy footfalls and shouts as the Nevisians approached from the other side.

Even though Stella was only an android, and Captain Kirk had evidently ordered her eliminated, Lebrun was reluctant to leave without her. She had come here to save her husband, after all. Whatever had happened on the ship could have been a big misunderstanding, or a case of divided loyalty. After all the thinking Lebrun had done about marriage—and despite Harry's insistence that his and Stella's was a match made in Hell—Lebrun didn't feel that she could just abandon Stella after watching her try so hard to save him.

But the Nevisian battle gods took the matter out of Lebrun's hands. Just as she was steeling herself for a rescue attempt, Stella's body faded away, leaving a six-inch-deep depression in the ground: a perfect mold of her features in crushed fern.

A Distrellian soldier skidded around the front of the shuttle, saw Lebrun, and fired wildly toward her. She leaped back inside and punched the door closed, then jumped toward the controls and lifted off without even sitting in the pilot's chair. Bracing herself against its back, she slapped the control for maximum lift, then when she was high enough not to be a target anymore she struggled into the seat and steered for orbit.

Her breathing had just begun to slow when the shuttle rocked under heavy fire, and a black wedge-shaped fighter screamed past only inches from the viewscreen.

Spock had been watching the ground battle at high magnification on the main viewer. It was difficult to identify individuals from the overhead angle, but he saw the shuttle land, saw the Stella android emerge and chase after someone on the ground and nearly reach them before the security team fired on her. When she had fallen he had recalled the security team, then watched as a Prastorian entered the shuttle and moments later took off. That seemed odd; shuttle controls were deliberately designed for ease of use, but a Prastorian shouldn't have been able to figure them out that quickly.

It looked like their cleverness might not save them even so; while the shuttle was still only a few miles above ground, five sleek interceptor craft rose from the spaceport to the north of the city and streaked toward it, firing as they lanced past, then arched around for another run.

He was just turning to Lieutenant Uhura to request that she contact the shuttle when she said, "We're being hailed. It's—it can't be. It's Ensign Lebrun."

"On screen," Spock ordered. Uhura routed the signal to the viewer, and sure enough, there was Ensign Lebrun seated before the shuttle controls.

"I'm under attack," she reported. "Shields deteriorating, and I took some engine damage before I got them up. I'm not sure I can make orbit."

"Acknowledged," Spock said, suppressing the urge to ask her how she had survived the disruptor attack that he had watched vaporize her in the Grand General's palace. First things first. "Get a tractor beam on that shuttle," he ordered the helmsman. "And lay down a burst of phaser fire around those interceptors. Lieutenant, tactical view again."

The viewscreen shifted back to the overhead view, and Spock watched phaser beams stab down into the atmosphere toward the swirling specks of the fighter craft.

"They're not leaving," Lebrun reported a second later. "They're fire—" Her signal washed out in static, then came back. "—down to twenty percent now. I don't think I can take another hit."

Spock considered using the tractor beam to push the attackers away, but they couldn't simultaneously lift the shuttle and push away five other objects. Nor could they simply beam Lebrun out of the shuttle, not without her lowering her shields and risking instant annihilation with the next attack before they could lock on to her.

Spock could see only one solution and he didn't hesitate to order it. "Target the interceptors," he said. "Shoot to disable if possible, but don't let them attack the shuttle again."

More phaser fire lanced down into the atmosphere as the helmsman and navigator complied with his order. Three explosions lit up the screen, and the two surviving craft tumbled out of control. Before Spock could order the pilots beamed to safety, two parachutes opened. Good; that was one less thing to worry about.

"Pull the shuttle to safety," he ordered. "Put Ensign Lebrun back onscreen." Her image replaced the planetscape. She looked a bit disheveled, but not injured. "Ensign, report," Spock said.

"Yes, sir." She ran a hand through her hair, leaving portions of it to resemble the Nevisian style. "Wow, where to begin. Let's see—"

"Begin with how you survived the attack on Distrel, and how you came to be on Prastor," Spock advised.

"Right. Well, apparently what happened was . . ."

Spock listened, fascinated, as she described how she and Harry Mudd had both survived and had been forced into the Nevisian society. If she weren't there onscreen before him, he wouldn't have believed it for a moment. But she was, and her story even answered one mystery that had been bothering him since they had arrived. He had wondered how two planets kept apart by millennia of war could have maintained a single language, and now he knew. The population of both planets apparently mixed so thoroughly that no linguistic split could develop.

That it happened through apparently supernatural means bothered him, but he was sure there was a rational explanation for that as well. In the meantime, Lebrun's very existence implied still further miracles. "If I understand correctly," he said, "then the captain and the others are probably alive on Distrel. And Harry Mudd as well, if he hasn't been killed yet again after arriving in mid-battle."

"The captain?" asked Lebrun. "Was he killed?"

"Yes," Spock said. "And Scott, Sulu, and Chekov as well. But apparently that was not as permanent a condition as we believed." He realized as he spoke that he was uncomfortably close to grinning. Really, these emotions were getting out of hand. He would have to meditate for a week once this was all over.

But that wouldn't be for a while yet. The captain and the others were still at large on Distrel, and it would take hours to search the entire planet for them. Unless he could get some help from the Distrellian government.

"Contact the Grand General," he said to Uhura.

It took a few minutes, during which the shuttle docked with the *Enterprise* and Spock heard cries of joy and laughter and weeping over the intercom as Ensign Lebrun and her husband, Lieutenant Nordell, were reunited. Shamelessly emotional, Spock thought as he switched off to give them privacy.

The Grand General looked even more wide-eyed than usual when he finally appeared onscreen. He was seated in a much smaller chair than the throne in which Spock had last seen him, and in a much smaller room, by the looks of things. Evidently the Prastorian invasion had forced him to retreat. He didn't wait for Spock to greet him, but immediately demanded, "What have you done?"

"I have rescued one of my officers from Prastor, and learned that more of them are being held against their will on Distrel," Spock replied. "I demand that you release them to us immediately."

The Grand General looked surprised. "I don't know a thing about that. Were they killed on Prastor?"

"Yes."

"Then they're probably here somewhere. And yes, you can have 'em back." He scowled at Spock and leaned forward into the video pickup. "You could have just asked. You didn't have to threaten us."

"I have made no threats," Spock said.

"No threats? Then what do you call what you've done?" The Grand General's voice rose to a shout. "What about your precious Prime Directive? If this isn't interference with a society, I don't know what is."

"Calm yourself," Spock told him. "We fired upon five interceptor craft that were threatening the life of one of our crew members. We regret that three of those craft were destroyed before their pilots could eject, but I hardly consider that a violation of the Prime Directive. It was an act of self-defense."

"I'm not talking about interceptors!" the Grand General shouted, rising from his chair.

"Then what *are* you talking about?" asked Spock, frankly puzzled by the man's behavior.

"I'm talking about the resurrections! They've stopped. People are dying for real, and you're responsible for it."

The resurrections had stopped? Spock had found them hard enough to believe in to begin with; could his skepticism have influenced something? It hardly seemed likely. "I fail to see how any of our actions could have affected your . . . peculiar adaptation to an afterlife," Spock said. "In any event, we have done nothing intentional to upset it. Perhaps if you could provide us with more information, we could—"

"I don't have any more information," the Grand General snapped. "The resurrections just stopped. I've contacted Prastor and they've stopped there, too. We've called a halt to the fighting, at least for the moment, but of course the Padishah thinks *I'm* behind it all, so he's threatened to attack us anyway if I don't make things right again. And thousands of people died before we issued the order, and they're still dead. Including two bathhouse receptionists who were electrocuted when your damned mechanical copy of Stella Mudd appeared in the water with them."

"The android was resurrected?" Spock asked. That seemed even stranger than the human resurrections, though they were all decidedly strange.

"Twice," the Grand General said. Someone approached and whispered something to him, then he looked back to Spock. "Make that three times. What's going on?"

"I don't know," Spock admitted. "I will endeavor to find out. But first I would like to recover my captain and crew members."

The Grand General sat back down. "Fine," he said. He beckoned someone close, whispered to them, and when they hurried away he said, "We'll search our records and see where they appeared. *If* they appeared. In the meantime, I want you to undo whatever it is you've done and get *our* people back."

Spock nodded. "If we are in fact responsible in some way for the problem, we will attempt to rectify it, but we must first learn what caused it."

"You people caused it. You and Mudd, messing around in other people's business where you didn't belong."

His assessment did carry a certain logic with it. Mudd and the *Enterprise* crew were probably the biggest disrupting factor Nevisian society had seen in recent times; it stood to reason that they might have inadvertently influenced something. But what could they have done to affect something as unusual as this? Had they angered a vengeful god? Disrupted the collective unconscious? Where did you start looking to find out why people weren't reborn anymore? As far as Spock knew this was the only spot in the universe where it actually happened in the first place.

"Helm, take us to Distrel," he said. "We will beam the captain and the others aboard as soon as they are located. Perhaps, since they have experienced the phenomenon directly, they will know something that we do not."

And if they didn't? Spock didn't know what he would do then. He was sure there had to be a logical explanation for all this, but he had no idea what it might be.

Onscreen the Grand General's messenger approached him again and whispered in his ear. The Grand General scowled at the news, then turned to Spock and said, "Apparently they *were* here, in the same reception center that your android appeared in, but they attacked one of the instructors and ran away. They could be anywhere on Distrel by now."

Chapter Nineteen

THE NICE THING about stealing a spaceship, thought Scotty, was that you only had to point it at the sky and light it up; you could learn to steer it later. And these fighter craft were already resting at about a thirty-degree angle. Good thing; the Nevisians didn't use a control yoke or a joystick or any other method Scotty was familiar with. They did use ignition keys, for which he was grateful. That meant all the important wires came together in one spot, which saved looking all through the control panel to find the pair that needed shorting out.

The toughest part of the whole job had been climbing into the cockpit in the first place. Since it was raining, the fighter ships had been parked with their canopies down, and it had taken him a few seconds to figure out how to raise one. The guards had caught up with him by then; only the captain's diversion kept them from looking up and spotting him as they ran past.

Once inside he had lowered the canopy again and found the engine start wires, but no obvious steering controls. He had wasted a few more seconds looking for them, but a glance out the window made him decide to launch without. A red-clad Prastorian lay on the ground between the guards and the *Enterprise* crew, and Captain Kirk, heedless of the danger to himself, was trying to drag him to safety.

Time to provide a diversion for *him,* Scotty thought. He shorted the ignition wires together and the tiny cockpit rumbled alarmingly as the fuel pumps and ignition chamber came to life right under his feet. It didn't come fast enough for the captain, though; Scotty saw a disruptor bolt strike him square in the side of the head before the guards turned to see who was in the fighter.

"Captain!" he yelled, his instincts telling him to jump out and rush to his friend's aid, but he knew he would never make it. And a second later Kirk vanished anyway, no doubt spirited back to Prastor by whatever strange agency had brought them here.

One of the guards fired at the canopy, and his disruptor charge blew an inch-wide hole in the clear plastic. Scotty didn't give him time for a second shot; he stabbed the big green button in the middle of the control panel with his thumb and shoved the slide control beside it all the way forward. He was instantly slammed back into the seat as the fighter took off under full thrust. The city streaked past below him, then disappeared behind. These ships might be primitive, but they were *fast.*

Air whistled through the hole in the canopy. That would be a problem in a few more seconds. Scotty looked for something to seal it with, saw a plastic ball dangling just about eye level from an overhead mount, and tugged on that. Silly place for an ornament anyway; it would work much better as a plug.

But the ship veered down hard and left when he pulled on the ball, and he realized belatedly that he had found the steering mechanism.

The ground became a flat wall in front of him. Scotty pushed the ball upward and to the right and the ship veered back around, shoving him down into the seat with four or five g's of force. No internal gravity! He would have to watch how hard he turned, then, or he could easily black out.

Now that he knew how to steer, though, there was one more thing he could do for Sulu and Chekov before he went after the *Enterprise*. He pulled the ball down and left again, more gently this time, and held it while the fighter angled around and headed back toward the spaceport. He aimed straight for the spot he had taken off from, leaving the throttle all the way forward, and only leveled out at the last second. For an instant he saw the upswept tails of the ships parked on either side of his flash past his canopy; then he was rising back up into the sky again.

Another pass showed him the effect of his barnstorming buzz; the two fighters he had flown between had been tipped onto their wingtips by the sonic boom and the jetwash, and the guards had scattered for ships farther down the line to chase him with.

Good. That meant they would leave Sulu and Chekov alone. Scotty lifted the steering ball up again and held it until he was aimed straight into the sky, then centered it and waited until he punched through the gray cloud layer.

The hole in the canopy still needed plugging. There was nothing else loose in the cabin, so Scotty held his left hand over it, flying with his right. The sky turned deep blue, then black, and the canopy grew cold. The vacuum just outside sucked at his skin, and Scotty knew he was going to have a hell of a bruise there, but if that was the worst of his troubles then he would be lucky.

He wondered how he was going to find the *Enterprise* up here. For that matter, he wondered if he could find Prastor. There were a couple dozen bright points of light out there, one of which was no doubt the planet, but most of them were probably nearby bright stars. If he picked the wrong one, it could be a *long* flight.

There had to be some sort of navigation equipment. Scotty leaned forward and inspected the control panel, looking for anything that looked like sensors. He punched a few buttons experimentally, finding the disruptor cannon and activating some kind of heads-up display, but it just presented him with multicolored static.

"Come on, I know you're here somewhere," he muttered, punching another button, the first of a row of five under the one that had turned on the display.

The static swirled into the image of a Nevisian woman's face. "Turn back at once or we will shoot you down," she said.

Aha! That was progress of a sort. "I'm trying to," Scotty told her. "But I nearly crashed the first time, and now I can't find the navigation controls to guide me back."

"Oh." She thought it over for a second, then said, "Top right panel, the yellow button labeled 'locate.' Push that, and while you're still holding it down tell the computer you want the Kelso spaceport. Then push the blue button below that and tell it 'autoland.' After that, keep your hands off the controls."

"Got it," Scotty said. "Thanks."

He pushed the button that had turned on the comm screen, and smiled as it faded away. Then he tried the yellow navigation button—he couldn't read the label, but there was only one button it could be—and said, "Computer, find Prastor." Another heads-up screen shimmered into existence, and on it a crosshaired targeting circle winked on and off in the upper left-hand corner of the screen, surrounding a bright red dot that had to be the planet. Scotty moved the steering ball until the circle was centered and had stopped blinking, then he punched the comm screen again, this time pushing the second button in the row below it.

The screen lit up with static again. Before anyone could come on the channel, he said, "Scotty to *Enterprise,* come in *Enterprise.*" Then he pushed the next button in the row and tried it again, and then the next.

Uhura answered on the fourth channel.

"Enterprise to Scotty. Where are you?"

"Somewhere between Distrel and Prastor," he said, feeling an immense weight lift off him. "Where are *you?*"

"En route from Prastor to Distrel. Wait a second

while I get a lock on your signal . . . all right, we see you. Come around and wait for us to pick you up."

"Sorry, I'm being chased," Scotty said. "You'll have to match my course and pick me up on the fly."

"Yes, sir. Stand by."

Scotty waited in the rumbling fighter ship, his hand pressed against the hole in the canopy and the g force still pushing him back into the seat, for what seemed like five minutes, but was probably more like five seconds. Then a streak of white burned across the blackness of space ahead of him and came to a stop less than a hundred yards away on his right: the familiar saucer and warp nacelles of the *Enterprise* matching velocity with him. Scotty felt as if he could reach out and touch it.

"Cutting engines," he said, pulling back on the slide control for the throttle. The *Enterprise* slowed to keep pace without shifting more than a few yards ahead of him.

"Locked on," Uhura said. "Ready to beam you aboard."

He was floating free now in the cockpit, held in place by his left hand stuck to the canopy. This wasn't a bad ship, primitive as it was. He hated to see it go to waste. "Just a second," he said. He pushed the navigation button again and said, "Computer, find the Kelso spaceport." Then he pushed the blue button below that and said, "Computer, autoland." Then he let off the button and, sighing deeply, said, "*Enterprise,* beam me home."

McCoy scowled at the monitor over the exam table where Ensign Lebrun lay, her husband still clutching her hand and spoiling the biometry readings. They weren't telling him anything he didn't already know anyway. She was healthy as a cadet. No sign of disruptor wounds, no sign of trauma of any sort; not even the mental distress that should have shown up ike a neon light on the psychological profile of someone who had gone through a near-death experience.

He was beginning to wonder if she actually had. She reported no memory of the actual event; just of going into danger and a moment later arriving in a tub of hot water halfway across the Nevis system. If she was suppressing the memory of death McCoy should have been able to see the neurological effects of that, but it looked to him as if she had never actually died.

The door slid open and Scotty stepped in, cradling his left hand in his right.

"Good, lie down here," McCoy said, patting the exam table next to Lebrun's.

"Nice to see you again, too," Scotty said.

McCoy grinned. "Sorry. Glad you're back. But I've got a mystery on my hands."

"And I've got a bruise the size of Mars on mine." Scotty showed him his hand, which did indeed sport a large red circle over most of the palm.

"How'd you get that?" McCoy asked him.

"Exposure to vacuum," Scotty said. He sat on the edge of the exam table and told McCoy about his adventures while McCoy treated his wound with a Wasner-effect antiinflammatory protoplaser.

"Do you remember dying?" McCoy asked him.

Scotty shrugged. "I was curled around an overloaded phaser. I don't remember the actual explosion, but then I doubt if anyone would. We're talking nanoseconds between then and complete disruption."

"Ick," Lebrun said.

"That's—" her husband began, but he stopped himself.

"What?"

"Uh, that's apparently what happened to you, too. Completely disintegrated, they told me."

"That's supposed to make it less icky?"

"I didn't mean it that way," he said. "I meant . . ."

"You meant what?" she insisted when he fell silent.

"I don't know. I was just talking."

"Well talk about something else. This gives me the creeps."

McCoy shook his head. These two were incredible. Reunited less than ten minutes, and they were already bickering again. They were still holding hands though; that was a good sign. "Go home," he told them. "Hang a 'do not disturb' sign on your door and don't come out for a week. Doctor's orders."

They both blushed, but Nordell helped Lebrun down off the exam table and they headed arm-in-arm for the turbolifts. Before the door swished closed behind them, McCoy heard Lebrun say, "I've been thinking about last night, and I think I owe you an apology," and Nordell answered, "No, no, it was all my fault."

McCoy smiled. Oh yes, there was hope for them yet.

He turned back to Scotty and made him lie back on the exam table, but he learned no more from him than from Lebrun.

"I don't know what happened to you two, but I can pretty confidently rule out death."

"You should examine Sulu and Chekov," Scotty told him. "I *know* they died. I saw it with my own eyes."

"And I saw Lebrun," McCoy said. "She was hit twice, but she was dead after the first shot; I'd swear to it." He began to pace the floor. "Yet you all came back, and you don't show any sign of trauma. I tell you, it gives *me* the creeps, too. I want to know how this happened."

"Don't look a gift horse in the mouth, Doctor," Scotty said. He swiveled his legs around off the table and stood up, then flexed his fingers. "Thank you for fixing my hand. Now if you'll excuse me, I should go see how things are goin' in engineering."

"Right," McCoy said distractedly. "And welcome back!" he called out as Scotty disappeared through the door.

Then he turned to the intercom. "Sickbay to Spock. Have we picked up Jim and the others yet?"

"We are just now beaming them aboard," Spock said. "Stand by." A moment later he said, "We have recovered Sulu, Chekov, and Harry Mudd, but the captain was apparently killed again during their escape attempt on Distrel. We are en route to Prastor to search for him."

"Jim's dead *again?*" McCoy asked. "Good grief, isn't once enough?" He was appalled at himself for sounding so flippant, but the knowledge that the captain would survive the experience apparently none the worse for wear did soften the blow considerably.

But Spock shattered his confidence with his next words. "I am sure it was unintentional, Doctor. However, I am far less sure of his chances for recovery this time. He apparently died after the resurrections stopped."

"What?" McCoy had to grab the edge of the exam table for support. This couldn't be. Jim couldn't be snatched away again, not after all he had been through already.

Just then the door opened and Sulu and Chekov entered sickbay, bearing Harry Mudd between them, his arms over their shoulders.

Harry Mudd. He was at the heart of this, McCoy was sure of it. "What have you done this time?" he growled.

All three men seemed taken aback by McCoy's outburst. Mudd cringed and looked to either side as if searching for something to hide behind, but he was in no shape to go anywhere. And like a cornered rat, he switched to bluster. "What have I done, Doctor? I have been fired upon, that's what. I have been kidnapped and subjected to indignities too numerous to count, but the one that concerns you is my leg. I believe they have broken it."

Indignities too numerous to count. Sure. Lebrun had told McCoy all about the Roman-style baths. But Mudd did indeed seem to have a leg injury. "On the slab," McCoy told him, gesturing toward the exam table Scotty had just vacated.

Chapter Twenty

SUCH A JOYOUS REUNION, thought Mudd. He should have been used to it by now, especially from the *Enterprise* crew, but he had allowed himself to hope that their shared experience would provide some camaraderie this time. Wrong. McCoy had healed his damaged knee, all the while complaining that Mudd had somehow engineered this whole sorry state of affairs simply to annoy him; and as soon as McCoy had finished his harangue Spock had summoned him to an inquisition.

Mudd took some joy in seeing that everyone else from the ship who had died on Distrel or Prastor was also seated around the long, oval conference table in the briefing room. And that the damnable android wasn't. She was apparently stuck in some kind of transcendental do-loop, appearing and disappearing again and again in the same pool of water on Distrel, a condition which Spock seemed to think was connected somehow with the halt in resurrections elsewhere.

"I think it's divine retribution, myself," Mudd said.

Spock, at the head of the table, looked exasperated, but then he always did. He said, "We cannot rule out the influence of a higher power; however, I suspect that once we uncover the nature of that power, we will find that it is no more divine than we are."

"Could be," said Mudd. "The locals refer to 'the Gods' whenever they talk about it, but whatever the cause, this whole situation reaffirms my faith that there is justice in the universe after all."

"Harry, I remind you that the Nevisians are poised to go to war on an unprecedented scale over this, and if they do, millions of them will die for real. Also, the captain is still missing and must be presumed to be in danger, if not dead himself."

"Yes, there's that, too."

That earned him no points with anyone at the table, not even with Ensign Lebrun. And McCoy, directly across the table from Mudd, looked as if he might re-break the leg he had so recently healed. Mudd held out his hands and said, "All right, all right, personal differences aside, I'm sorry he's in trouble. But what do you expect me to do about it?"

Spock glowered at him like a Federation Court judge. "I expect you to tell me the real reason why you came here. And anything else you know about the Nevisians."

"I was *brought* here," Mudd reminded him. "I've been shuttled back and forth completely against my will, and I'm getting—"

"To the Nevis system itself," Spock said. "What enticed you to come here?"

Mudd considered his response. He was a complex man; certainly Spock didn't expect him to explain everything. So he simply said, "The war. It was a chance to prove to those—those *androids* that I wasn't the person you had convinced them I was. I came here to help negotiate peace."

"And make a fortune on Palko distribution," Chekov said.

"Pah," Mudd said contemptuously. "A drop in the bucket to a man with vision."

"Your vision seems extraordinarily acute when profit is involved," Spock said.

"Why, thank you," Mudd replied, genuinely surprised to receive a compliment from the Vulcan, of all people.

But of course Spock couldn't let it go at that. "I cannot believe that a man of your . . . talents . . . would come here without an ulterior motive. Perhaps you could tell us about the other potentially profitable ventures your educated eye may have spotted in the Nevis system. With an emphasis on anything that might shed light upon our current situation."

He wasn't going to give up, was he? Well, then, Mudd would throw him a bone and see what he did with it. In fact, maybe he could get Spock to lead him straight to his own quarry. It might be worth a try, since Mudd had no interest in returning to either planet to continue the search on his own, especially if another war was brewing. "Hmm," he said, pretending to come up with it on the spot. "Well, when you put it that way, maybe I could point out a thing or two. For instance, their interplanetary transporter. I realize Prastor and Distrel are relatively close as far as distance goes, but they're still farther apart than our technology would allow us to beam. And rumor says they once had interstellar capability. The design for that would be worth a bit if we could come up with it."

"Aye, that it would," Scotty said from halfway down the conference table.

"Or take this resurrection business," Mudd went on. "If there does turn out to be a mundane explanation for it after all, then we could certainly find a market for it elsewhere. The Klingons, I imagine, would pay handsomely for a device that would allow them to die gloriously over and over again."

"Such a device would upset the balance of power throughout the galaxy," Spock said.

"Not if I sold it to everyone else as well," Mudd pointed out.

McCoy could sit still no longer. "Dammit, this speculation is pointless. We've got to do something to get Jim back, not just sit here and scheme up plans to rob the locals of their technology."

Spock said, "The bridge crew is searching for the captain at this very moment. The Prastorians and the Distrellians are also conducting their own search. We are doing all that can be done directly, which leaves us with indirect methods, such as determining what else Mr. Mudd knows about this society. And you, Doctor. What have you discovered in your examinations?"

"Well," McCoy said, mollified somewhat to be asked for his expertise, "I can pretty confidently state that these people didn't actually die. I found none of the toxins or enzymes normally released during death in their tissues."

"But we know we did," Scotty said. "Maybe whatever brought us back to life cleaned out those enzymes."

"And repaired all the damage done by the disruptors? I don't think so. Sulu's still got the scar he's had since childhood; why didn't it repair that while it was at it?"

"Maybe it's a time machine," said Sulu. "It backspaces just a few seconds until the subject is alive again."

"But it would have to have a subject to send back," McCoy protested. "Scotty was a cloud of elemental particles after that phaser overloaded, yet here he is. I can't imagine a time machine that could reassemble him from *that*."

"It wouldn't matter," Sulu said. "If it went back a few seconds and beamed him away before he—oh. Paradox."

"Indeed," said Spock. "If a time machine were employed, bystanders would not remember seeing a person die. Victims would simply disappear moments *before* death seemed imminent, which is not the case."

"So we're looking for something that can actually resurrect a corpse and edit out the trauma of death," said McCoy. "Sounds to me like we're looking for divine intervention after all."

"We are looking for anything that might shed light on this phenomenon," Spock said.

Scotty leaned forward. "Then I'd suggest studying it in action. We've got the perfect opportunity to do that on Distrel. From what you've told me, that Stella android keeps reappearing every few minutes We should go see if we can figure out where it's coming from."

"We must finish scanning Prastor for the captain first," Spock said. "As soon as we have established to my satisfaction that he is not here, we will return to Distrel and examine the android."

Mudd suddenly realized he had an opportunity to improve his odds of escape tremendously. "You forget the android's own ship," he said. "It should still be orbiting Prastor, shouldn't it?"

"It should," said Spock.

"Then we can go back to Distrel in that while the *Enterprise* continues to search here." Yes, indeed they could. And the moment the landing party beamed down, Mudd would blast off at warp ten for some other part of the galaxy.

Spock raised an eyebrow appreciatively. "That is an excellent suggestion."

Mudd couldn't resist. "Well of course it is, laddie-buck. I made it."

The problem with Mudd's idea, Sulu realized when he got back to the bridge and scanned Prastorian space for the android's ship, was that it required that ship to be in one piece. But whatever agency was responsible for the resurrection of individual warriors, it apparently didn't resurrect spacecraft, for Sulu found only a tumbling collection of debris where it should have been.

"That's" what they were shooting at," Uhura said when he brought it up on the screen.

"What who was shooting at?" Sulu asked.

"The fighters that attacked us after you went down to the surface. When we backed off, I saw them fire at something else before they returned to base. I didn't think anything of it at the time, but that's what it had to be."

"Friendly lot," Chekov muttered. He turned to Spock, who looked uncomfortable in the command chair. "So what do we do now, sir?"

Spock considered that for a moment, then said, "We will leave a shuttle here to continue scanning for the captain, and take the *Enterprise* back to Distrel and examine the android. Mr. Chekov, you will remain here in the shuttle. Contact us immediately if you discover anything."

"Aye, sir." Chekov got up from his workstation and strode for the turbolift. He didn't look happy about being left alone in hostile territory, even if there was a cease-fire in effect. Everyone knew how long the previous one had lasted, and the Padishah was already threatening to end this one. But he didn't question his orders.

"Mr. Sulu, take us back to Prastor as soon as he leaves the shuttlebay," said Spock.

Sulu laid in the coordinates, then watched his monitors until he saw the shuttlecraft dwindle against the starfield. "Shuttle away," he said. "Engaging engines."

The interplanetary flight took just a few minutes. Sulu brought the ship into orbit around Distrel, a bit less elegantly than he might have if Chekov had been feeding him navigation data, but he got the job done. He brought them to a halt over the city where the android kept reappearing, and said to Spock, "We're in position, sir."

"Very well." Spock punched the intercom button. "Spock to engineering. Mr. Scott, meet me in the transporter room." He let up on the button and said, "You have the conn, Mr. Sulu. Set up a planetwide scan for the captain while we are away."

"Yes, sir." Sulu felt a surge of relief that he wasn't being ordered down to the surface again. What a change from when they had first arrived here. He remembered being disappointed that he hadn't been selected for the first landing party, but after what he'd gone through when he *had* beamed down, he was glad to stay on board this time.

What had happened to his sense of adventure? He was usually first in line for planetside missions, the more dangerous the better. Was he scared? He didn't think so; if he had been asked to beam down, he would have gone without protest and done whatever was required of him without hesitation. But despite what Dr. McCoy had said, he felt as if he had been given a second chance on life, and he didn't intend to squander it.

That must have been how Chekov had felt when he realized he would be left behind; he was reluctant to risk losing what he had so recently regained.

Sulu wondered if the Nevisians felt this way after they died, too.

The bathhouse was uncomfortably hot, even for a Vulcan. The temperature was actually about the same as home—it wasn't the heat, but the humidity that made it unbearable. Spock considered disrobing for comfort, but practicality won out; he needed his belt to hang his recording instruments from. And with luck they wouldn't be here long anyway.

Harry Mudd seemed even less comfortable than Spock, though whether that was because of the heat or the proximity of over a dozen armed Distrellians, Spock couldn't say. He wasn't even sure why he had brought Mudd along; he would probably be useless in an investigation like this, but there was a chance that his time with the androids had given him some useful knowledge about them.

Scotty approached the whole venture with characteristic determination, ignoring both heat and guards as he headed straight for the pool in which the android kept reappearing.

"She should show up any time now," said one of the guards, a woman who wore a practical, if scant, blue uniform. "She appears every ten minutes or so."

Spock and Scotty set up their tricorders and waited. "I'm getting something," Scotty announced a minute later. He was monitoring for Chi band phased matter emissions; Spock switched over to that mode himself and scanned around from side to side to see where they were coming from. It was hard to trace; he found over a dozen separate sources in the walls, ceiling, and floor.

Then the android flickered into being, and the emissions stopped. A second after that a bright blue flash lit up the inside of the bathhouse, and the sizzle of a high-voltage short circuit echoed from the walls. Spock's inner eyelids slid closed, preventing him from seeing the android itself. The flash lasted only a moment, but by the time he could open his eyes again the android was gone.

Spock replayed his tricorder readings: there had been more phased matter beams just after the flash.

"It appears to be a variant of a standard transporter," Spock said.

"Aye," Scotty replied. "Except we're under an

energy shield at the moment. No transporter I've ever heard of can penetrate a shield."

"Unless the phase transition coils are within the shield as well," Spock said. He walked around the pool to the wall where the nearest of the emission sources had been and examined the area with his tricorder. Energy readings were high in several high-frequency ranges. "There is a scanning device here," he reported. "In fact, there are several of them."

"Gods' eyes," the woman guard said. "We put them in all our buildings."

Yes, that would be an appropriate name for them. Spock remembered finding an elaborate worldwide sensor network during his first survey of the planet; these were undoubtedly part of that network. And whoever they reported to would certainly know all and see all, if they could process the volume of data they received.

"Where do they send their information?" he asked the guard.

She looked puzzled. "To the Gods, of course."

Spock suspected they were dealing with a semantic problem rather than a theological one. "Where is the gods' physical location?" he asked.

"They're everywhere," the guard said. "Watching over us and protecting us from harm."

Then again, maybe it was a theological problem. He tried a different tack. "Where do these gods' eyes come from?"

"From the Gods?"

Scotty said, "I think what Spock means is, when you put up a new building, where do you get the new gods' eyes to put in the walls?"

"Oh," she said. "I'm not sure. From the palace, I think."

"See if you can find out," Spock told her. She turned away to go ask someone, but he stopped her before she could leave. "What have you done with the bodies of the two attendants who were electrocuted?"

"The Gods took them away," she replied.

"I see. Thank you." When she was gone, he said to Scotty, "Apparently the sensors and dematerialization subroutine continue to function, but the rematerialization process has been interrupted somehow."

"Except here," said Mudd, nodding toward the pool. He wiped sweat from his brow with the back of his sleeve.

Indeed. This locus seemed to be the single anomaly.

Scotty looked at the water, then back at Spock. "I wonder what would happen if we drained the tub so the android didn't short out."

"That should be easy enough to test," Spock said. He looked down into the water. Yes, there was a drain at the bottom of the pool, stopped with a simple plug. He looked around for a rod to dislodge it with, but saw nothing. The attendants probably did the job manually.

Well, so could he. He set his tricorder down and pulled off his shirt.

"You're not going in there, are you?" Scotty asked him.

"That seems to be the simplest way to remove the plug," Spock replied. "If we wait until after the android appears again, I should have more than adequate time."

"Aye, but if you don't . . ." Scotty left the rest

unsaid, but Spock knew what he meant. If he was wrong, then he would join Kirk and the others who hadn't rematerialized—wherever they might be. Spock tried not to think about where that most likely was: nowhere at all.

He stripped down and waited for the android's next reappearance, averting his eyes this time to avoid the flash. When he looked up again the android was gone, so he stepped into the pool, wincing at the sudden increase in temperature, and held his breath while he reached down for the plug and pulled it free. Water gurgled down the drain and Spock climbed back out of the pool, glad to be out of the heat. He had forgotten that the electrical discharge would warm the water even more than normal.

He dried off and dressed again while they waited. The pool was still half full when the android appeared the next time, so it disappeared with the same blue flash. The next time, however, the last of the water was just swirling around the drain when the android materialized in midair, then landed with a thud on the wet tile bottom. It was a mess. Phaser burns all along the front and right side and a disruptor burn on the left shoulder had exposed its inner workings, and its left arm was missing below the elbow. Much of the exposed circuitry was charred and crackling with sparks even without water to help short it out. Amazingly, the android struggled to raise its head, spotted the three men watching it, and croaked out, "Harcourt Fento—" before slumping back down, inert.

A second later it vanished again.

Mudd sniffed. Spock looked over at him, and was startled to see a tear run down his cheek. For an android? Perhaps it was the similarity to his wife that brought on the emotional response. Whatever the cause, Mudd noticed Spock's attention and immediately turned away, and when he turned back he had composed himself again.

"So, what do you think?" he asked gruffly.

Spock said, "I think we should look for the source of the transmissions. The Grand General's palace would be a logical place to start. What do you know of its secret byways?"

"Me?" Mudd protested. "Why do you think I'd—" He looked from Spock to Scotty, then blushed. "Never mind. All right, so I had a look around. And yes, there's an almighty big network of catacombs underneath it."

"That sounds like just the sort of thing we're looking for," Spock said. "Come on."

Chapter Twenty-one

SCOTTY COULD TELL that the Grand General was not happy to see them again. He was busy preparing for a major battle, and he made it clear that he only allowed them into the palace again because he needed their help in preventing it. Even then he insisted on accompanying the humans on their investigation.

"But you're wasting your time," he told them as they walked along the corridor from his temporary throne room toward the stairway. Blast scars pocked the surface at random all along its length, evidence of the fighting that had raged here only hours ago. "You won't find the Gods skulking around in the cellars. And they're most certainly not the mechanical mockery you suggest." He seemed personally offended at the very idea. Scotty wondered how much of that was righteous indignation, and how much was embarrassment over being fooled by the Stella android.

"Perhaps not," said Spock. "But there is the matter

of the 'gods' eyes' that are installed in buildings throughout the planet. Those are mechanical, are they not?"

"Yes, but they're provided directly by the Gods. We certainly couldn't build something like that ourselves."

"No?" Scotty asked. "Then how do you get them? They don't just magically appear in the walls, do they?"

"No," the Grand General admitted. "They magically appear here in the palace, in the Gods' Eye Shrine."

That sounded promising. "Let's have a look at that first," Scotty said.

The Grand General sighed. "Very well." He turned left at the next cross-corridor and led them through a maze of hallways and rooms to a small but lavishly decorated shrine. It looked at first glance like an insignificant religious altar, but upon closer examination Scotty recognized the pedestal in the center of the room as a raised transporter pad. The Grand General stepped around it to a glowing panel on the wall and waved his hand in front of the light. "Arbiters of fate," he said, "watch over us and guide us."

There was a soft whir and rush of displaced air; then a cylinder about six inches thick and a foot long, rounded on one end, appeared on the pad. Scotty scanned it with his tricorder. It was a sensing device, all right, already activated and beaming a steady stream of data—where? Nowhere in particular, it seemed. It just sent it out in all directions. Apparently these things worked like a decentralized computer network, sending out information through whatever route was open until it reached its intended target. It was a good design for multiple redundancy, but it made tracing things difficult.

Spock had taken a different approach; he had monitored the pad at the moment of beam-in. "The matter stream came from beneath us," he said. "I believe Harry's guess was correct: the machinery—or whatever—we seek is in the catacombs." He nodded to the Grand General, removed the sensor from the pedestal, and backed away out the door and down the hallway a few yards, saying, "If you could activate it again, I will attempt to triangulate."

The Grand General scowled at the notion of "activating" the gods, but he turned back to the control panel and waved his hands in front of it and beseeched the arbiters of fate again, and another "gods' eye" appeared on the pedestal.

Spock consulted his tricorder. "The source lies five hundred feet below us, and twelve hundred fifty feet to the northwest."

Scotty had been monitoring it this time as well, and his reading backed up Spock's. "All right," he said. "Now we're getting somewhere. Let's go have a look."

It was a long descent. They could probably have used one of the palace transporters, but Scotty didn't trust the alien machinery through so much rock, especially now that some of that machinery was malfunctioning. If the transporter web was tied together like the sensor web, there was no telling what might go wrong.

But when they neared their destination, he wondered if they would have to use a transporter after all. A hundred feet short of their goal the stone-lined corridor they were in came to a halt against solid rock, and Scotty's tricorder showed no cavities within scanning range beyond it. That was only about fifty feet, but they couldn't cut through fifty feet of rock without special equipment. All of which would have to be carried down again after they climbed back up the stairs to get it.

This was the only corridor they had found that led even this close to the transmission source, and the tricorder revealed no more levels below them, either. "Looks like a dead end to me," Scotty said. His voice echoed in the long expanse of stone. They were well below the level that had been lit by overhead panels; they were proceeding by flashlight now. The dancing shadows and the echoes made Scotty's neck hairs stand out.

Mudd was panting from all the walking and descending of stairs. "Of course it looks . . . like a dead end," he said. "If I were trying to hide something I'd make it look like one too. That doesn't mean it *is* one."

"Then where is the passage?" Scotty asked him a bit testily. He was tired too.

"Back there somewhere," said Mudd, waving off down the corridor the way they had come. Doors opened off to the left and right every dozen feet for a hundred yards or more. "One of those rooms obviously has a hidden passageway that bypasses this false lead."

"That is entirely possible," Spock said. "It would be a simple but effective diversion."

Scotty sighed. "I guess there's an advantage to thinking like a crook," he muttered.

"I am not a crook!" Mudd spluttered, his jowls quivering as he shook his head in vehement denial.

Scotty and Spock both looked at him without

speaking a word, and after a moment Mudd said a bit sheepishly, "All the charges have been dropped. Check and see."

"We already have," Spock said. "But at the moment your criminal record is irrelevant, except where it helps us find our objective." He moved back down the corridor, scanning each room as they passed it. Scotty followed along, checking for forcefields, trapdoors, or anything else Spock might have missed.

"Here," Spock said a moment later. He opened the door before him and entered the room. It looked like an empty stone cube, maybe a dungeon cell, but Spock walked confidently across to the far wall and pushed against a protruding rock, and a panel slid aside to reveal another even smaller chamber.

"Doesn't look like it goes very far," the Grand General observed.

"No, it doesn't." Spock stepped into the room. It was more of a closet, really, with just room enough for one person to stand in comfortably. Scotty shined his flashlight through the doorway to help Spock see, but there was little to examine. The wall opposite the door had been scribbled on by a child, or so it seemed, though someone would have had to hold him up to do it, since the scribbling was chest-high.

"This appears to be a map of the tunnel system," Spock said. Scotty looked at it again, and realized that Spock was right. "However," Spock went on, "it shows no passageway to the area we want to reach, which I estimate to be about here." He poked his finger at the wall to the left of the squiggles.

"No, wait!" Scotty shouted, but it was too late. There was a flash of light, and Spock disappeared.

"Now what?" groaned Scotty. He checked his tricorder, attempting to measure any residual radiation from the phased matter beam that might give him a clue where Spock had been taken, but he hadn't been looking for transporter traces. He already knew where Spock had gone anyway. This was the same kind of system that the Nevisians used in their public transporters. Just touch the map where you wanted to go, and they would send you there. Except this one would send you to places not on the map. Like into solid rock, if Spock had guessed wrong.

Cautiously, like a cat in a roomful of dogs, Scotty entered the transporter chamber and scanned the map for clues. Maybe there was a way to bring someone back from wherever it had sent them, or—

When his communicator beeped for attention, he nearly dropped his tricorder. He took a deep breath, unclipped the communicator from his belt, and flipped it open. "Scott here."

"This is Spock. I believe I have found what we are looking for."

Mudd hesitated at the edge of the transporter chamber. He didn't like this blind leap into nowhere. But Spock had assured him that it was all right, and Scotty wouldn't leave him behind, and the Grand General wouldn't go until he had seen a second person do it—which left Mudd to make the leap.

It seemed like it always came down to something like this. A life-or-death choice made at somebody else's urging, the real choice lying not in the act itself but in whether or not to trust people who openly disliked him. And of course if he declined, they would think him a coward. How did he keep winding up in situations like this? Really, he would have to put an end to it before it killed him.

This seemed as good a time as any. If he merely pointed to a spot at the top of the map, the transporter would take him upstairs again, where he could contact the *Enterprise* and have them beam him back to safety.

Whereupon he would still be at the mercy of these same people, who would dislike him even more for skipping out on them.

A bad choice was no choice at all. And Mudd *was* curious to see what was hidden behind all this subterfuge. He might even find the interstellar transporter he had been looking for, or something else equally valuable.

"Well, are you going or not?" Scotty asked impatiently from behind him.

"Nothing ventured, nothing gained," he muttered, and he reached out to the spot of bare rock that Spock had touched. It was cold and rough beneath his fingertip.

An instant later, light flooded his eyes. He blinked and waited for them to adjust to the brightness, and slowly the scene around him resolved. He was in a long, high-ceilinged corridor that seemed to stretch on toward infinity. Unlike the hallways he had just been in, this one was brightly lit from overhead, though Mudd noticed that at least a third of the panels were flickering as if about to burn out, and maybe one in ten had already done so. This place hadn't seen maintenance in a long time.

Nor ventilation. The air smelled stale, and there

was an unpleasant tinge of burned electronics just at the edge of detectability.

Machinery lined the walls on both sides of the corridor. Unlike the lights, most of the tall, rectangular racks of components still seemed functional. A few banks were dark, but most of them hummed softly, and activity lights glowed on front panels that were labeled in Nevisian script. Mudd didn't need labels to recognize what he saw, though. This was a computer system. A *big* computer system. Just the part that he could see from where he stood made it easily the biggest Mudd had ever seen, and he had the feeling that this corridor went on for miles.

And now that he looked, he could see side passages leading away, probably to still more corridors like this one. And stairways at the junctions led downward again to even more.

Big didn't always mean sophisticated, he reminded himself, but even if these things used vacuum tubes and relays, there was a lot of computing power here.

"Impressive, isn't it?"

He flinched at the voice, then turned and saw Spock standing a few feet away. The Vulcan was as poker-faced as ever, but Mudd thought he could see a gleam in his eye that betrayed his excitement. He was a technophile, and this sort of thing was techie heaven.

The corridor ended a few dozen yards beyond him, and occupying most of that space were pedestals and low platforms bearing various pieces of hardware. It looked like a shopping display, only none of the goods were familiar. No, Mudd recognized one item: a gods' eye just like the one that had materialized upstairs in the altar.

"Mudd has arrived successfully," Spock said into his communicator, and a moment later the Grand General blinked into existence next to him. And a moment after that, Scotty showed up.

He whistled softly when he saw what they had discovered. "Well now, would you look at that," he said.

Spock was already examining the artifacts at the end of the corridor with his tricorder. "This gods' eye is identical to the one we saw upstairs," he said. "Down to the molecular level. I suspect it is the template from which all gods' eyes are created." He moved over to another device, a mushroom-shaped business with a stem about the size of a man's chest and a flat-topped cap twice that diameter. "This appears to be a modular transporter platform. Also a template, I suspect. Grand General, am I correct in surmising that the 'gods' provide you with your transporter technology as well?"

"What?" he asked. He had been staring in rapt fascination at the endless rows of humming machinery. "Oh, yes." He turned around to see what Spock was looking at. "Yes, that's a transporter module. And that"—he pointed at a rectangular box with a glass screen on one end—"is a communicator, and you of course recognize a disruptor."

Indeed, there on a pedestal of its own was the same hand weapon that Mudd had seen in the hands of so many armed fanatics, including the ones who had fired on him upstairs in this very palace. The *very* same weapon, apparently, duplicated over and over again each time someone asked the "gods" for a gun.

Now he began to recognize some of the other items. Shield generators, laser cutting tools, microfusion power packs . . . in fact, nearly every technical gadget he had seen during his entire stay on Distrel. All ready to be reproduced over and over again, as often as a person could push the button.

"Do you actually manufacture *anything* on your own?" he asked.

"Of course we do," said the Grand General, but he didn't elaborate. He had gone back to staring wide-eyed at his surroundings, still unable to quite believe what he saw. He looked, Mudd thought, a bit like an old-world Catholic suddenly discovering a mechanical Jesus.

Spock moved back down the corridor to the first of the rack-mounted computer elements and examined it with his tricorder. "Molecular circuitry," he said, obviously impressed. "And holographic memory. There is considerable computing and storage capacity here." He looked off into the distance and said, "Enough, I believe, to direct the affairs of an entire civilized race."

Calling the Nevisians "civilized" might be pushing the definition, Mudd thought, but he couldn't deny there was a lot of computer power here. One might even say an almighty lot.

And there was enough profit potential to tempt a saint.

Chapter Twenty-two

SPOCK HAD NOT BEEN entirely surprised to find the computer. After listening to the experiences of the people who had been killed and resurrected, and after watching the android Stella reappear again and again, he would have been surprised to find anything else. But figuring out how it worked was another matter. He could guess some of the general principles, but the specifics would require more study.

Scotty stepped up next to him and said, "Do you really think this thing's behind all the resurrections?"

"It seems the only logical explanation for the phenomenon," Spock replied, glad for the opportunity to check his reasoning with someone who could detect any flaws in it. "To bring someone back to life without the memory or the biological effects of dying would require a sensor array that could record a person's entire subatomic structure while they are still alive and in good health, plus the ability to store that information until the next scan."

"So the computer could use the previous pattern to regenerate the person from if they were suddenly killed," said Scotty. "Aye, that makes sense. It could also explain why they use disruptors to fight with, too. Doesn't take long to die after you're hit with one, so a person wouldn't lose much subjective time in the resurrection."

"I hadn't thought of that advantage to disruptors," Spock said. "I was considering the memory requirements of storing multiple scans. That amount of data would take up considerable memory, so I had assumed disruptors were used to reduce the number of past samples required to ensure a healthy subject."

"Could be," Scotty agreed. "But how do you explain the android? *It's* certainly not a healthy subject."

Spock felt the thrill of the logical chase coursing through him. "Precisely," he said. "The android is damaged because the computer falsely assumed it was healthy when it overwrote the previous scan with the current one. It was still moving, after all, and speaking. But it was already damaged beyond repair. So when the computer detected its 'death,' it attempted to restore it to life by using the previous pattern, but that pattern was nonviable."

"Why would that lock up the whole system, though?" asked Scotty. "This can't be the first time it's lost a resurrection subject. I'd imagine people die of heart attacks and such all the time."

Hmm. That was another good objection. "A valid criticism of my theory," Spock said. "Unfortunately I do not have a good answer for you, other than that the android is not a person."

"That's not the only problem with the theory," Scotty said, almost apologetically. "Those bathhouses where we wound up were shielded from transporters."

Spock nodded. "That much, at least, I believe I can explain. If the data-gathering devices—the 'gods' eyes'—also function as transport signal emitters, which we have already observed that they do, then the pattern stored in the computer's memory could be sent to them over conventional communication channels, to which the shield is transparent. No phased matter beam needs to penetrate the barrier, because the transporter is already inside it."

Scotty rubbed his chin thoughtfully. "The bandwidth would have to be incredible to carry that much data."

"The sensor network would provide multiple transmission pathways," Spock replied.

"There'd have to be all sorts of error-correction techniques to make sure nothing got scrambled along the way."

"Requiring massive amounts of computing power." Spock gestured down the seemingly endless corridor lined with computers.

"Aye, but enough for everyone on two *planets?* Could anyone build that much hardware?"

"That's the beauty of it," Spock said. "Given the technology to replicate anything they have a template for, the sheer volume of computers becomes a trivial production problem. Storage space would have been the biggest obstacle, but transporter technology would make carving these tunnels a simple process as well.

For that matter, I imagine the caverns provided the raw material to build computers out of."

"Well, it's a passable theory," said Scotty. "Barring the problems I pointed out. And there's no denyin' they've got plenty of equipment here. If you're right, then somewhere in here should be a control station. Let's see if we can get it to talk to us."

They found the control computer easily enough, by the simple expedient of looking for the one that was physically different from the others. Interfacing with it was more difficult, since it apparently didn't accept verbal input and there was no keyboard or other input device that either of them could recognize. The Grand General tried the laying on of hands and beseeching the gods to respond in their hour of need, and Mudd poked about in the nooks and crannies between consoles for an operator's manual, but neither approach was any more successful than Spock's or Scotty's.

At last Spock gave up and simply began monitoring the state of the internal electronics with his tricorder. It was a slow, tedious process, and he was keenly aware of the mounting political tensions overhead, but he could think of no better course of action. This computer was the key to everything, of that he was sure. He just needed to find out how it worked.

Scotty had moved on down the line of identical substations, scanning each one in turn. After a few minutes of that he returned to Spock and said, "Well, I've got one bit o' good news. It looks like there's still transporter patterns in some of these buffers. It takes about ten racks per person, by my guess, but there's plenty of 'em to go around."

Spock looked up from his tricorder, real hope filling

the emptiness inside him for the first time in hours. "Is the captain in any of them?"

Scotty shook his head. "It'd take decades to scan 'em all, and even then we have no idea what kind of data compression techniques they're using. All I can tell you for sure is there's something in those memory banks."

"And it's stuck there until we can figure out how to unlock the computer," Spock said.

Mudd had been poking around among the artifacts at the end of the tunnel, asking the Grand General what each one was. Now the two of them came back to Spock and Scotty and Mudd asked, "Making any progress?"

"Some," Spock admitted. "I have discovered a periodic data flow that seems to match the resurrection cycle of the android. I suspect it's a self-check routine, since it seems to involve the entire processor and program storage areas, but I have not yet determined what it is checking for." He didn't mention his growing suspicion that the computer was trying to figure out what had gone wrong with the android.

"Grand General," he said. "Is anything other than a Nevisian—or humanoid alien—ever resurrected?"

"What do you mean? Other animals? No, the . . . the Gods . . ." He hesitated, then squared his shoulders and said, "The Gods bring back only people. People killed in battle, at that."

Spock nodded. He had suspected as much. "Something apparently filters the input for a 'humanoid' signature, and disregards all else, probably at the source. That would cut down on the amount of data flow necessary for the central processor to handle. But since the android was also considered humanoid, the definition must not be too strict."

"Certainly you can't believe that the android fooled the Gods!" the Grand General said indignantly.

"It was good enough to fool you," Mudd reminded him.

Spock ignored them both. He was speaking mostly for his own benefit, and for Scotty's. "The rematerialization process, however, must be considerably more sophisticated. It must check for transmission errors that could damage the subject. It no doubt scans a newly revived being's medical condition before it considers the restoration complete."

Scotty nodded. "Aye, that makes sense. But that still doesn't answer my original objection. This can't be the first time it's lost a patient."

"No," said Spock. "But I am willing to bet this is the first time a patient, as you call it, has turned into a robot."

Scotty laughed softly. "It probably thinks it got an order for a gods' eye confused with a person."

"Actually," said Mudd, "that's not a bad description of the original Stella."

Spock looked up at him, unsure what he meant. He had the uncomfortable suspicion that he was missing something obvious, but only to a human. "How is that a good description of your wife?" he asked.

Mudd rolled his eyes upward in their sockets. "It was a joke," he said, confirming Spock's guess. "I just meant that she certainly *thought* she was God."

"Ah." Spock turned back to the computer with his tricorder. It didn't take long to confirm his other suspicion as well: the computer thought that the android was a mistake. He couldn't tell that directly, but the evidence seemed overwhelming. It kept running a self-check, and finding nothing wrong with its programming or hardware, it attempted another resurrection. But the pattern stored in the buffer could produce only an android, which triggered the self-check routine again. It was caught in an endless loop.

"Can't you bypass it somehow?" Mudd asked when he heard Spock and Scotty discussing the situation.

Spock tried to mimic the expression Mudd had worn earlier when Spock had failed to get his joke. It seemed to be the appropriate expression here as well. "There is no provision for input," Spock told him. "The computer was hard wired for this task and no other. And even if there *were* an input device, we do not understand the programming language. Nor would we know how to alter it without causing conflict with other subroutines, of which I identify at least twenty-five. Plus there is the matter of—"

"All right, all right," Mudd said, holding out his hands. "I get the picture. So if we can't bypass it, how can we convince it to give up?"

How indeed? Spock shook his head. "I do not believe the original programmers considered giving up to be an option."

"Then what do you suggest?"

He examined the possibilities. Logically, there was only one good alternative. "I suggest we convince it that it has succeeded."

Mudd had his hands on his hips, clearly enjoying the game of baiting Spock. "How do you plan to do that?" he asked.

"By providing it with the real Stella," Spock said. "We will have to find her and bring her back here for the computer to scan the moment after it resurrects another copy of the android."

He was embarrassed to admit that he derived some small satisfaction from watching Mudd turn absolutely white.

The argument burst onto the bridge with the suddenness and fury of a thunderstorm. A Harry Mudd–sized thunderstorm, to be sure, but in an enclosed space he was more than enough to rattle the furniture. Sulu winced as the turbolift doors slid open and Spock stepped out, chased by Mudd in mid-rant.

". . . won't cooperate for a minute!" Mudd was saying. "She's a witch and a shrew and I have no intention of getting within ten parsecs of her ever again."

"Not even to save the lives of everyone caught in the Nevisian computer's pattern buffers?" Spock asked him.

"They put themselves there," Mudd protested. "I *stopped* the war; I didn't start it again."

"No, but you brought the android that locked up the computer. An interplanetery court would no doubt find you responsible for their deaths."

That made Mudd pause. Even if the Prime Directive didn't apply to him, murder was a capital crime no matter where it took place.

"All right," he said, "I'll tell you where she is, but only if you promise to drop me off somewhere else along the way."

"I make no such promise," said Spock. "You could lie to us about Stella's location. And until we know if bringing her here will work, you are responsible for the situation down there." He sat in the command chair and swiveled it sideways toward Mudd. "Captain Kirk's death will no doubt be the first one prosecuted, and that will be done in a military court."

Sulu heard Uhura gasp, and felt his heart skip a beat. "The captain is dead? I thought—"

"Unless he was resurrected before the android was damaged," said Spock, "which seems unlikely since we have not yet found him on either planet, then he is apparently in a state of suspended animation, stored as data encoded in the computer system that has, unfortunately, locked up."

"And bringing Stella Mudd here will unlock it?" Sulu asked.

"It might," said Spock. "We have no way of knowing for certain without testing the hypothesis directly. Unfortunately, we require Harry's cooperation, which he is reluctant to give."

Mudd laughed shrilly. "'Reluctant' isn't the word for it, Spock old boy. I'm not going back to her, and that's that."

Spock frowned. "You are not being logical." He said it as if he expected Mudd to collapse in shame at the accusation, but Mudd merely snorted.

Sulu saw the problem here: Spock was arguing like a Vulcan and trying to appeal to Harry's sense of responsibility. But Harry *had* no sense of responsibility. Only self-preservation.

"Mr. Spock," Sulu said, standing up from his duty station. "With all due respect, let me show you a better method of getting what we need."

Spock looked at him quizzically, one eyebrow raised, then said, "Proceed."

Sulu stepped closer to Mudd, who backed warily away, but he wasn't nearly quick enough. Sulu grabbed his right arm and spun him around to face the wall, yanking upward on it just as he had done with the Nevisian who had shot Chekov. Mudd yowled inarticulate protest, but Sulu didn't stop until he heard bones creak under the strain.

"Where is she, Harry?" he asked quietly.

"Spock! You can't allow this!" Harry screeched, trying to turn his head to catch Spock's eye, but Sulu kept him facing the wall. "This is an outrage!"

Spock did indeed seem uncomfortable with the spectacle of a Starfleet officer manhandling a civilian on the bridge of a starship, but Sulu held up his free hand, palm out, and shook his head. *I won't hurt him,* he mouthed silently.

Much, he added to himself.

He turned back to Mudd, who was flailing about ineffectually with his free hand. "The coordinates, Harry," he said, adding a bit more strain on his arm.

Uhura snickered.

"I'll file a protest! You'll be the ones facing the court-martial!"

"You'll be signing the papers with two broken arms and ten broken fingers," Sulu told him, never raising his voice. "Or you can give us the coordinates." He yanked upward again on Mudd's arm.

"Ow! You're—ow! All right, all right, but I demand—ow! I mean it. I demand separate quarters, and an armed guard for me at all times. If you don't promise me that much, I'll take the broken arms and fingers, because Stella will give me worse than that."

By the quaver in his voice, Sulu wondered if he was exaggerating. He must be . . . mustn't he? But they would provide Mudd with a guard anyway, just to make sure he didn't skip out, so it really didn't matter one way or the other. Sulu lightened up the pressure on his arm. "Deal," he said. "Now where do we find her?"

"The Hoffman system," Mudd said resignedly. "She's on York Three in the Hoffman system."

"Very good," said Spock. "Lieutenant Uhura, recall Ensign Chekov from his search. We will leave as soon as he arrives."

"Yes, sir," she said, but she hesitated before turning back to her comm panel. "Mr. Spock? While you were gone, our new orders came in from Admiral Tyers. We're supposed to rendezvous with the *U.S.S. O'Halloran* in the Duval system."

Spock nodded. "I see. I'm afraid we will have to miss that rendezvous. I will send her an explanation en route, but for now we will proceed to the Hoffman system."

Chapter Twenty-three

KIRK RECOILED WILDLY, trying to keep his balance. What had happened? A second ago he had been dragging Harry Mudd to safety, and now—

Water sprayed everywhere with the force of his reaction. Water. Dammit, he had been killed again!

He spluttered as he slipped under the surface, then he found his footing and stood up, shaking wet hair from his eyes. "All right," he said, looking around for the naked ladies, "where am I this time?"

"Arnhall," said a voice off to his left. He looked through the steamy air and saw what he had expected, but then the word she had said struck home.

"Where exactly is that?" he asked. "In relation to Distrel."

"Certainly that's not the most important question you—oh." She stopped as the mist parted and she saw who had arrived. "You're one of the aliens," she said after a moment.

"James Kirk, captain of the *Enterprise*," he told her. He climbed out of the pool and walked toward her. Other Nevisians in the tubs all around him stared openly, but he ignored them. "I don't care where Arnhall is; I just want to go back to my ship. And I'm not taking no for an answer."

"I, um, you'll have to talk to the Council of Heroes about that," she said.

"Fine. Let's go."

She didn't move. "Don't you want to relax first? After their second death, most people need some time to think things over and consider the changes in their lives."

"That's just it," said Kirk. "My life isn't going to change. I'm going back to the *Enterprise* and gather up my people and we're leaving you and your silly war behind."

"I don't think going back is allowed."

"Then you'd better change your rules, because that's just what I'm going to do."

She took a deep breath. "You definitely need to talk to the Council of Heroes." This time she turned away and led him past the other attendants who were waiting for more people to appear, and on out of the bath chamber.

Ten minutes later, clothed in a soft rainbow-colored sweat suit and his hair still damp, he was ushered into the council chamber. It was more of a council cottage, actually, with the transporter in the front hallway and a living room to one side and a dining room on the other. He had no idea where it was on the planet; he and his bathhouse guide had made three transporter jumps to get here. It was not close to the equator, judging by the angle of the sun and the cool air, but that was about all he could guess. It really didn't matter, because he still had no idea which planet he was on. The gravity seemed lighter than either Prastor's or Distrel's, but it was hard to judge for sure. He was still on an adrenaline rush.

The Council turned out to be three white-haired Nevisians, two women and a man, who sat in soft chairs around a fireplace in which a couple of burning logs gave off a sweet aroma and enough heat to knock the chill out of the air. A wide window in the wall to the right of the fireplace provided a wonderful view of a lake and snowcapped mountains off in the distance. Off to the side a pile of old masonry might have been the remains of an ancient castle. Only portions of two walls still stood, and trees growing inside its perimeter sent branches out through the windows.

"Welcome to Arnhall," the woman in the middle said.

"Thanks." There was a fourth chair by the fire, obviously for Kirk, but he didn't sit down. "I'd love to stay and visit, but I've got pressing business back home."

The man on her right laughed softly. "This is your home now. What's behind you is behind you. That's the whole point of the war, you know."

Kirk disliked this guy immediately. "Is it? Looks to me more like you're training an army. What's the plan? Galactic conquest? Or just this quadrant?"

The man laughed again. "I'm afraid we would make rather poor warriors. People who have died twice already are much less willing to do it a third time, especially when they know it would be permanent. That, too, is the point of the war."

"I've heard people talk about fighting for peace

before," Kirk told him. "Usually right before they invade their neighbors."

The woman in the middle said, "We already tried that, millennia ago. We discovered that once you start fighting, you never stop. There's always someone else to attack or defend against, some ideological struggle or another to whip people into a frenzy. As a people we realized it was a pointless way to live, but as individuals we each still yearned for glory."

"So you went to war with yourselves?"

"Exactly. We learned that people can outgrow their violent tendencies, but they need a defining event in their lives. A redefining event. We found that death works quite well in that regard." She nodded toward the empty chair. "Sit."

Kirk sat. His chair was next to the other woman's, the one who had not said anything. She nodded to him, but remained silent.

"It's really the loss of everything a person holds dear that matters," said the first woman. "It gets them to thinking. We try to spread the fighting around to give them time to establish a second life before we send them into battle again, so they have even more to lose. We hardly ever have to send someone back for a third life."

"That's . . . a pretty harsh system," Kirk said, trying to be diplomatic.

"Life is harsh. And it gets worse the more you give in to violence. Unfortunately most beings don't have a chance to learn that until they've already squandered most of their time."

"That still looks like the case," Kirk observed, noting the white hair and wrinkled skin on all three of the Nevisians—or was it Arnhallians now?

That drew a response from the quiet woman. She tilted back her head and laughed, not the soft chuckle of the other two, but a loud, raucous laugh that set Kirk's teeth on edge. "Score one for the alien," she said. "He saw through you two relics in a flash."

Kirk said to her, "I take it you disagree with their assessment of the situation."

"Slightly." She held out her hand. "I'm Narine, the First Advocate. They keep me around for laughs."

Kirk gripped her forearm in the fashion he had learned from the Grand General of Distrel. She seemed pleased that he knew the gesture.

She pointed to the man. "This is Kenan, Second Advocate, and beside him is Hadock, Third Advocate."

"What's the significance of first, second, and third?" Kirk asked.

"Stages of life," Narine said. "I speak for the people who haven't died yet. Kenan speaks for those living their second life, and Hadock speaks for those who have come to Arnhall."

Kirk felt a bit surprised. "Yet *you're* the one who doesn't like this system? From what you've told me, the young are the most aggressive. And from what I saw, they certainly looked like they enjoyed the war."

"The young are the most impressionable. They also have the most to lose. I was nine when I came here. That was seventy years ago, and I still miss my mother."

Kenan said, "Oh, don't go on about your mother. She was here on Arnhall for years. You could go see her any time you wanted to all that time."

Narine frowned. "And she didn't care a bit whether I did or not. By the time she got here she had brought up a second family—and lost that one, too. She didn't want to form any more close attachments. That's what your precious resurrection system creates: cold-hearted fatalists who don't want to be hurt again. Sure they don't fight anymore. They don't *live* anymore."

"Yes, yes, that's what Ginn Donan said five millennia ago, but it's better than the alternative."

It sounded like they'd argued this out many times before. They might have gone on at length rehashing it again, but there was a knock at the door and the bathhouse guard who had escorted Kirk there stepped into the room. "Excuse me," she said, "but we seem to have a problem. There've been no more resurrections since the alien arrived."

The Council of Heroes all turned toward Kirk. "Did your people talk ours into peace again?" asked Hadock. "I thought we'd convinced them it was against the will of the Gods."

"As far as I know, they still think so," Kirk said. "The war was still going on strong when I left."

"Then one of your people has interfered with the machinery," said Kenan. "That's the only other explanation."

"What machinery?" Kirk asked.

Narine laughed, then told him about the cavern beneath the Grand General's palace on Distrel and the transporter buffers and computers there that revived people killed in the war. Kirk wasn't surprised to learn about them; he had suspected something of the sort. And if someone had tinkered with them, he could just imagine who it had been.

"My first officer, Mr. Spock, might know something about it," he said. "If you would let me use a communicator I could contact him and find out for you."

Kenan and Hadock exchanged a glance, and Hadock said, "I believe it would be more efficient to simply send you back. You or your first officer can undo whatever you have done to our resurrection machinery; it doesn't matter to us which of you restarts it."

"Could you let me talk with him first anyway?" asked Kirk. "He probably doesn't even know I'm still alive."

"No," said Hadock. "We can't do that."

"Can't, or won't?" asked Kirk.

Narine laughed again, and said, "Gods, but you're a refreshing voice. I'd like to keep you here just to hear you question authority. But in this case, Hadock is telling the truth. We have no subspace radio, and through normal communications channels it would take several years for your message to reach your ship."

"Years?" asked Kirk. That would put Arnhall in a completely different star system. Could that be possible? He had arrived here by transporter, and that usually had a very limited range. This was alien technology; there was no telling what it could do, but to have that sort of transport capability and no subspace radio seemed a bit fishy. Something wasn't adding up here.

"Why don't you have subspace radio?" he asked.

"We never needed it," Hadock replied. "We can go anywhere we want instantaneously."

Kirk looked over at Narine, and she nodded. "True enough. But an equally true answer would be that we don't have a clue how to build it. If our ancestors didn't leave us a template for something, we don't have it."

"That's enough," Kenan said sternly. "You disapprove of everything we stand for; fine. But you don't control this council. Captain, it's time for you to go." He nodded to the woman who had brought the message. "Send him back to the Grand General's palace on Distrel. And Captain, when you get there, see that you restore our computer just the way it was before you arrived. We may not be members of your Federation, but we know of it, and we will make our presence known in a most unpleasant fashion if you violate your Prime Directive."

"He's bluffing," said Narine. "Blow the whole mess to bits for all I care. They can't do anything about it. They're a couple of tired old farts who hate the idea of change, that's all."

Kirk smiled at her. "I tend to agree. But it's not my place to force it on them. I believe that's your job."

"Hah. Right again, much as I hate to admit it. Go on, then. Go back to your people and keep on *living*." She turned away and sank back into her chair, once again a wizened, silent old crone.

Chapter Twenty-four

McCoy HATED THE NOTION of leaving Kirk behind while the *Enterprise* went off in search of Stella Mudd, but if he truly was trapped inside that infernal computer as Spock seemed to believe, then McCoy supposed there was little more they could do for him on Distrel. Spock was the computer expert, and if he said Kirk couldn't be sprung from his prison without Stella, then it probably couldn't be done.

It gave McCoy the creeping jeebies just thinking about it. Stuck in a transporter buffer, not even as a beam of elemental particles, but just as information in storage. A cosmic ray could flip a bit somewhere and he could emerge with purple eyes or an extra nose—or far more likely as a blob of unrecognizable gray goo. McCoy had attended the autopsies after a few transporter accidents, and he didn't want to see any more.

And then, as if having Kirk stuck in there wasn't

enough, there were all the Nevisians who had died after the android had locked things up. A couple thousand of them at least. They weren't as dear to McCoy as Kirk was, but a couple thousand lives was a couple thousand lives, and McCoy was a doctor. If there was anything he could do to help save them, he was morally obligated to give it his best shot.

And on top of all that there was the Prime Directive problem, though McCoy wasn't so sure how he felt about that. On the one hand, the Nevisians' perpetual war disgusted him as few things he'd seen in his travels had, but on the other hand it was *their* war, and they had every right to keep on with it if that was what they wanted to do. No doubt a Starfleet tribunal would think so, and even though Mudd and his android had caused the actual damage, the *Enterprise* was so inextricably tied to them that everyone would go down in flames over this.

So here they were on this wild goose chase. He just hoped they could actually find Stella. They had no idea where on York III she was, or what her living situation might be. Harry wasn't cooperating at all, and Spock was reluctant to turn Sulu loose on him again until they knew whether or not they needed any more information from him. It might be a simple matter of accessing a database and calling her comm number—or it might not.

When the *Enterprise* dropped out of warp McCoy went up to the bridge to see which it would be. Lieutenant Uhura was already busy at the comm station talking with the local government authorities, and Spock was back at his science station poring through planetary records as fast as Uhura could access them for him. For lack of a better place to sit,

Harry Mudd occupied the captain's chair, and while he no doubt would have relished the position in other circumstances, he was clearly uncomfortable there now. He fidgeted and examined the controls in the armrest, as if looking for the one that might get him out of the situation.

McCoy felt a bit uneasy at seeing him there, too, though he knew full well that Mudd could cause no more mischief from the command chair than from anywhere else. It was the authority, not the chair, that gave a captain control of the ship, and Mudd had none of that.

"How goes the search?" McCoy asked, taking his usual stance beside the chair.

Spock looked up from his monitors. "I find no record of Stella Mudd more recent than three years ago, at which time she applied for a legal divorce in absentia."

"She divorced me?" Harry asked indignantly.

Spock said, "Yes, but that was two years earlier. This appears to be the second husband to abandon her."

"More like dropped her like a pound of antimatter, you mean," Mudd said. "I wonder who the poor bugger was."

"His name was Bischoff," Spock told him.

"Bischoff!" said Mudd. "Hah! Serves him right. He conned me out of a starship once on Silva Five."

"It appears he turned that starship into quite a fleet," Spock said, examining the database again. "He is listed here as one of the wealthiest people in the system, former owner of an interstellar cargo and passenger transport service that spanned most of this sector."

"Hah," Mudd sniffed. "It was all my ideas that got him there." He frowned. "You say 'former owner.' What happened to him?"

"He apparently took his flagship on a personal cruise to an unstated destination, and never returned."

"He'd had enough of Stella," Mudd said. "I suppose she got everything in the divorce?"

"Yes," said Spock.

"So she's rich again, is she?" Mudd rubbed his jaw thoughtfully.

"Again?" McCoy asked him. "Did you marry her for her money?"

Mudd laughed. "Me? Doctor, I'm surprised at you. Of course I married her for her charming personality."

"Unfortunately," said Spock, "she used some of her newfound wealth to purchase a new identity, which is apparently legal here. We cannot learn that identity unless we show conclusive evidence of past criminal activity."

"Yes, that was always one of the things I liked about the Hoffman system," Mudd said, leaning back in the captain's chair. "Unfortunately they kept raising the price, but they're true to their word. You really can't find someone's new identity once they've cleared their felony check and paid the fee." He sighed. "Too bad. We probably could have located her otherwise."

McCoy snorted. "Spare us the crocodile tears, Harry."

"Sincere or no," Spock said, "he does seem to be telling the truth about the procedure for penetrating the new identity. Unless we can convict her for a felony crime committed in her previous life, the government will not release her new name to us." He paused, thinking, then said, "I can scan through news records of the past three years and correlate them for matching photos, but it will take days, and the odds of success are slim."

"I've got a better idea," said McCoy.

"Oh?"

"Yeah. Uhura, get me the head of this identity bureau. Not some flunky, but the top person. Tell them a Starfleet medical officer wants to talk to them about a priority-one contamination problem."

"Yes, sir."

"Doctor," said Spock. "May I remind you that misuse of your rank is grounds for your own arrest?"

"Who said I was going to misuse it? I'm just going to— Hello." The main viewscreen lit up with the image of an impeccably dressed man in his forties or fifties, seated behind an enormous wooden desk. No papers marred the glistening surface. Good. That meant he was probably a figurehead. But one with power, McCoy hoped. He said, "I'm Chief Medical Officer Leonard McCoy, aboard the *U.S.S. Enterprise.* I'm investigating an outbreak of Nevisian Stasis Syndrome in a nearby star system, and I need to talk to one of your citizens."

"Nevisian Stasis Syndrome?" the official said, frowning. "I have never heard of it."

"Not surprising," said McCoy. "I just discovered it. It's a completely debilitating condition that until now had always been mistaken for death. I've discovered that the victims can be revived, but I'm missing one crucial piece of information."

"Information which our citizen possesses. I see. And this citizen has no doubt purchased a new identity, or you wouldn't be talking to me about it."

"That's right."

The bureaucrat leaned forward. "Nice try. Yours is one of the more inventive I've heard recently. Nevisian Stasis Syndrome; that's one for the memoirs. But we take privacy quite seriously here. Sorry." He reached forward to cut off the signal, but McCoy stopped him before he could touch the switch.

"And Starfleet takes epidemics quite seriously," he said. "I have the authority to quarantine this entire star system indefinitely to prevent health risks to the rest of the Federation. I hate to do that, since I know how hard it can be on commerce, but galactic security has to come first. Sorry." He mimicked the bureaucrat's insincere apology. Spock looked like he was about to protest, but McCoy shut him up with a warning glare.

The bureaucrat leaned back in his chair and pursed his lips. "Hmm. Well, under the circumstances, I suppose I could contact the person you are looking for and explain the situation, and let *them* decide whether or not to reveal their identity to you."

"That would be a start," McCoy said. "Make sure you impress upon her the seriousness of the situation."

"You can be sure I will. What is this person's former name?"

"Stella Mudd."

He narrowed his eyes. "That name seems familiar. Just a moment." He tapped his desktop a few times, and McCoy realized he had a built-in data monitor. It took him a second to find the information, but they knew when he'd done it by the involuntary gasp he made.

"Looks like you've found her," McCoy observed.

"Unfortunately, I have." The man took a deep breath, squared his shoulders, and said, "Just a moment." This time when he reached for the comm switch, it was merely to put them on hold. Instead of the usual still picture of most hold screens, his was a running ad for the Hoffman system, showing barely clothed people strolling along a beach, dining by candlelight, shopping in a busy market filled with goods and alien proprietors from throughout the Federation, all over a caption reading, "Business as usual on York III."

"You used to live here?" McCoy asked Mudd.

He squirmed, embarrassed at having yet another aspect of his past exposed. "Well, everyone needs a place to hang his hat, you know. This was . . . convenient."

"I'll bet it was."

Mudd laughed. "Don't get all high and mighty. You'd fit right in here, the way you handled that situation. Nevisian Stasis Syndrome. An excellent story. I didn't know you had it in you."

McCoy shrugged. "You do what you have to do."

"Doctor," said Spock, "surely you're aware that you have no basis for quarantining this system."

"I never said I did," McCoy told him. "I just said I had the authority to, which is true."

Mudd stood up from the captain's chair. "It looks like you won't be needing me any further," he said nonchalantly. "So I'll just nip down to my quarters for a quick—"

"Sit down, Harry," said McCoy.

"But—"

"Sit."

Harry sat. A moment later the screen came to life again, not with the bureaucrat, but with the living, breathing—no, *wheezing*—face of Stella Mudd. The years had not been kind to her, or else Harry had been when he'd provided the androids with a description of her to build their replica from. Her hair was now an improbable color of reddish purple that could only have come out of a bottle, and her skin had the artificially tight sheen of someone who had been under the protoplaser a few times too many. Behind her, dozens of white-clad people—they looked like maids—scurried back and forth with towels, sheets, and cleaning equipment. It looked like she was in a hotel laundry room, though what a wealthy person would be doing there was hard to imagine.

"All right," she screeched, her voice like a sliding door with a piece of metal caught in the crack, "what's going on he— Well, if it isn't my long-lost Harcourt. I was wondering how long it would take you to find out I was rich again. Come back for another slice of the pie, have you?"

Mudd seemed to shrink in his chair. "Um, hello Stella. I, um, well, actually, that was the furthest thought from my mind."

"I bet it was," she said. "Well let me tell you, you no good, gold-digging, sorry excuse for an ex-husband, I'm back on top again and I'm going to stay there this time. Without you."

"Yes, dear. That's quite all right. In fact, I'm very happy for you." Harry seemed to perk up again at the thought that the feelings might be mutual.

She squinted at him. "You seem to be fairly well off

yourself, though captain of a Starfleet ship doesn't exactly seem like you. How'd that happen? I'd have expected to see you in the brig instead."

"My dear," said Harry, puffing himself up and sitting straighter in the chair, "perhaps you have forgotten your own gentle words of advice, given to me so long ago, but I assure you I have never forgotten that I should always attempt to make something of myself. This is just a temporary phase on the way to far greater things." He looked over at McCoy and winked ever so slightly with the eye that faced away from the viewscreen.

"Very temporary, if I know you," Stella said. "Well if you didn't come slinking back for a handout, then what did you come for?" Behind her, a woman carrying a pile of towels collided with a man carrying a tray of wineglasses. Both towels and glasses went to the floor, the glasses smashing into glittering shards. Stella whirled around, appraised the situation instantly, and shouted, "You're both fired! Get out of my hotel! You—" she pointed at another woman who cowered nearby, a hypersonic cleaner in her hands, and at another man holding a sheaf of papers "—and you, you've just been promoted. Clean up that mess. And the rest of you, get back to work!" She turned back to the viewscreen. "Sorry, but you know how it is. You just can't find good help these days."

Mudd looked to Spock, and then to the rest of the bridge crew. "Yes, it's difficult, isn't it?" he said.

McCoy couldn't tell if he was being snide to her, to the bridge crew, or both, but in any case he ignored the slight and said, "Speaking of help, that's why we're here. We need your assistance in a matter of life and death."

"You do?" Stella seemed genuinely surprised to hear that. Evidently she had thought the whole story was fabricated just to reach her.

"We really do," McCoy told her. "We've got thousands of people whose lives depend on taking you back with us to the Nevis system."

"Why me?" she asked suspiciously. "What can I do that you can't?"

"You can be yourself," McCoy said. "You don't have to do anything but go there and beam down to the surface with us. It'll be perfectly safe, and we'll bring you right back. But we've determined that of all the people in the galaxy, you're the one we need to solve our problem."

"You're kidding. Somebody needs me?" She was shocked at the very concept, and obviously flattered. Apparently nobody had ever told her they needed her before.

"Lives depend on you," McCoy said.

"Well . . . I don't know." She preened herself and gestured over her shoulder. "I'm needed here, too, you know. This place would fall apart without me."

McCoy suspected it would run considerably smoother without her hand in all the details, but she obviously loved micromanaging dozens of employees. She had found the perfect position for a woman who loved to tell people what to do. But McCoy knew where the chink in her armor had to be. He said, "Oh, certainly someone with your managerial skills has a second-in-command who could look after things for a few days."

She nodded slowly. "Of course I do. It's just that it's such short notice, and I—"

"And you would have the chance to catch up on old

times with Harry," said Spock. "Certainly there must be some things you wish to say to him after all this time."

Harry blanched at the suggestion, but he smiled bravely.

Stella smiled back, but it was the smile of the leopard just before the pounce. "I just might at that," she said. "Let me pack a bag and I'll be right up."

When she switched off, McCoy turned to Spock and said, "Spock, that was inhuman. Even Harry doesn't deserve that."

Spock replied, "It appeared that she was about to back down. I achieved our objective, did I not?"

"Yes, but the price . . ."

Harry slumped down in the captain's chair. "Bodyguard," he whispered. "You promised me a bodyguard."

Chapter Twenty-five

KIRK ARRIVED in the throne room. The place looked like a war zone, and in fact it was. The Prastorians had gutted it, set afire everything that would burn, and smashed the rest. The Grand General would be a long time rebuilding from this invasion.

If he was even alive. Was anybody left in the palace? It seemed deserted. "Hello!" Kirk called out, his voice echoing off the soot-blackened stone. He wished he had some kind of weapon to defend himself with in case the wrong people answered his call, but that fear vanished when a Distrellian soldier stepped into the throne room and immediately bowed low.

"My lord hero," he said, still looking at the floor. "Welcome."

Must be the rainbow robe, Kirk thought. They apparently didn't see many of them around here. "I need to talk with the Grand General," he said. "And with my—the *Enterprise*."

"Yes, sir," the guard said. "The Grand General is right this way. Unfortunately the *Enterprise* has gone away."

Gone away? Had they given up searching for Kirk and the others already? That didn't seem like Spock. Or McCoy. They would stick around until they were absolutely sure there was no hope that anyone had survived. Of course the evidence probably looked pretty overwhelming, but still.

He followed the soldier, who looked straight ahead as if afraid the sight of a genuine Arnhall Hero would blind him, through blast-pocked hallways to a much smaller throne room where the Grand General sat directing repairs to his palace. He looked up when Kirk entered the room, then scrambled to his feet.

"You've come! Thank the Gods. We . . . wait a minute." Recognition wiped away his relief. "Captain Kirk?"

"The same," Kirk said.

"But . . . are the comp—uh, the Gods awake again?"

"The computers?" Kirk asked.

"The, uh, the arbiters, yes." He waved his hands toward the door and said to his court, "Leave us, please."

Silently, everyone got up and walked out the door, and the soldier who had escorted Kirk there closed it behind him on his way out.

When they'd left, Kirk said, "You don't want your people to know that their fates lie in the circuits of a computer in your basement? Why not?"

"Because I just learned of it myself, and I'm trying to decide what to do about it," said the Grand General. "Sit, please." He waved at a chair, and sat back down in his own. "I take it you have been to Arnhall, then. I hadn't expected that, since you were killed trying to escape. When you didn't reappear on Prastor, we assumed you were stuck in the—your Mr. Spock called it a 'pattern buffer'—along with everyone else."

"I was dragging Harry Mudd out of the line of fire when I got hit," Kirk told him, settling down across from him. "Apparently your computer thought that was heroic enough to send me on."

The Grand General nodded. "Yes, that would probably do it. And it must have happened just before the android ruined everything." He looked a dozen years older than when Kirk had last seen him, but he brightened now and said, "The Heroes must know about it, though, mustn't they? Did they send you back to fix the problem? Did they tell you how?"

"Well, yes and no," said Kirk. "They want me to fix it, all right, but it's pretty clear they don't know how to do that. They don't even know what happened to it. They just told me to undo whatever we'd done and get it working again."

"I see. Well, Mr. Spock and the rest of your crew are trying to do just that, but it all seems very improbable to me. They need to find Harcourt's wife—the real one—and bring her back here to fool the computer into thinking it has resurrected her."

Kirk tried to picture it, but couldn't. "Wait a minute," he said. "What does Stella Mudd have to do with anything?"

"It's a long story," said the Grand General. "Perhaps it would be easier to just show you."

He got up again and led Kirk into a back room,

which turned out to be a local transporter that took them to the palace's outer wall, where they stepped across the shield boundary into another transporter which took them to another one in a different city, which deposited them outside a bathhouse. Apparently only the resurrection system could beam through shields, thought Kirk. Transporters that weren't hooked into the network had to do it the normal way.

Inside the bathhouse he saw the Stella android, still reappearing and disappearing in her dry hot tub every few minutes. Then they beamed back to the palace and went into the caverns, through the blind transporter in the hidden closet, to look at the computers. Kirk gazed down the seemingly endless line of memory banks, each one complex enough to store an entire person's molecular pattern, and shook his head in amazement.

"Quite a setup," he said. "But not quite the 'gods' you'd been led to believe in, eh?"

"No," said the Grand General. He looked up at one of the flickering overhead lights. "It all seems a bit . . . tawdry compared to the legends."

Kirk nodded. "The truth usually does. I guess that's why legends are so popular among the masses." He looked back at the computers. "Narine, one of the leaders of Arnhall, told me I should blow all this to bits."

"I have considered it," said the Grand General. "But I'm not sure if I want to take responsibility for ending a system that has served us for so long."

"Served you, or enslaved you?" Kirk asked.

"That does seem to be the question, doesn't it?"

The Grand General shook his head. "But whatever else we may think about it, it has kept us from actually killing each other in warfare for millennia. And now with another battle waiting for the slightest pretext to erupt, I am reluctant to cast away that safety net."

"It's the safety net that keeps you fighting," Kirk said.

"I wish it were so, but the Padishah threatens to attack us even though the . . . 'Gods' no longer protect our warriors. One final, glorious war to end all wars."

Kirk sighed. "I've heard that phrase before. We number our 'wars to end all wars' nowadays. We're up to three and still bickering." Though he had to admit, war—on Earth, at least—was less likely now than ever before. Humanity finally seemed to be learning.

Unlike the Nevisians. They were an old enough race to be one of the galaxy's wisest, but they had stagnated instead.

"Have you and the Padishah ever talked peace?" he asked.

The Grand General nodded. "Certainly. And you saw how well that worked."

"Not that." Kirk waved his hands dismissively. "I'm not talking about trade agreements; I mean have you ever talked peace because you don't want to shoot at each other anymore?"

"That would have been against the will of the Gods."

Kirk kicked at one of the metal consoles with his toe. The hollow bonk echoed down the corridor. "Yeah," he said, "I know what you mean. It's hard to buck authority. But sometimes that's what you've got to do if you're going to grow up."

* * *

Ensign Lebrun stood just inside the door to Harry's quarters, watching him pace nervously back and forth in front of the bed. He'd been fidgeting for hours. If he kept it up much longer he would wear through the deck plating—and through Lebrun's patience.

"Would you calm down?" she said finally. "She's not going to hurt you."

Mudd stopped pacing, but didn't sit down. "That's easy for you to say. You haven't been married long enough to know all the ways a wo—a spouse can hurt another."

"I'm learning," Lebrun said. "But making up is half the fun. Heck, with Simon and me it's *all* the fun."

"I wouldn't know," said Mudd. "I don't believe Stella and I ever 'made up.' "

"Well good grief, don't you think it's high time you tried?"

"No." Mudd turned to his viewport and looked out at the stars. "In fact, I believe it's time to move on. The Andromeda Galaxy might be far enough, though perhaps I should go for something on the other side of the Virgo cluster. What do you think?"

Lebrun laughed. "I think you're being needlessly melodramatic. She's a perfectly nice woman."

"For a targ."

"Harry, you're impossible."

"So I've been told. Repeatedly."

"Sorry." Lebrun realized she was browbeating him just as badly as anyone. She stepped toward him, but just then the door chimed.

"Don't open it!" Harry said, shrinking back.

"Oh, for crying out loud." Lebrun turned toward the door. "Come."

* * *

It slid aside to reveal Mudd's worst fear: Stella, standing there and tapping her toe impatiently.

"Hello," Lebrun began to say, but Stella spoke at the same time.

"There you are, Harcourt. Consorting with children again, I see. Well, First Officer Spock has just informed me that we're approaching the Nevis system, and will be beaming down so I can save Captain Kirk and the other people trapped by your ridiculous android. Don't ask me why, but he wants you to come along as well."

"I'd just as soon not," said Harry.

"That goes without saying," said Stella. "Since it wasn't your idea. But perhaps you had best listen to good advice for a change."

"Oh, I would listen to it if I ever heard any. But good advice seems to be in such short supply in your vicinity." Harry took a cautious step closer to her. "It's almost as if the abundance of witchon particles in the air cause it to evanesce."

"Witchon particles? Is that some kind of slur? Because if it is—" Stella took a step into the room.

"Please, stop it, both of you." Lebrun held out her hands. "You don't have to do this to each other."

Stella looked as if she might bite Lebrun's head off, and for a second Lebrun thought she might have to go for her phaser, but then Stella blinked and smiled. "You're right, dear. We don't. I've divorced the old windbag."

"Windbag?" protested Harry. "Now just a minute."

"No." Stella turned to go. "I'm needed elsewhere. I'm *appreciated* elsewhere. Come watch or not; it's up to you." She looked back to Lebrun. "A word of advice, miss. Whatever he promises you, be sure you get it in writing."

Lebrun blushed. "It's not like that."

"I'm sure it isn't. Nothing with Harry is ever quite what it seems."

"No, really, I'm already married and everything." Lebrun held out her hand to show Stella her ring.

"More's the pity," Stella said, as she sashayed off toward the turbolift.

"But—"

Harry laughed. "Don't even try," he said. He watched Stella round the corner and disappear, then hitched up his pants and said, "You know, that was just like old times. And I'd forgotten how refreshing it is to watch her depart. Come on, let's go watch her do it again."

Chapter Twenty-six

THE BEST SEATS in the house, it turned out, were in the bathhouse, where she would arrive. Harry didn't particularly care; perhaps he could take some amusement at seeing Stella slip in the tub.

He had already witnessed perhaps the most amusing spectacle of all: Spock trying to hide his emotion when he discovered that Kirk wasn't trapped in the computer buffer as they had thought. Dr. McCoy at least had the grace to weep for joy, though why anyone should shed a tear for the likes of Kirk was beyond Harry. But Spock had been forced to stand there like an android himself and say, "I am pleased to see you, Captain," and shake his hand like a politician stumping for votes.

Ah, what fools these mortals be, Mudd thought. Always hiding this, apologizing for that, bickering over something else. No one could say or do what they really wanted to, and all for what? Some misguided sense of duty or honor or decorum? What a crock! Far better to just let it all hang out, thumb your nose at phony obligations, and concentrate on what mattered. Like getting rich and having fun. If everybody did that it would be a merrier galaxy, that much was certain.

The Distrellians had shut down their shield generator so the *Enterprise* could beam the android away and beam Stella directly into its place. Spock and Scotty were monitoring the "gods' eyes" for their particular emission signature, while Kirk and the Grand General and the Padishah stood beside the empty pool. The Padishah looked a bit stunned— apparently they had shown him the face of God just a few minutes earlier and he was still trying to decide what to think. He kept wiping his face with the backs of his decorative gloves, even though the heat in the room had long since dissipated.

Mudd and Ensign Lebrun and her husband, Lieutenant Nordell, stood on the other side of the tub, while a few dozen Distrellians had gathered around a bit farther back.

"Transporter sequence starting," Spock announced, his voice loud in the tiled bathhouse.

"Get ready," Kirk said into his communicator.

"Matter stream initiated," said Spock.

Kirk waited while the flickering shape in the tub took on form. The moment it solidified, he said "Now!" and the *Enterprise*'s transporter locked on to the android, which shuddered and sparked in the confinement beam but didn't fall to the floor. It faded away, and right on its heels—beaming in from the other transporter on board the ship—came the real Stella. She was in the same orientation as the android, angled slightly backward in a position that would be comfortable in water, but was awkward as could be in air. Even though she had been told to expect it, she flailed her arms and squawked like a surprised chicken before landing with a thump on the thick pad they had placed on the bottom of the tub.

She stood up and brushed off her dignity, then accepted the Grand General's hand out of the tub. He was smiling at her again, Mudd noted. The old goat. Well, if he kept her out of Mudd's hair as well as he'd kept the android, then he was welcome to her.

"Well," she asked. "Did it work?"

Everyone turned this way and that, looking expectantly into the other pools for the host of soldiers who should be materializing in them at any moment. Someone coughed, and after a few seconds, whispering started up, but nothing appeared in the water.

"What's wrong?" asked the Grand General.

"I don't know," said Kirk. "Spock? Scotty?"

"It shoulda worked, Captain," Scotty said, thumping his tricorder and taking another reading of the gods' eye.

"It obviously didn't."

Spock said, "I will go see if I can determine what has happened." He headed for the transport station, and presumably the palace.

There was an embarrassed silence while they waited for him to reach the computers in the caverns. The Padishah finally broke it, saying to the Grand General, "If this is a trick, I promise you will be the first one we send into oblivion when we annihilate your entire planet."

"If this is a trick," said the Grand General, "you

can *have* this planet, because I and everyone else here are heading for Arnhall, with weapons drawn."

"And just how do you plan to get there?" asked the Padishah.

The Grand General laughed halfheartedly. "I hadn't thought of that. If it's a trick, we're stuck here, aren't we?"

Kirk's communicator chirped at him. "Kirk here," he said.

"Spock here. I am in the computer center, and I believe I have found the problem. The system is no longer running its self-test program. It has apparently reloaded its main program, and awaits only the proper input to resume processing."

"So what's the input?" Kirk asked.

"It appears to be . . ." Spock hesitated.

"What?"

"Unfortunately, it appears that someone must die in battle."

"Oh," said Kirk.

"That is not the worst of our problems," said Spock. "I have examined the transporter patterns in storage, and have discovered an alarming degradation of the signal. Apparently these memory devices were never intended for long-term storage. There was an error-correction routine in effect while the self-check was active, but now that the main program is back on line, the error-correction routine is no longer operating. By my calculation, we have less than ten minutes before the signal degradation becomes too severe to allow reconstruction of the stored patterns."

Kirk looked unbelievingly at his communicator. "Any more bad news?"

"Yes," Spock said, apparently unaware of the concept of a rhetorical question. "The way the memory devices are configured, all of the patterns are decaying at the same rate. Whoever dies to restart the resurrections will stand the same risk as those people already here."

The Padishah looked at Kirk, then at the Grand General. "I can arrange plenty of deaths just as soon as you like."

"No, no, please," said the Grand General. "There's got to be a better way." He looked at Kirk imploringly.

"Spock?" asked Kirk.

"I wish there were, Captain, but this computer is hardwired. There is no altering its program. And it requires a death to trigger the resurrection process."

Kirk looked over at Harry, and Harry could see the gleam of the wolf in his eye. "Who, me?" he asked, backing away, but Kirk had already looked away. Mudd nearly went over backward into the next pool of water, but Lebrun rescued him from that indignity.

Kirk said, "I can't ask anyone else to do this. And I can't let your two planets go back to war to solve a problem that was brought on by outsiders. But it doesn't matter whose fault this is"—and he looked at Harry again—"it's the duty of a Starfleet officer to give his life for the cause of peace if that becomes necessary. We all know the risks, and we all know it could come at any time, no matter . . ."

What a blowhard, thought Mudd, tuning him out. Kirk was going to puff himself up to heroic proportions and then get someone to shoot him, and he'd come out of this with a commendation and a cushy desk job back home. Mudd knew his type. He'd probably set this all up with Spock ahead of time. There was no more danger here than trimming a fingernail.

Well, okay, trimming it with a phaser set on high, but really. And the rewards—dear lord, the rewards!

Almost against his will, Mudd found himself edging forward. Kirk was winding down now, saying, ". . . and so I say look not to the past, but to your future, and remember the sacrifices of the people who have come before you. As long as you build on the foundation they lay, as long as—"

Mudd cleared his throat. "As long as you keep blathering on about it, Kirk, we'll never get the job done. Do please close your face and let a real man show you how it's done."

Kirk couldn't believe his ears. Mudd was going to take responsibility for something? It was almost worth the insult just to witness it. And if Harry meant what Kirk thought he meant, this could be a red-letter day indeed. "What do you want, Harry?" he asked. "You and me, mano a mano?"

Mudd looked at him disdainfully. "I wouldn't give you the satisfaction, Kirk." He stepped past—shoved Kirk aside!—and reached instead toward the Padishah. The Padishah looked as astonished as Kirk. What could Mudd want with him? But that became clear when Mudd took his gloves from his unresisting fingers, separated one out and returned it, then turned with the other to the Grand General.

"You've been paying far too much attention to my wife," Mudd said. "Where I come from, that's a matter of honor." And he slapped the Grand General in the face with his glove.

The Grand General narrowed his eyes. "What is the significance of this?"

"He's challenged you to a duel," Kirk said, awe-struck.

Stella looked as if she might faint. "Harry . . . I didn't know you cared."

Harry smiled an enigmatic little smile at her, then said to the Grand General, "Well, are you willing to fight for her?"

The Grand General looked out at the faces turned toward him, especially at the Padishah and his reti-nue, suspicious and ready to go to war at a moment's notice. The logical choice would be for the Padishah and the Grand General to fight the duel, but that would only trigger the war no matter who won. "Yes," he said. "Yes, I see it now. This is the way it must end. Very well."

Mudd returned the Padishah's other glove and asked, "May I borrow your weapon, sir?"

"What? Oh, yes, certainly," said the Padishah. He drew his disruptor pistol from its holster and handed it over.

"Thank you." Mudd stepped back to the walkway between tubs. As he passed Lebrun and Nordell he said, "Be good to each other. Don't make the same mistakes Stella and I did."

Nordell put his arm around Lebrun. "We'll try," she said.

Mudd turned to the Grand General. "We start out back to back, take ten paces, turn and shoot. Come on, we're about out of time. Kirk, you may count."

Kirk couldn't believe this was the same Harry Mudd he had come to know. Fighting a duel? Impos-sible! But he and the Grand General moved into position, and everyone else moved away to give them room. Kirk said, "Harry, I can't let you do this. You've never fired a weapon in your life, have you?"

Mudd aimed at the ceiling and pulled the trigger. A bright white bolt of energy caromed off the tile, showering everyone with debris. "Sure I have," said Mudd.

"But—but—"

"Okay," Mudd told the Grand General, "each time he says 'but,' we take a step. When we get to ten—"

Laughter drowned out whatever else he said.

All right then, if this was how he wanted it, who was Kirk to stop him? It *was* Harry's responsibility, after all. It was just such a shock to see him actually admit to it. Kirk waited for the laughter to die down, then said, "Ready? One . . . two . . . three . . ."

Mudd and the Grand General took slow, even steps. When they got to ten they turned, and everything seemed to freeze for a moment as they eyed one another across twenty yards of space. Then both men raised their weapons and fired. Kirk flinched as Mudd's shot went wild and blew more tile off the wall just over his head, but the Grand General's aim was true: Mudd fell to the floor with a smoking hole in the center of his chest.

"Harry!" screamed Stella. She ran to him, bent over his inert body, and said, "Oh, my poor Harry, oh, my dearest—"

Harry raised his head, struggled to speak, managed to croak, "Goodbye, cruel world," then fell back to the tile.

Everyone rushed forward, but before they could reach him he shimmered into a column of light and was gone.

"Something has happened," Spock said through Kirk's communicator. "I'm reading massive memory transfer out of the buffers."

As he spoke, there was a splash off to Kirk's left, and a Nevisian woman appeared in the water. Another splash, and a man appeared just beyond her. Then another and another beyond them.

A babble of voices broke the silence that had followed Mudd's death, but Stella's shout overrode them all. "You idiots!" she screamed. "You let him get away again!"

Kirk looked at her, then at the spot where Harry had been. Of course she was right; in their fear of the worst-case scenario they had overlooked the most likely outcome of all this. Everyone but Harry, who was no doubt reappearing in a tub of his own somewhere. Not on Prastor, either, Kirk suspected. This was Mudd's third time through the system, and though his second time hadn't been heroic enough to send him to Arnhall, this one certainly qualified.

And from there Mudd could beam to any planet he wanted to, no doubt taking as many secrets of Nevisian technology with him as he could carry. Kirk really should try to stop him, but there was just one problem with that: he had no idea where Arnhall was. And he really didn't want to die again to find out. Too many people in the Nevis system had already died trying to reach Arnhall.

Epilogue

The soft blue and white clouds of York III shone brightly out of the viewscreen, lighting the *Enterprise*'s bridge like sunlight through a large bay window. The familiar sounds of the crew at work were also a comfort, as was the presence of Captain Kirk in his command chair again. Everything seemed to be in its proper place at last; even, Spock reluctantly admitted to himself, McCoy standing beside the captain's chair.

The intercom whistled, and Ensign Vagle said, "Transporter room one. Stella Mudd is away." He sounded considerably relieved to be delivering the news, as well he might. Stella had been rather unhappy with the outcome of things on Distrel, and had made sure everyone on the *Enterprise* knew it. Spock felt sorry for her employees in the hotel when she returned, but he was glad to have the last remnant of this whole situation off the ship. Harry Mudd's influence spread chaos wherever it went, and Spock was eager to put it all behind him.

Captain Kirk's thoughts evidently paralleled his own. He sighed loudly, then said, "Well, gentlemen, I hope that's the last we'll see of either Mudd for a while."

McCoy nodded. "Forever would be just about long enough for me. But somehow I doubt we'll be that lucky. Harry has a way of popping up just when you need him the least."

"Indeed, Doctor?" Spock asked him. "Ignoring the mysticism and psychotic sense of individual persecution inherent in your argument, a look at the facts of the matter show that his influence in this case was, in fact, of considerable benefit."

"Only you would defend Harry Mudd," McCoy said. "All right, I'll bite. What good did he do us?"

"He provided the Federation with three prospective new member worlds."

Both Kirk and McCoy looked at him in surprise. "Did I miss something in the confusion?" Kirk asked. "I thought Distrel and Prastor were still independent. Defiantly so. And as for Arnhall, one crochety old lady on the Council of Heroes isn't exactly a revolution."

"Yes," said Spock. "But how long do you imagine the current situation can continue? The leaders of Distrel and Prastor both know the truth about their 'gods' now, and a growing number of citizens have also learned the secret. I do not believe the current system can survive that knowledge. And when the Nevisians begin looking for a new direction, the Federation will be there to welcome them."

"I don't know," said McCoy. "People are reluctant

to change. It wouldn't surprise me a bit if they kept right on fighting with each other even if they do know what's behind their afterlife."

Spock nodded. "Perhaps. If history is any guide— or for that matter, if personal experience is any guide—then people will always fight. But generally they make up again. Harry Mudd reminded the Nevisians that they can make peace if they want to, and the complications that arose from the android proved to them that they can make peace when they need to. I believe that is an important lesson for anyone to learn, and one which will eventually lead them to a less violent way of life."

McCoy shook his head. "I hope you're right, but you've got more faith in human—or should I say humanoid—nature than I do."

"Perhaps it is not entirely faith," said Spock. "There is one other detail I failed to mention while I was in the caverns below the palace."

"What?" Kirk asked.

Spock realized he had to back up a bit to make his point. "The lights were not on when I beamed in the first time. They responded automatically to my presence, and presumably turned off again when I and Scotty and the Grand General and Harry Mudd beamed away. In any case, they were off when I went back alone, and they again turned on automatically upon my arrival."

"So the lights are automatic," McCoy said impatiently. "So's everything else in the Nevis system. What's the point?"

"The point, Doctor, is that everything is also old. The computer was designed for longevity, but the lights apparently were not, and they have lost a great deal of their original efficiency. They now generate nearly as much heat as light, and the heat they produced the first time we were there apparently loosened a fixture, for the light over the central processor was hanging a bit askew. I would never have noticed it had I not heard a somewhat ominous creak from overhead while I was scanning the computer with my tricorder."

"You're saying the light is going to come down on the computer?" Kirk asked. "The *main* processor?"

"That seems likely," Spock replied. "Perhaps not immediately, but soon. Within another three or four visits, I imagine. And I did not see a template for another one among the items stored for duplication, so I suspect the main computer is irreplaceable."

Kirk said, "You know the Grand General won't be able to resist going down for a peek once in a while. Why didn't you tell him?"

Spock had the attention of the entire bridge crew now. He felt a bit uncomfortable under their scrutiny, for he knew that humans could react unpredictably when he explained a logical decision, but the captain had asked for his reasoning so he forged ahead. "I decided that informing him of the imminent failure would have violated the Prime Directive."

"How could warning him that the whole computer system is in danger violate the Prime Directive?" asked McCoy. "When that light falls, it'll change everything."

Spock nodded. "Indeed it will, provided they have not changed already. But the light fixture was old before we arrived, and would almost certainly have failed within a few hundred more years even if we had not activated it. Therefore, I reasoned that by alerting anyone to the danger and giving them the opportunity to repair it, I would have artificially extended the amount of time the resurrection system dominated their society. So I remained silent."

So did the bridge crew for a few seconds. Then Chekov could contain himself no longer. He snickered, then Sulu chuckled, which set Uhura into a fit of giggles, which in turn brought out McCoy's patented goofy grin, all of which made the captain shake his head and laugh out loud.

"Spock," he said when he could catch his breath, "that's the most amazing line of doublethink I've ever heard."

Perplexed as usual around displays of mirth, Spock said, "Then you disapprove?"

"Disapprove? Of course not. It's perfect. It's just so . . . so devious. I think you've been spending too much time around Harry Mudd."

"The association was entirely involuntary, I assure you," Spock told him.

"I'm sure it was. But just this once, I think it was a good thing." Kirk sat up a little straighter in his chair. "And now I think it's time we left the Nevisians to their own devices, and Harry Mudd to his. We're late for our rendezvous with the *O'Halloran*. We wouldn't want Spock to get into trouble for dereliction of duty, now, would we?"

"That would be unfortunate," said Spock, relieved that his logic hadn't gotten him in trouble this time.

"Indeed it would. Plot a course for the Duval system, Mr. Chekov."

"Laid in, sir."

"Mr. Sulu, take us out of orbit. Ahead warp factor seven."

279

"Aye, sir."

Spock watched the viewscreen as the planet slid aside and the distant stars filled the view. When Sulu engaged the warp engines they turned to streaks, but Spock shivered as an entirely different picture flashed before his eyes. For just an instant it had looked to him as if someone had reached out and *stirred* the stars. He knew it was illogical, the product of an overworked brain and nothing more, yet for that moment he had even known who had done the stirring. Harry Mudd, of course, who was once again free and no doubt dreaming up his next bit of mischief somewhere out there in the vastness of space.

"This is Captain Kathryn Janeway of the Federation starship *Voyager*," Janeway said, pitching her voice to carry to the communications relays. "We come in peace, and would like to establish trade relations with the inhabitants of this planet. Please respond."

Paris fixed his eyes on the main screen, waiting for it to dissolve into the familiar larger-than-life figures of full communications. Instead, the complex of buildings remained on the screen, empty of life and movement. Their surfaces shone in the local sun's pale light, an odd, oily brilliance that was like nothing he'd ever seen before. Stone or metal, the shapes were graceful, weirdly beautiful—they looked, he thought, like the city sculptures he'd seen once on Delphis IV, celebrations of the Delphians' crowded, transurban world.

After a moment, Kim said, almost apologetically, "There's no response, Captain."

"Keep trying." Janeway pushed herself out of her chair, stood hands on hips, staring at the screen with narrowed eyes. "And carry on with the science scans."

"Yes, Captain."

"Check for any sign of recent fighting, too," Chakotay said, and came to stand beside Janeway.

She lifted an eyebrow at him. "Surely if the Andir-rim had done enough damage to prevent the Kirse responding to our hail, we'd be able to see signs of it from space."

Chakotay shrugged. "We don't know how large a population the Kirse actually have. One good reason for spending resources on an automated defense system as elaborate as this one could be a small or a declining population."

"It's possible," Janeway said, but shook her head. "And right now, Mr. Chakotay, we've got too many possibilities to be useful."

She sounded almost Vulcan as she said that, and Paris hid a grin, imagining Tuvok's startled approval. He realized that Chakotay was looking at him then, and hastily fixed his attention on his own controls, running an unnecessary diagnostic just to have something to do. The navigation sensors were as empty as the rest of the sensor screens, only the phaser platforms moving in their careful orbits, chattering to themselves, apparently oblivious of the ship hanging just outside their range. *Or I hope we're outside their range,* Paris amended. *At least they don't seem all that interested.*

"I'm not picking up any tracks of recent phaser fire," Kim said. "Or anything else that could mean a recent attack."

"The defense platforms do not seem to have fired recently, either," Tuvok said. "Their current configuration suggests that they have been on standby for some time."

"The preliminary science scan shows that nearly ninety percent of the land in the temperate zones is under cultivation," Kim said, "and we haven't even begun to classify everything. It looks as though there are plenty of plants carrying hexuronic acid, though, so we ought to be able to get everything we need. I am picking up what might be lower life-forms, but my readings are inconclusive. It could be sophisticated organic-based machinery."

"What about the citadel?" Janeway asked.

Paris could almost hear the shrug in Kim's voice. "I'm not picking up anything there, Captain. There is power in some kind of storage cell, but it's very low level. No life-forms at all."

"Captain, the pattern of power use suggests that the building may be on standby," Tuvok said. "Its condition is similar to that of the platforms."

Janeway was silent for a long moment, so long that Paris ventured another glance over his shoulder, to see her staring at the screen, a faint, thoughtful frown on her face. "Very well," she said at last. "We'll give the Kirse another chance to show themselves. Mr. Paris, put us into orbit outside the optimum range of those platforms, and, Mr. Kim, set up an automatic contact transmission. We'll give them twelve hours to respond, and then we'll see. In the meantime, keep scanning. Let's get as complete a picture as possible of this planet."

"Aye, aye, Captain." Kim's response was still Academy-perfect, and Paris knew his own acknowledgment sounded even sloppier by comparison. He felt his cheeks burning, and turned his attention to his console, fingers moving easily over the complex controls, setting up the optimum orbit. *At least I know how to do this,* he thought, *and there's not an Academy graduate who can match me.* The bravado rang a little hollow even in his own mind; he made a face, and touched the controls again.

"Moving into orbit now, Captain."

"Excellent, Mr. Paris," Janeway said. "Twelve hours, gentlemen. Let's see if we can find the Kirse."

Not entirely to Janeway's surprise, the twelve hours passed without any further sign of life from the surface. In part, she thought, it was a good thing—she had been able to get a full eight hours' sleep for once—but all things considered, it would have been simpler if they had made some sort of contact. She pushed Neelix's latest effort at breakfast aside and concentrated on her datapadd. The reports flashed past as she scanned through them, all monotonously the same, except for the doctor's. More than half the human crew were seriously affected by the deficiencies, and the level of supplemental dosage needed to stave off problems for the rest of the crew was approaching toxicity—and even that would be impossible to sustain without using the replicators. At least the news from the science scan was good. The Kirse world was lovely, filled with vegetation that would almost certainly supply their every need, but there was no sign of the inhabitants, no sign of the sophisticated culture that had built the citadel. She touched controls on the datapadd to recall the report that covered the massive structure, and the image filled the little screen. Towers rose from a central hexagon, each one different from the rest—one topped with thin structures like old-fashioned radio antennae, another glittering as though sheathed in ice or glass, still another sporting a bulbous, gold-washed shape that looked vaguely familiar, if only from holograms—and dozens of outbuildings spread from that center, creating a pattern like a slanted spider's web or early frost on a windowpane. It was strikingly beautiful, an artificial structure as lush as the flourishing plant life, and obviously the work of skilled engineers, the same skilled engineers who had created the network of defense platforms—who were nowhere to be found.

She shook her head, leaving the image on the screen, and addressed herself to the plate in front of her. Neelix had done his best to create something both palatable and nutritious that didn't use too much of the defective foodstock, but his best efforts still left much to be desired, and she regarded the grainy mess—roughly based, she suspected, on Tom Paris's unenthusiastic description of oatmeal—without pleasure. Still, it was carbohydrates, and she took a careful bite. It was less sweet than she had expected, and bland to the tongue; she swallowed hard, almost wishing for some of Neelix's more dramatic spices, and reached for the vitamin supplement the doctor had provided from his dwindling supplies. It was orange, a failed attempt to mimic a natural juice, and she drank it as quickly as she could, putting aside the glass with a grimace of distaste. Here in the privacy of her quarters, she could at least indulge her own dislike without worrying that she was setting a bad example, and she tossed the glass into the collection bin with more force that was strictly necessary. Even taking into account the fact that the doctor was a hologram, without taste buds and not yet used to full-time interaction with human beings, it simply tasted bad. She drew a glass of water to wash away the bitterness, and turned back to her desk.

"Computer, contact the duty officers, and tell them I want them in the ready room in—" She glanced at the nearest chronometer. "—fifteen minutes."

"Confirmed," the computer answered, and Janeway reached for her datapadd. She glanced at her image in the mirror beside her cabin door, making sure that she looked as collected—as unaffected by mere human frailties—as a Starfleet captain should be. Especially now, it was a necessary illusion.

She was the first one in the ready room, as she had intended, but almost as soon as she had seated herself at the head of the table the door opened and Chakotay appeared. She nodded a greeting, and he gave her one of his rueful smiles.

"Nothing new so far," he said. "Either no one's

home, or they're hiding from us. Kim hasn't been able to raise anyone on the planet, except the machines, and they don't want to talk to us either."

"So what do you think?" Janeway asked.

The first officer shrugged, and took his place at the table, adjusting his datapadd as he did so. "As I said before, it could be that the Kirse have been eliminated—I don't know why else they wouldn't respond at all to our presence. If they think we're hostile, well, they've got that defense system just waiting for us, and if they think we're friendly, there's no reason not to respond to our overtures." He spread his hands. "Except, of course, that there's no sign of damage to the citadel or to anything on the planet."

"I suppose something else could account for the disappearance," Janeway said, halfheartedly. "Disease, natural waning of the population—for all we know, they could have emigrated en masse, we'd never know the difference." She touched her controls, projecting the image of the Kirse world onto the larger of the viewscreens. The blue-green disk, cloud-streaked, seemed an almost mocking presence behind the cage of its defense network. "One thing I am sure of, though, Chakotay. We're going to have to get supplies here."

"I agree." Chakotay nodded, his tattooed face somber. "I've been over the latest figures with the doctor twice already. We don't have a choice anymore."

"No." Janeway broke off as the ready-room door opened again, admitting the rest of the junior officers in a cluster. An instant later, a second viewscreen lit, and the doctor looked out at her, Kes just visible over his shoulder. Janeway squared her shoulders and folded her hands on the table. "Gentlemen," she said. "Let's have your reports. We'll start with yours, Mr. Kim."

The young ensign glanced quickly at his datapadd, then back again. He looked exhausted, Janeway thought, and he moved with a care that suggested that his joints ached. "I can go into details, Captain, but it's pretty much what we saw in the first scan. There's plenty of food down there, food that we can eat which also contains hexuronic acid—that's the precursor to vitamin C—and most of the other elements we need. Most of it seems to have been cultivated, at least originally. The whole planetary land mass, except for the area around the citadel, is like one big garden, or at least a series of linked gardens. It looks almost as though the continents have been modified to provide specific habitats and microclimates to grow the various plants. I think I've picked up traces of irrigation systems and artificially created land forms—mostly barrier hills and things like that, but some of the lakes look artificial, too." He touched his datapadd and a holographic globe appeared to float above the tabletop. "Of course, the area right around the citadel—" As he spoke, colors brightened on the image. "—there, for about a hundred kilometers all around, is heavily cultivated, and there are definite irrigation channels just under the surface. Some kind of sophisticated drip system, I think."

"But no sign of the builders," Janeway said.

Kim shook his head. "None, Captain."

Janeway studied the image, trying to imagine what

could make a people abandon a world like this. "What about life-forms? Any more detail?"

To her surprise, it was Chakotay who answered. "Nothing conclusive. Mr. Kim and I have been over the readings a couple of times, and Lieutenant Torres rerouted systems power to try to improve the resolution, but we're still pretty much where we started. There are things that might be animals down there, but they could be complicated machines."

"Organic-based machines," Torres corrected. She looked at Janeway. "I think Neelix was probably right about the Kirse needing to trade for metals. There doesn't seem to be a whole lot on the planet."

"But no intelligent life?" Janeway asked.

Kim shook his head. "Not that we can find."

"You're sure these are animals?" Paris asked. "I mean, if you can't tell for sure what they're made of, how can you tell if they're smart?"

"They're engaged in what looks like highly repetitive, probably food-gathering activities pretty much all the time," Kim answered.

Paris gave a fleeting grin. "So if they are intelligent, they're probably bored?"

Kim smothered a smile of his own. "Probably."

Janeway allowed herself a smile as well—after all, if they could still make jokes, however bad, they had to be doing better than she'd thought—and looked at Tuvok. "Have you been able to find out anything more about the defense platforms, Mr. Tuvok?"

"I've run a complete analysis," the security officer answered, "and I've been able to make a partial assessment of their capabilities. Our present orbit is just outside their optimum focus, which means that, should the Kirse or their machines decide that we are a threat, our shields would be able to withstand their strongest attack for the time needed to take us out of orbit."

Paris cleared his throat, the smile vanishing from his face. "Mr. Tuvok and I have programmed an escape pattern into the navigational computers. If we're fired on, that'll take us out of range by the quickest route."

"Excellent," Janeway said, and meant it.

"Also," Tuvok went on, "the spacing of the orbits and the weaponry aboard the platforms suggests that they are designed to intercept an attacking force by phaser fire only. In other words, they have no shields."

"How do they defend the platforms themselves, then?" Chakotay asked.

"Each platform is heavily armored," Tuvok answered. "It appears to be a collapsed metal sheathing. Also, there are molecular differences among the various pieces of armor that suggest they were installed at different times."

"So what you're saying," Janeway said, "is that they don't have the transporter, either."

Tuvok nodded. "That is correct, Captain. Neither the defense platforms nor what I assume to be the citadel's defense mechanisms are configured to block a transporter beam."

That was good news, and Janeway leaned back in her chair. An away team on the Kirse planet would have the margin of safety that the transporter had been invented to provide. For an instant, she felt as though she were caught in a timeslip—her crew suffering from scurvy, the transporter a significant advantage, the Federation out of range even of subspace radio—and then put the feeling firmly aside. The transporter was only an advantage as long as they were able to lower their own screens to receive the crew, but there should be enough of a communications lag between the planet and the defense systems to allow *Voyager* to retrieve the away team before it came under attack.

"Very well," she said aloud. "I assume you've all seen the doctor's report?" There were murmurs of agreement around the table, and she went on, "The gist of it is that we have to replenish at least some of our supplies here—we have no choice in the matter."

"Based on the estimates Lieutenant Torres gave me," the hologram said, "and the observed frequency of M-class planets in this sector, there will not be enough healthy crew members left to collect the food once we find a suitable planet if we don't resupply here."

"Exactly." Janeway gave a rueful smile. "So I intend to take an away team down to the planet—to the citadel, for a start—and see if we can find the Kirse. Mr. Paris, Mr. Kim, Lieutenant Torres, you'll accompany me."

"Captain," Tuvok said. "May I suggest that I be part of the team as well?"

Janeway shook her head. "I want you on the ship, Tuvok, where you can keep an eye on the defense platforms."

The Vulcan nodded, his face as impassive as ever, but Janeway thought she caught a hint of disapproval in his eyes. "Then may I suggest you take a larger security contingent?"

"I will take two more people," Janeway said. "But I don't want to suggest that our presence is hostile." She looked around the table. "Any further comments? Then let's go find what's happened to the Kirse."